Born in Sheffield, Ernest Barrett was the eldest of seven children. He was called up for National Service in 1948 and after signing on, spent six and a half years in the R.A.F.

After leaving the forces he took a job at the steel works in Rotherham. He later moved to Lincolnshire after suffering a life changing accident at the steel works in 1968. After struggling to cope with his injuries he eventually got a job with the Skegness council, where he stayed until his retirement in 1995.

After an Open University course he took up writing poetry and short stories. Although he didn't complete the course (much to his regret) it was a great help. This was followed by him joining the Skegness Writers.

The Lincolnshire Wolds

By Ernest Barrett

I've roamed the lakes and dales.
Seen mountains that reach the skies.
But never has a more beauteous sight,
been set before my eyes.
Rolling hills and sweeping valleys,
carpeted with golden corn.
Drifting clouds casting shadows,
on gentle winds are borne.
As I look around, it's a pleasure to behold
The peaceful serenity,
that is the Lincolnshire Wolds.

Gazing upon this tranquil scene,
my heart is filled with joy.
The winding brook, that drove the mill
when I was but a boy,
smoothly gliding round gentle bends,
as it wends its way to the placid fens.
Now as the shadows lengthen
and the evening sun turns gold.
I breathe a heartfelt sigh,
at this view of the Lincolnshire Wolds.

BLIND STAB

I wish to dedicate this book to my children and step children,

Stephen Ernest and Sarah
Keith Lawrence
Marlene Angela Rose and Michael
Charon Elaine and Mark
Yvonne Michelle
Deborah Jayne and Ian
Christine Anne and Clive
Pauline Jean and Steve

Ernest Barrett

BLIND STAB

AUSTIN MACAULEY
PUBLISHERS LTD.

A CIP catalogue record for this title is available from the British Library.

ISBN 978 184963 413 7

www.austinmacauley.com

First Published (2013)
Austin Macauley Publishers Ltd.
25 Canada Square
Canary Wharf
London
E14 5LB

Printed and Bound in Great Britain

Acknowledgments

I would like to take this opportunity to thank the nursing staff of Boston Pilgrim Hospital and Lincoln County Hospital Radiography Department for the care and devotion that they have shown during the eight weeks of treatment given to me and the good friends that I have made. i.e. Noel. David. Terry and others. I would also like to thank the voluntary drivers who spent hours taking us there and bringing as back every day without complaint. It was really appreciated. Great job boys and girls.

Ernie

Chapter One

Richard Moristone played nervously with the pile of chips in his hand; repeatedly rippling them through his fingers as he made his mind up where to place them. He had already lost five grand in small wagers. This time he was going for broke. His eyes were almost closed as he made his decision. It was entirely his choice. Which was it to be, red or black? Black had come up three times on the trot and he'd bet on red each time.

'Surely,' he told himself, 'black couldn't come up again. According to the law of averages it has to be red this time.'

'Ladies and gentlemen,' bellowed the croupier, his dickie bow almost hidden by his double chin, as he addressed the group of well dressed punters who were crowding around the roulette table.

'Place your bets.'

Moristone's heart was pounding as he reached out with a shaking hand; he hesitated for a couple of seconds, his mind in turmoil as his fingers, gripping the stack of chips, hovered indecisively over the table. Then, with a feeling of abandon, he placed his last five thousand on red. The croupier spun the wheel and sent the small metal ball on its way, bouncing and dancing over the apertures as the wheel slowed down. Moristone closed his eyes, not daring to watch. He took a deep breath; so much depended on the result. A fifty-fifty chance, black or red. He'd gone beyond his means on this one. Already five grand down, he desperately needed red to come up for him to break even. He mentally made himself a promise; if this went his way, he was finished with gambling. The wheel stopped; he breathed out slowly as he opened his eyes, hardly daring to look. The croupier called it, his voice seemingly indifferent to the consequences.

'Twenty, on the *black*.'

Moristone swayed imperceptibly; his knuckles white as he gripped the edge of the table to steady himself, beads of sweat standing out on his forehead. He felt physically sick, as he watched his five grand raked in unfeelingly by the croupier. Shaking his head from side to side, and with a look of disbelief on his face he slowly turned away from the table. There was a strong smell of nervous sweat mingled with tobacco smoke permeating the air of the large gambling hall as he pulled a handkerchief from his pocket and mopped his brow.

Dejectedly, he pushed his way through the eager punters that were crowding round the roulette table, almost fighting to throw away their money. His debt was now ten thousand pounds. The enormity of what he had done came home to him. He felt a churning in his stomach as he wandered aimlessly among the various gambling activities that were going on. He'd taken a chance and signed a cheque for ten thousand pounds for the amount of chips he'd received, when there wasn't enough cash in his bank account to cover it.

The strong overhead lights cut a swathe through the pall of blue tobacco smoke that hung like a mantle over the gambling activities in the casino in Hull. Gregory Mendois, his eyes half closed, looked down from his office at the potential speculators that were meandering around the diverse forms of gambling that was going on. The roulette wheel looked to be particularly busy. He sucked at the cigar in his mouth, as he watched with interest, at what he liked to describe as, 'the mugs', parting with their cash; especially. Richard Moristone.

Moristone's mind was in turmoil as he reached into his inside pocket and pulled out a silver case; opening it, he took out a cigarette and placed it between his lips; flicking his lighter with his thumb, he lit it. Taking a deep drag, he closed his eyes and slowly exhaled, blowing a thick stream of smoke towards the yellowed ceiling, as he attempted to come to terms with the desperate situation he was in. His eyes narrowed as he made his mind up. He had to get out of here, he told himself. Taking a quick look around the crowded casino, he swiftly made his way to the exit. A burly doorman, on orders from the office that overlooked the tables, moved to block his way. Moristone turned, only to see Arnie, the six-foot-two floor manager, who was built like a brick outhouse, elbowing his way through the excited gathering as he approached him; his shoulders sagged when he saw the determined expression on the big man's face. Arnie's beady eyes were unblinking, as he looked down at Moristone.

'The boss wants to see you,' he snapped, in a tone of voice that wasn't going to take no for an answer. Arnie nodded his shaven head in the direction of a flight of stairs that led to the manager's office.

'Okay,' he replied, looking up at the big man, with a weary air of resignation. 'Let's go.'

Moristone raised his eyebrows and glanced up at the long window that overlooked the large gambling room. A man with black slicked down hair, smoking a cigar looked down at him. With a feeling of trepidation he followed the big man up the flight of stairs.

Gregory Mendois, the owner of the casino, was of Portuguese origin; he had lived in Britain for thirty-seven years, having arrived at the age of four with his parents who were immigrants. They gained entry into Britain in nineteen forty-five, just after the war. His father George opened a furniture shop in London, which he ran until nineteen seventy, when he retired. He worked hard to ensure that his off springs wanted for nothing. After selling the business, he and his family moved to Hull.

In the meantime his two sons, Gregory and Jonathan went to university to study law. Jonathan, the younger one, passed with flying colours and was offered a position with a law firm. Gregory failed miserably, then much to his father's dismay, took up activities on the wrong side of the law. Five years later their father died of lung cancer. The doctor blamed his heavy smoking, but their mother believed much of it was down to worry over Gregory's behaviour. When the will was read out, the two sons were left one hundred thousand pounds each.

Gregory Mendois inherited most of his father's attributes, hard working and a will to make something of his life. The exception was his dishonesty and a cruel streak, which he used to great advantage. After receiving his inheritance he made a couple of bad investments on the stock market. Then he formed a syndicate of likeminded investors and started the backstreet unlicensed casino in Hull, which he ran with some success. He knew it was illegal but that did not stop him, although he had to be careful. If the cops found out it could mean a lengthy spell in prison. He would be finished. He hired cardsharps for the card games and the roulette table was rigged. He smiled inwardly.

'Well,' he told himself, taking a long pull on his cigar and blowing out a thick stream of smoke. 'Why give the suckers a chance? If they want to get rid of their money, I'm quite happy to oblige them.'

He'd been watching Richard Moristone night after night, recklessly gambling. Up till now he'd always covered his debts. Mendois watched through the window as he signed a cheque for a sizeable amount of chips. He picked up the internal house phone and spoke into it.

'Mike,' he grunted, 'how much has Moristone signed for?'

'Ten big ones boss,' replied Mike the banker.

Mendois chewed on his cigar as he studied the situation, an inscrutable look on his swarthy face; something didn't look right, he told himself. He didn't like it. Moristone had seemed unusually nervous as he signed for his chips with a cheque for ten grand. It wasn't like him; he always had a confident superior attitude.

'Arnie,' he called over his shoulder to his manager as he watched Moristone placed his last wager. 'Give our contact at the bank a call and ask him to check Richard Moristone's account.'

The big man picked up the phone, dialled a number. A few minutes later, after making the enquiry, the answer came back. Moristone was almost insolvent. His total assets amounted to five hundred pounds.

'Boss,' called Arnie, from across the room as he was about to replace the receiver. 'He's got five hundred quid in his account.'

Mendois, who had been pacing up and down the office floor as he waited for the call, took the phone from him and spoke into the receiver.

'Does that constitute all his bank assets?' he enquired.

He grimaced as he heard the answer.

'Arnie, go down and tell Moristone I want a word with him,' he snapped.

The big man nodded and went through the door.

Mendois had his back to Richard Moristone as he entered the room; the air was heavily tainted by cigar smoke as he turned to face him. Moristone could almost feel his cold piercing dark brown eyes pinning him down. A shiver went down his spine as he looked away, avoiding eye to eye contact.

'Ah, Mr Moristone!' exclaimed Mendois courteously, as the troubled man entered his office. 'My manager has informed me that you are ten grand in our debt.'

He paused for a moment, concentrating on the cigar in his fingers, as he reached out to the ashtray that lay on the highly polished desk. Then he looked up, his eyes cold and unfeeling, despite the polite expression on his face and told him, lowering his voice for effect...

'When you drew your chips, you signed a cheque for that amount, thereby assuring my manager that you were good for the money; when in reality, you were almost broke.'

'I've always paid my debts to you before,' argued Moristone, his hand shaking as he took out a handkerchief and wiped his brow, adding with some conviction,

'As a matter of fact you've had over twenty grand out of me in the last six weeks.'

Mendois nodded in agreement as he carefully tapped the ash that hung precariously from the end of his cigar, on to the ashtray, then placed it between his lips and took another deep drag; after blowing a stream of smoke at the man in front of him, he replied, 'That may be so, but we've been in touch with our contact at your bank and made enquiries about your present finances.' He stabbed the air with his cigar to emphasise the point. Then he went on... 'He's informed us that you do not have the necessary amount in your account to cover the cheque you gave us.'

He waved a well manicured hand as Moristone opened his mouth to say something.

'In fact, except for the small amount shown, you don't have any money at all, do you?' he hissed almost inaudibly.

The assertion was more an accusation than a question. Moristone's face paled as the statement struck home. He shuffled his feet uncomfortably.

'You now owe the casino ten thousand pounds,' Mendois snapped meaningfully, his eyes never leaving the hapless man's face.

Running his fingers nervously through his hair, Moristone looked away as he tried desperately to think of something to say,

'I have other assets I can fall back on,' he lied.

'I'm not interested in where you get the money from,' countered Mendois. 'Just get it.'

Richard Moristone didn't like his tone of voice. He pulled himself up to his full height and squared his shoulders.

'You'll get the money when I'm good and ready to pay you,' he asserted belligerently.

Mendois gazed at his cigar for a moment, as he rolled it slowly in his fingers. He looked up; there was a cruel glint in his eyes as he replied.

'You don't seem to realise the seriousness of your position,' he snarled, pushing his face up close, until their noses were almost touching. 'You knowingly gambled with money that you didn't have. I don't take kindly to that and I don't like being taken for a fool. Make no mistake we'll recover the money you owe us one way or another.'

Moristone was visibly shaken by the savageness of the inferred threat, as Mendois turned and nodded to his manager, who at eighteen stone, dwarfed Moristone.

'Arnie,' he grunted in a low voice, 'Mr Moristone doesn't seem to understand the trouble he's in. Show him we mean business.'

The big man swaggered across the floor, opening and

closing his hands as he flexed the muscles in his brawny arms. Reaching out, he grabbed Moristone by his lapels, picking him up bodily and throwing him across the office. He groaned in agony, as he bounced off the wall and landed with a thump on the floor. Mendois looked down at the stricken man, a cruel smile on his face as he saw Moristone's eyes screw up with pain,

'Let's see now. It's the fourteenth of October today.' He paused for a moment as he counted on his fingers. 'You've got fourteen days to find the money,' he snapped unfeelingly.

'Okay! Okay! You've made your point,' Moristone gasped, holding his hand up in submission, as he struggled to his feet. He raised his arms to fend off another expected attack, as Arnie, his fist raised, approached him again. Mendois stepped between them, his arm outstretched, restraining the big man.

'Steady on, Arnie, we don't want to cause him to have an injury,' he declared mockingly. 'Show him out, I think he's got the message,'

'Don't forget, my friend, you've got fourteen days to pay up,' Mendois called after him as Arnie bundled him unceremoniously out of the office.

Richard Moristone was taken to the rear exit of the casino, where he was propelled through the door with the aid of the big man's size twelve boot in his back, then he was slammed against the wall, face first. A strong smell of garlic mixed with tobacco permeated the air as Arnie pressed his mouth close to Moristone's ear.

'This is a sample of what you'll get if you don't pay up,' he growled, taking a step back.

Two heavy punches slammed into Moristone's kidneys bringing him to his knees. He slumped to the floor and the lights went out, as his face hit the wall. Arnie, a mirthless grin on his face, went back into the casino, the heavy doors banging shut behind him.

Chapter Two

Moristone opened his eyes slowly; he looked down and saw that he was sat in a puddle of rainwater, his legs were stretched out on the asphalt path, as he leaned back against the wall, his head throbbing. He could just make out the outlines of the big door, (through which he had been kicked) in the inky blackness around him. Turning his head sideways, he could see bright lights at the end of the alley. The distant wailing of a police siren broke the silence of the night, as it sped through Hull city centre. Massaging the back of his neck to ease the pain, he struggled to his feet and stood for a moment swaying from side to side as he regained his balance, then he staggered towards the bright lights that beckoned him. Stopping for a moment where the alley met the main street, he leaned dizzily against the wall for a couple of seconds, as a feeling of nausea swept over him.

After regaining control of himself, he looked up and down the main road to get his bearings; then shaking his head to clear it, he weaved his way to where he'd parked his car. Opening the car door, he collapsed into the driving seat exhausted. Taking a deep breath he reached up and massaged the back of his neck with the palm of his right hand and closed his eyes for a few seconds, his body racked with pain. He shuffled his backside in the car seat, the seat of his pants were wet through after sitting in the pool of rain water in the alley. Reaching up he turned the driving mirror towards him and looked into it. He grimaced. What he saw when he checked his face wasn't a pretty sight; his top lip was swollen and a bruise was beginning to show just below his right eye, evidently where his face had made contact with the brickwork.

'Ouch!' he grunted, his face screwing .up in pain as he gingerly touched the nasty bruise just above his cheek bone. He was going to have a lovely shiner in the morning, he told himself. A small area under his eye was already beginning to turn blue.

Gritting his teeth, he took a handkerchief out of his pocket, and dabbed at the graze on his cheek before fastening his seat belt. Starting the engine, he switched on the headlights, engaged the gear, and pulled out into the late night traffic. He'd plenty to think about as he returned to his flat in Anlaby Road, not least, how the hell he was going to find money that he didn't have, to pay off his debt to Mendois. He toyed with the idea of refusing to pay; after all it was a gambling debt, and there was no law that said that he had to pay. For one thing the place was illegal. Okay they could ban him. That didn't bother him, he wasn't going there again anyway. If he was threatened he could report them to the police.

Shaking his head, he inwardly smiled to himself.

'Who am I kidding?' he muttered out loud, suddenly banging his foot down on the brakes at a pedestrian crossing, to allow an elderly couple to cross. Going through the gears, he continued on his way out of the city centre.

He knew he had to find the money somehow. The alternative didn't bear thinking about, he told himself; drumming his fingers on the steering wheel as he stopped at a red light. There was a worried frown on his forehead, as he pushed the gear into first and accelerated, when the lights changed to green. He had a grim look on his face as he arrived at his flat in Anlaby Road. Clambering out of the car, he unlocked the outer door and splashed through a large puddle of water that had formed in the door well. Limping painfully, he wearily climbed the concrete steps that led to his flat. Monica his girlfriend was stretched out on the settee watching the television, as he entered the entrance hall and slammed the door behind him. She had a cigarette in her fingers, her long blonde hair half covering her face, as she lay cross legged, her short skirt exposing her shapely thighs.

'Where have you been all this time, Richard?' she called out, tossing her hair back over her shoulder and uncrossing her legs as she sat up. She heard the door close with a bang, followed by his faltering footsteps, as he made his way along the hall.

Richard Moristone ignored her question as he staggered into the lounge and flopped down beside her on the comfortable settee, his clothes soiled and in disarray. Leaning forward he held his head in his hands and ran his fingers through his unkempt black hair, as he looked down at his feet. His head was throbbing as he groaned and closed his eyes.

'Pour me a drink, Monica,' he gasped, as she looked at him, her lovely blue eyes full of concern.

'My God, Richard!' she exclaimed in a shocked voice, when she saw his bruised face and the condition his clothes were in. 'What the hell's happened to you? You look as though you've had a right going over.'

Getting to her feet, she went into the bathroom and returned with a bowl of warm water and a flannel. After tenderly bathing his bruised face, she lit him a cigarette and placed it between his lips. Thanking her, he straightened up and leaned his aching head back on the rear of the settee. He took a deep drag of the cigarette, and relaxed as the soothing smoke filled his lungs. Then he slowly blew it down his nostrils and watched it drift to the ceiling through half closed eyes. He was beginning to feel a little better as she poured him a whisky and handed it to him. He tossed it straight back. The burning liquid going down his throat felt good; he held out the glass for another one.

'I'm in serious trouble,' he confided to her, in a low voice, as she handed him another drink, then sat down on the thick pile carpet, at his feet, as he swirled the amber liquid round in the bottom of the glass for a couple of seconds, before tossing it back.

She cocked her head on one side and looked up at him, her brow furrowed questioningly.

'Trouble. What kind of trouble?' she asked him, her voice full of concern.

He hesitated for a moment as he gathered his thoughts, then he went on to tell her about losing at the casino and the threats he'd received.

'I can't understand you, honey,' she told him, her American accent showing through as she shook her head in disbelief.

'You've told me time and time again, that they're nothing but a bunch of cheats, yet you will keep going there chasing your losses when you know you can't win.'

He didn't like her reminding him what an idiot he'd been, but deep down inside him, he knew she was right, he just could not resist the temptation. It was like a sickness in him. Getting up from the settee, he walked over to the large mirror on the wall above the fireplace and surveyed the damage done to his face by Arnie.

'I know, I know,' he admitted grudgingly. 'But it's done now and somehow I've got to find a way out of the mess I've got myself into.'

'Can you raise the amount of money necessary?' she asked him, an anxious look on her face as she passed him another tot of whisky. He looked into the glass of amber liquid for a few seconds, then he returned her worrying look, ruefully shaking his head.

'What can I do?' he asked her, tipping his head back and swallowing the fiery drink. He screwed his eyes up as it burnt its way down his throat. Moristone grimaced as he shook his head from side to side; he was beginning to feel the effects of the strong drink.

Monica, an attractive twenty-five year old, frowned as she looked at him, a thoughtful expression on her face. She'd never seen him like this before. He was usually cocky and arrogant. She'd known him since she'd come over from America in nineteen eighty, to study economics at Hull University. He had been in his last year of business studies. He'd told her he wasn't really interested, but he'd promised his grandmother, his only relative, that he would try his best. It seemed the only things he showed any interest in were his Harley Davidson motor bike and gambling. The latter being his biggest failing. She'd met Richard at one of the University dances, and had instantly fallen for his charm. He'd followed this up by asking her out a few days later. After three months they'd decided to form a serious relationship; she'd taken a flat of her own in Hessle, an attractive little village close to the Humber Bridge. Monica often stayed with him at his flat in Hull during the week when she was studying. Its close proximity to the University was much more convenient than her flat, which was a good half hour away, taking into account the heavy morning traffic.

She chewed her bottom lip as she looked at him reflectively. He'd always seemed capable and confident; at the moment he looked beaten, not knowing what to do next about the situation he was in.

'Is there any way I can help?' she offered, as he stood in front of the mirror taking a close look at his bruised face. 'I've got five hundred pounds in my bank account, Richard, you can have that.'

Turning away from the mirror, he looked down into her eyes and laughed mirthlessly.

'Five hundred pounds?' He snorted derisively. 'Monica, that's chicken feed. I've got to get my hands on ten grand somehow, in the next two weeks. If I don't get it…'

The sentence went unfinished as he shrugged his shoulders dejectedly.

'What will happen to you if you can't find the money?' she asked with an exhale.

'The consequences don't bear thinking about,' he replied in a low voice, as he reached out for the cigarette that was burning in the ashtray where he'd left it. Placing it between his lips he took a long drag and blew it towards the attractively patterned ceiling, which was beginning to take on a slightly yellowed hue.

Her hands went to her mouth in shock; she knew he gambled, but not to this extent.

'Where will you get that amount of money from?' she asked in a hushed voice.

There was a scraping sound as he scratched the stubble on his chin. He paused as he studied the cigarette in his fingers, and thought for a moment; he raised it to his lips and took another pull on it.

'To be honest, my love, I don't know,' he admitted, letting the smoke trickle slowly down his nostrils. 'I'll have to see if I can get some help from my friends.'

His tone of voice displayed little confidence. 'If that fails, I'll go and see if my grandmother will help me out of the trouble

I'm in.'

'Didn't she tell you not to come again, after the last time she helped you?' Monica reminded him as he sat back down on the comfortable settee, pulling his face as his wet trousers stuck to his thighs.

'Yes, I know what she said!' he exclaimed irritably. 'She always tells me that, but she eventually gives in.'

She placed her arm around his shoulder affectionately.

'Richard, you could refuse to pay it. After all it is a gambling debt. As far as I know it isn't enforceable by law,' she told him.

He turned to her, a serious look in his brown eyes.

'Monica my dear, you don't know who I'm dealing with,' he confided.

'These people have no regard for the law. They are not to be taken lightly. If I refuse to pay it will mean at least a couple of weeks in hospital, or worse.'

'There's no need for them to know,' she put to him.

He looked at her over the rim of his glass, as he finished his drink; there was a questioning look in his eyes.

'I don't get what you mean,' he rejoined, giving a slight shrug of his shoulders.

'Well, if I go to the police and explain to them your predicament, they might help you,' she suggested hopefully.

'Don't you think that I've already thought of that?' he told her, a mirthless grin on his face. 'The syndicate that Mendois runs would look into it and they would soon find out that I had shopped them.'

He paused for a moment before telling her...

'My life wouldn't be worth that.' He clicked his fingers.

'Anyway,' he continued, laying the back of his head on the settee and half closing his eyes, as he gazed tiredly up at a moth as it seemingly attacked the light bulb, only to fall beaten to the carpet, 'the police can't act without proof, and with his contacts Mendois wouldn't easily be caught out, and where would that leave me?'

'What are you going to do then?' she asked him in a low voice.

'As I've told you. I'm going to see if any of my friends will help me. If I don't get anywhere with them, I will have to go to my Grandma,' he replied as he took one last deep drag of his cigarette, then, with the smoke trickling down his nostrils, he stubbed it out in the ashtray that lay on a small highly polished coffee table.

'After that I'll take it from there,' he added with a shrug of his shoulders.

With this he walked into the bathroom to get a hot shower and a shave.

Chapter Three

It was dark as Richard Moristone drove along Beverly Road in Hull. It was the twenty first of October. It had been raining on and off all day. The overhead street lights were reflecting off the puddles of rain water that lay in the road side. A week had passed since his unfortunate encounter with Mendois. Attempts to raise the amount of cash he needed to pay off his gambling debt from his friends had failed; when it came to parting with their money, he'd discovered that he hadn't as many friends as he thought he had. He laughed to himself. The blunt truth was, he hadn't any friends. The only thing he could do, he figured, was to get in touch with Mendois and ask him to give him more time to get the money. If he refused his request he could threaten to go to the authorities and expose the casino which was operating without a licence.

'That's it, that's what I'll do. I'll threaten to expose him,' he muttered to himself, as he changed gear and slowed down to negotiate a corner. He was taking a short cut to where his flat was situated. Deep down inside himself, he knew he was playing a dangerous game. Gregory Mendois wasn't a man to be trifled with.

On arrival back at his flat he lit a cigarette and poured himself a double scotch. He tossed it straight back, wincing as it stung his tonsils. A heavy frown creased his forehead, as he thought about what his next move should be; he nervously paced up and down the large lounge, drawing deeply on the cigarette in his mouth as he made up his mind. Suddenly he came to a decision. Blowing out a thick stream of smoke, he picked up the phone, and rang a number. Arnie answered it.

'Arnie,' he said, in a business-like voice. 'This is Richard Moristone. Can you tell Mr Mendois I'd like a word with him?'

He heard a muttering at the other end. A few seconds went

by as he held the receiver to his ear. The phone eventually being handed over.

'Hello,' a cold unfeeling voice said. 'This is Mendois. What do you want?'

'I'm ringing to let you know that I'm having a lot of difficulty in raising the cash that I owe you.' He paused and took a deep breath, then blurted out, 'You'll have to give me more time to get hold of it.'

'Now look here,' snapped Mendois, a note of annoyance in his voice, 'I gave you two weeks; that's ample time to raise the cash. You've got one more week to go. I expect the full amount in repayment of your debt on my desk by the twenty-eighth, seven days from now. I've already spelled out to you the consequences if you don't comply.'

Moristone chewed on his bottom lip nervously as he took in the underlying threat in Mendois's words. He had no doubt that the man would fulfil his promise. The hand that was holding the phone was shaking as he decided to take a chance.

'What if I inform the police that you are running an illegal casino?' he retorted defiantly.

There was the sound of a long indrawn breath on the other end of the phone.

'My advice to you, my friend,' snarled Mendois, 'is, if you want to stay healthy. Don't go to the police.'

The phone went dead. Moristone's heart was pounding as he stared at the receiver in his hand for a moment, before placing it back on the hook. 'Had he gone too far?' he asked himself; instantly regretting his outburst.

There was a thoughtful look on Mendois's face as he paced the length of the floor in his office. His eyes narrowed as he weighed up the consequences of what he'd just heard.

'Is it possible that Moristone would have the guts to shop me to the police?' he asked himself.

His brow furrowed as he took a long drag on the cigar in his fingers and looked up at the ceiling; then slowly exhaling, he blew a long stream of smoke into the air.

'Okay I've got connections,' he muttered, but he knew he

dare not take the chance. Stopping his pacing, he came to a decision He turned to Arnie.

'Richard Moristone is threatening to shop me to the police for running the casino, if we don't give him more time to repay his debt,' he told the big man. 'I want you to find him and let him know what will happen to him, if he does go to the police.' He stabbed at the air in front of him with his cigar for emphasis.

'I want you to get hold of Carl and take him with you.' Then as an afterthought he added, lowering the tone of his voice, 'Tell Moristone I've decided to be generous. Tell him that I'm going to give him an extra seven days to come up with the cash, but let him be in no doubt what will happen to him if he goes to the cops.'

The big man stood with his arms folded as he listened intently to his boss's instructions. He had a grim look on his face as he got the message; his eyes were cold as he nodded his shaven head in acknowledgement of his orders, then turned to leave.

'Oh by the way, Arnie,' Mendois called after him, 'shake him up a little, but don't knock him about too much.'

Arnie smiled mirthlessly as he went through the door.

The wipers were fighting a losing battle with the torrential rain that lashed against the windscreen as Moristone approached his flat. It had been almost twenty-four hours since he'd phoned Mendois. He'd heard nothing in return since. A black Ford car followed at a discreet distance behind him. The occupants of the car were two tall men; one of them was heavily built, with a bullet shaped shaven head, the passing car lights reflecting off his shining skull. The other one was lean and angular, with a mop of unruly black hair. There was a cruel expression on his thin bony face; he opened a wrapper and popped a strip of chewing gum in his mouth as he leaned forward in his seat, his long greasy hair falling over his forehead, as he tossed the wrapper through the side window and peered through the heavy rain at the car in front of them.

'Don't lose him Arnie,' snapped Carl, the lean one, his jaws working overtime, chewing away excitedly, as he saw the car ahead was just turning off the main road.

Arnie's mouth widened in a grim smile as he put his foot down and accelerated to close the distance between them and the car they were following, its rear wheels creating a cloud of spray behind it, making it difficult for the wind screen wipers to cope with.

Moristone switched the rear wipers on to clear his view of the headlights of the black car that seemed to have followed him ever since he'd passed through the busy city centre. He pulled into a parking spot outside his flat. His heart missed a beat as the black car pulled up behind him and the two big men disembarked: He looked across at them nervously. He experienced a sinking feeling in the pit of his stomach as he recognised them as the two heavies who were employed by Mendois. Quickly clambering out of his car he hurried to the outer door that led to his flat. The rain was bucketing down as the two big men approached him. A feeling of panic went through him as he recognised one of them as Arnie. He well remembered the beating he'd received at his hands in the casino.

His hands were shaking as he fumbled nervously with the bunch of keys. He had just turned the key in the lock and pushed on the door, when the two shadowy figures stepped up behind him, one on each side. They lifted him bodily through the door he'd opened. It led into the stairwell at the bottom of some concrete steps. They spun him round and slammed him with his back against the wall. Carl held a knife to his throat as he struggled to free himself. Arnie held him by his lapels, lifting him until his feet were off the ground.

'What the hell do you want?' he croaked, as a big hand squeezed his throat until he was hardly able to breathe.

'Never mind what we want. Just shut your mouth and listen carefully,' growled Carl, who was holding the knife.

'We're here to give you a warning,' he added ominously. 'You owe the syndicate ten grand...' He paused to let the message sink in before going on...

'The boss has told us to inform you that he's giving you seven extra days to pay up. If it isn't settled by the fourth of November, we've got orders to cut your heart out and feed it to the dogs.'

He lowered the knife and pressed it into Moristone's chest to emphasise his point. He winced as he felt the sharp blade penetrate his clothes.

'Okay! Okay!' he babbled hysterically, as flecks of saliva showed at the corners of his mouth. 'You don't have to get rough.'

Arnie lowered him down until his feet were back on the ground, dusted him down and stood back, a leering grin on his face.

'Oh by the way, we've got a message for you,' said Carl, spitting the gum out of his mouth as they turned to leave. Don't even think of going to the police. That is if you want to stay healthy.'

Richard Moristone shuddered at the implied threat. He stood for moment catching his breath and massaging his throat, as the two of them left him alone standing in a pool of rainwater, at the bottom of the dark stairway. A minute later he heard the sound of a car engine starting up as the two big men drove away into the darkness. He was trembling as he pulled himself together, dragged himself up the stone steps and staggered into his flat. Slamming the door shut behind him, he made his way along the hallway and into the comfortable, lounge where he poured himself a shot of whisky; he lifted it to his mouth and tossed it back. Lighting a cigarette, he flopped down in one of the two easy chairs, and took a long pull on it; he lay back and rested his throbbing head on the back of the chair, as he thought over the predicament he was in. He knew one thing for certain now, his life wouldn't be worth tuppence if he didn't pay up, and there was no going to the police. Mendois wouldn't let him off the hook. He jumped up out of the chair puffing away at his cigarette nervously. Pacing up and down the flat, he tried to think of a way to extricate himself from the dire situation he was in.

'I've only one hope now,' he told himself, as he sat back down in the chair and ran his fingers nervously through his hair, 'my grandmother. Oh I know she's told me before that she wasn't going to keep on helping me, but the old girl's always coughed up in the end.'

With the extra seven days grace Mendois had given him, he had thirteen days left to settle up. Pouring himself another drink, he sat down again and stretched out in the armchair; taking another long drag on his cigarette, he rested his chin on his chest and looked down at his muddied shoes. He was deep in thought as he raised his eyes and looked up at the decorative Artex design on the ceiling; he watched as a smoke ring drifted slowly upwards, then broke up.

'Why did I have to start gambling?' he asked himself out loud. 'It wasn't as if I'd needed the money.'

Shaking his head in exasperation, he stubbed his fag out in the ashtray and prepared himself for a shower and bed. He sighed as he went into the bedroom, undressed and went into the shower; he cast his mind back over the last few years as the soothing hot water cascaded over him.

Since his parents had been killed in a car accident when he was a boy, he'd gone through the fifty thousand pounds of insurance money that he'd received on his twenty-first birthday. He'd spent it on the high life and gambling. First it was the horses and then the casino. He'd had no luck. Then he'd lavished presents on female company for sexual favours. In no time at all the money had gone. He'd taken one last chance at the casino by betting heavily, in the hope that he would recoup some of his losses. To no avail. The result was that he now owed ten grand to Mendois, a man who, he was certain, would stop at nothing to get his money. He realised now, what kind of men he was dealing with, after the going over he'd suffered. It was a painful lesson. He knew they were not to be fooled with. He had no doubt that Mendois meant what he'd said.

Somehow he told himself as he stepped out of the shower and towelled himself vigorously, he had to find the money from somewhere. After being let down by so-called friends there was only one avenue left open for him. He would have to go and see his grandmother tomorrow morning. She lived in a farmhouse on the outskirts of Lincoln.

It was ten a.m. on a cold, late October morning as Richard Moristone climbed into his car.

'Winter's starting early this year,' he mumbled to himself as he rubbed his hands together and took a deep breath of the cold air. He turned on the ignition; after a couple of false starts the engine burst into life. A few minutes later he was driving through the morning mist as he made his way to the Humber Bridge.

The sun, shining down from a misty blue sky, was just beginning to melt away the light covering of frost as he stopped the car at the entrance to Brambles farm. Climbing out of the car, he looked out over the open countryside as he took a deep breath of the fresh morning air. Opening the wide farm gate, he drove his car up the long drive, and parked it on the gravelled forecourt. He approached the thick oak front door and lifted the large brass doorknocker; after rapping on the door and getting no answer, he walked in.

'Grandma,' he called out loudly, as he closed the door behind him and entered the spacious hallway, his voice echoing around the one hundred and fifty year old farmhouse.

A dog barked incessantly from the rear of the house.

'Out here,' a woman's voice shouted.

Following the direction from which the voice came, he went through the well equipped, old fashioned kitchen and out into the garden, where his grandma was kneeling on a piece of wooden board, a small gardening fork in her gloved hand as she pottered about among the plants. A black Labrador stood beside her wagging his tail as Richard Moristone approached. The grey haired old lady raised her head and looked up at him out of the corner of her eye as he approached.

'Hello, young Richard,' she greeted him. 'To what do I owe the pleasure of your company?'

There was a hint of sarcasm in her greeting, as she straightened up and got to her feet. She gave a groan of agony, her hands holding her back. She had a good idea what he was after. He only came to see her when he was in trouble and needed money. Over and over again she'd told him.

'This is the last time I'm going to help you out.'

'If that's what he is here for,' she told herself, 'he's wasting his time.'

'Hello, Grandma,' he said, looking down at the ground and shuffling his feet self consciously, as he tried to avoid contact with her sharp blue eyes.

She stood looking up at him, with her hands on her hips; there was a stern expression on her lined face.

'What are you here for this time?' she asked him, a sharpness in her tone of voice.

He let the remark go, getting annoyed wouldn't help. He took a deep breath.

'Well, Grandma, I was wondering if you could...' he hesitated for a moment.

'Come on, young man, spit it out,' the grey-haired old lady commanded.

He ran his fingers through his dark hair self consciously, then blurted it out.

'Er, would it be possible for you to lend me some cash?'

She raised an eyebrow and studied him for a few moments, the frown on her forehead adding to wrinkles that were already there. It was as if she was trying to see into his soul, her eyes never leaving his troubled face. She'd helped him out before. He'd come to her numerous times with the same story and she'd been a soft touch, but it had come to her notice that he'd been doing quite a bit of gambling.

'*Lend you*?' she rejoined, a touch of scorn in her voice. 'Don't you mean *give* you?' she countered sternly, her compressed lips giving the impression of a slit in her face.

'If I don't find the money within the next two weeks, I'll be in serious trouble,' he explained to her, his voice dropping in volume as he tried to influence her.

'Have you been gambling again?' she snapped, giving him a meaningful look.

He shook his head and looked her straight in the eyes, feigning an innocent look.

'How did she know I'd been gambling?' he asked himself.

She ran her tongue over her dry lips for a moment as she thought over what he'd said. She had to admit, he did look worried; maybe for once he was telling the truth.

'How much money are we talking about,' she enquired, a

softer tone to her voice.

He looked away as he again shuffled his feet uncomfortably, then he took a deep breath.

'Ten thousand pounds,' he informed her in a low voice.

'*Ten thousand pounds*?' she gasped, a look of incredulity on her face. 'Where do you think I'm going to get that amount of money from?'

He shrugged his shoulders, a defeated look on his face, as he turned his head away from her and gazed out over the fields. He breathed in sharply, then bracing himself, he turned to face her again, his eyes hardening.

'I thought you might advance me some of my inheritance,' he suggested to her brazenly.

'If you'd looked after your money instead of squandering it on gambling,' she declared, 'you wouldn't have been in this predicament in the first place.'

'I suppose that means you're not going to help me then,' he snapped arrogantly; put off by her snotty attitude.

'No I'm not!' she exclaimed, shaking her head. 'And remember. You haven't got an inheritance until I'm dead and gone.'

She got down awkwardly on her knees again, and carried on gardening, then looked up at him over her shoulder as he prepared to leave.

'The way you're conducting your life my lad, my money may finish up at the dogs' home.'

The threat got home to him. He clenched his teeth as he turned away scowling.

'The only way out he'd got, as far as she was concerned,' he figured, 'was if she dropped dead in the next two weeks. Not much chance of that,' he thought, as he watched her working away in the garden. 'She's fitter than I am.'

He stormed back through the house, slamming the doors behind him.

Kicking out savagely at a stone on the driveway in frustration, he returned to his car. Climbing in, he took out a cigarette and lit it, his hands shaking. Taking a long pull on it to steady his nerves, he sat for a couple of minutes to gather his thoughts, then with a deep sigh he turned on the ignition and started the car; there was a screech of burning tyres as he gunned the engine and drove off at speed. Seething with anger, he gripped the steering wheel tightly as he negotiated the narrow country lanes on his way towards the Humber Bridge and back to his flat in Hull.

Fear gripped him at the memory of the drubbing he'd had at the hands of Mendois's two heavies. He'd got less than two weeks to get out of the mess he was in.

'What am I going to do?' he asked himself as he stopped the car outside his flat. Short of doing a robbery, he couldn't see a way out of his predicament.

If only he could get his hands on his inheritance, his problems would be solved. Suddenly a clever plan formed in his mind. The more he thought about it the more he liked it. There was a cruel glint in his eyes as he worked out how to go about it.

The next day he placed an advertisement in the local papers. It read:

To whom it may concern.

If you are in serious trouble and need a way out, contact box no 220.

The response was encouraging. Three days after the advertisement, he received six replies. After studying them all carefully, he selected what he considered were the three most desperate ones. They were from two men and a woman. He now had to choose a venue a good distance from Hull. After much consideration, he arranged to meet them at the Bell Inn, an out of the way pub in a small village, near Spawsby in Lincolnshire. He remembered calling there for a drink a couple of times in the past.

The Bell Inn was situated just off the side of a country road about two miles from Spawsby. The detached building stood out from the dark green leaves of the trees behind it, with its white painted front lit up with coloured lights adorning the door and windows. Inside it had 'olde worlde' charm, with its oak beams and large open fire place. On its walls were hung nineteen forties wartime photographs of Lancasters, with their bomber crews posing in front of the aircraft. It was said that they used to meet there for a drink between bombing runs over enemy territory during the Second World War. Over forty years after the Second World War, the ex-service men still held the 'get together' once a year. On the opposite side of the road from the Bell Inn was an imposing church that served the residents of the village. Weddings and funerals were held in turn, giving the two congregations a chance to either celebrate or commiserate in the pub.

Half a dozen cars were parked in the parking area outside the Inn. John the landlord, a six-foot-two lean man, his bit of a beer belly showing his liking for the occasional drink, was in his late fifties. He leaned over the bar, his bald head scarred by numerous encounters with the low beams that ran across the ceiling. Poking his head out, he glanced across the room to where a couple of customers were sitting, then he turned his attention to an alcove, where four individuals sat. Each had ordered their drinks upon entering the pub. They were comprised of three men and a woman. They were sat hunched forward around a table, in the dim light that came from a small lamp on the wall, strategically placed to light up a watercolour painting of the Inn. The woman wore a pink beret and a scarf that almost covered her face, her long blonde hair falling over her shoulders. The others had their coat collars turned up, and the three men all wore caps pulled down over their eyes, giving the impression that they were attempting to hide their identities. He saw there were four different coloured envelopes in the middle of the table. One of the men was speaking in a low voice, seemingly giving out instructions to the other three that were sat around the table.

'Are you warm enough?' called out John, puffing at a fat cigar. His cockney accent betraying the fact that he'd moved up from London with his family, along with the influx of southerners, who had settled in the area. There was a smell of burning wood and tobacco smoke permeating the room. He'd just stoked the fire: all that was coming from it was billowing smoke, some of it blowing back into the lounge. The man doing the talking nodded his head and waved his hand, acknowledging that they were okay. After each of them had picked up an envelope, they finished their drinks and walked out of the door without so much as a backward glance.

John shook his head as the four cars drove off. His wife Irene looked up at him.

'What's the matter, John?' she asked inquisitively, seeing his furrowed brow.

He scratched at a spot on his chin, then told her, in a low voice, 'There was something strange about those four that have just left.'

'Which four do you mean?' she asked looking over the bar and scanning the large room.

'They've gone out now,' he told her irritably. 'There were three men and a woman. They were sat in the alcove.'

'What do you mean by *strange*?'

He shrugged his shoulders. 'It's something I can't put my finger on, Irene.' He paused for a moment, then added, 'It was just as though they were using the pub as a meeting place. They were so secretive.'

'Go on with you.' She chuckled as the doorbell tinkled and two men came in. 'You've got too much imagination.'

'I still say they didn't look right,' he retorted, running his hand over his bald head.

Then with a shrug of his shoulders, he walked along the bar to where the two customers were waiting to be served.

Chapter Four

'Which one of the women that are working here is Rose Drawell?' enquired the man that was seated at a corner table in the Hotel in Skurness, a seaside resort in Lincolnshire. The sound of soft music and the haunting voice of Frank Sinatra singing, 'My Way' coming from a juke box that stood against the wall just inside the entrance, echoed around the spacious bar room.

The man was leaning on his elbows, clasping his pint of beer in both hands, his cold eyes almost hidden by the brim of his cap, which was pulled down over his forehead. He was addressing one of the waitresses as she leaned over the table to collect the empty glasses. Marjory Bane, her blonde hair showing dark roots, placed the empties on a tray and wiped the table before turning to face him, a quizzical look in her eyes.

'The woman serving behind the bar,' she told him, nodding indicatively to the barmaid, who was in the process of pulling a pint of beer for a customer. Marjory, being the nosey type, asked, 'Why do want to know that?'

'Just curious,' he replied, somewhat inadequately; giving a slight shrug of his shoulders as he reached into his pocket and pulled out a silver cigarette case. Taking one out, he placed it between his lips, then he flicked the lighter that was attached to it and lit the cigarette. After taking a long drag, he leaned back in his chair and blew out a stream of tobacco smoke, letting her know that the conversation was over.

Marjory stood for a couple of seconds, her eyes half closed as she tried to make him out. The clothes he wore were rough and ready. What you might call a working man's outfit, yet his hands belied this. They looked soft and unused to hard work, 'Like a toff's,' she thought as she watched him out of the corner of her eye, tapping the side of his glass nervously with his finger. She turned away and carried the tray of empty glasses to the end of the bar where Bill Coltern, the landlord, took them from her. She turned and called to Rose who was giving a customer his change.

'Rose,' she called, in a restrained voice from the opposite end of the bar.

'What do you want me for?' Rose called back, a trace of annoyance in her voice as she replied. She was in the act of pouring a martini from a bottle for another customer.

'I want a word with you,' said Marjory; there was a note of urgency in her voice.

Rose, an exasperated look on her face, finished serving the man, then came down to her from the other end of the bar where another customer was still waiting to be served.

'Marjory!' she exclaimed in a low voice. 'Can't you see I'm busy?'

Marjory leaned over the bar and whispered to her secretively.

'A man has just been asking questions about you.'

'Asking about me?' she said, a questioning look in her eyes. 'Why would he be asking about me?'

'That's what *I* thought,' Marjory replied. 'He asked me to point you out.'

'Which man was it?' enquired Rose, looking across the smoke filled room.

The man in question, put his cigarette to his lips and took another deep drag before reaching across the table and stubbing it out in an ashtray. Smoke trickled down his nose as he pulled back his sleeve and looked at his watch, which showed nine-forty-five p.m. Tilting his glass, he finished off his beer and wiped the froth from his lips with the back of his hand. Placing his hands on his knees he prepared to rise from his seat. He took one last quick look out of the corner of his eye at Rose, as he turned to go towards the large glass swing doors.

'That's him,' confided Marjory, indicating with a nod of her head to the man who was sat in the far corner of the room, adding, 'The one who is just getting up to leave.'

Rose, following her gaze, got a fleeting glimpse of the man

as he turned towards the exit and sauntered out.

'He's a stranger to me,' she said with a shrug of her shoulders. 'From what little I saw of him, he doesn't seem to me to be one of the regulars.'

'No!' exclaimed Marjory, shaking her head. 'I haven't seen him before either. And what's more. I don't like the look of him.'

Rose, her brow furrowed, had a thoughtful look in her eyes, as she turned to go back to serve a customer, who had been waiting patiently to order his drink.

At that moment Bill Coltern walked towards them from the other end of the bar, hitching up his baggy trousers as if attempting to cover up his beer belly.

'What have you two been whispering about?' he asked.

'It's Rose,' replied Marjory. 'A strange man has been asking about her.'

Bill listened attentively to Marjory's vague description of the man. He scratched the stubble on his chin thoughtfully as he studied the situation, then went to have a word with Rose, who was just finishing pulling the customer's pint. He waited until she'd finished giving him his change, then leaning towards her, he whispered in a low voice, 'Rose, have you noticed anything out of the ordinary lately?'

'It just depends. What do you mean by, out of the ordinary?' she replied as she placed the money in the till.

'Well…' he exclaimed. 'Have you noticed anyone following you? Things like that.'

'No,' she told him, shaking her head. She paused for a moment as she cast her mind back. 'There is one strange thing that has happened to me. But I don't think it has anything to do with the man asking questions about me.'

Bill leaned forward to get closer, as he cocked his ear towards her.

'Go on Rose,' he urged. 'I'm listening.'

'Well,' she began, 'yesterday morning I received a letter informing me that Jimmy, my husband has taken out a large insurance on me.'

'Who was it from?' asked Marjory.

Rose's forehead creased as she plucked thoughtfully at her bottom lip.

'I don't know,' she replied. 'There was no signature on the letter.'

'Was it hand written?' queried Bill.

'No,' answered Rose with a shake of her head. 'It was typed.'

'Mmm… It probably came from an office then,' rejoined Bill, running his fingers over his bald head and rubbing the back of his neck with the palm of his hand. Then he asked her, 'What are you going to do about it?'

'Nothing,' was her sharp reply. 'I don't want to have any contact with him again.'

Bill took a deep breath and once again adjusted the belt around his paunch.

'Rose, I think you'd better wait until I'm finished tonight,' he told her, a note of concern in his voice. He knew that she always took the short cut across the park gardens. 'I'll walk you back to your lodgings.'

'It's okay, Bill, I'll be all right,' she told him after giving it a little thought. She had visions of waiting till nearly midnight for him to lock up. 'Thanks for the offer.'

Finishing at her usual time, ten-o-clock, Rose pulled on her warm coat; then, bidding them goodnight, she turned to leave, her hands pushed deep into her pockets.

'Mind how you go,' called Bill as she left, lifting her coat collar up around her neck. She nodded to him as she stepped out of the door, leaning into the biting cold east wind that was being blown in from the sea. She could just hear the music from the nearby arcades, drifting in the wind towards her, as she set off for the entrance to the park across the road.

The man who has been asking after Rose, sat waiting patiently in his car in the hotel car park, as he observed her crossing the road and entering the gates which led into the gardens. After making enquiries, he had kept his eye on her over the last two days and discovered that she usually took this route. It was a short cut to her lodging which was situated in Algar

Road. He sat for a few moments, then after jotting down a few notes in a note book, he started the engine, pushed the gear into first and drove slowly away.

The following night the man sat in his car again; this time at the rear of the park, near the exit gates, and waited, the cigarette in his mouth glowing in the dark as he took a drag on it. Rose came through the park just after ten-o-clock. He looked away quickly as she suddenly stopped and turned towards him as she walked past. He hurriedly started the car and drove off. He sensed her eyes following him, as he turned the car and drove up towards the main road. There was a thoughtful expression on her face as she carried on walking towards her digs. The next day as she was working behind the bar, she called to Bill, who was squatting down on one knee as he tapped into a new barrel of bitter.

'Yes, Rose,' he answered, a little irritably, as he raised an eyebrow and looked up at her over his shoulder. 'What do you want?'

'Do you remember the other day when we were talking about that stranger asking about me?' she confided.

Bill paused for a second as he tightened the tap in the barrel, then looked up at her again and nodded his head.

'Well,' she went on, 'I noticed a man last night, on my way back to my digs, who seemed suspicious.' She paused for a moment as she cast her mind back.

'Go on,' urged Bill impatiently.

'Well,' she explained, 'I'm not certain if it was the same man who was asking about me, it was too dark to see him properly. He was sitting in his car outside the gates on the other side of the park gardens. As soon as I came out he seemed to give me a hard look. Then he drove off.'

'Did you recognise anything at all about him?' enquired Bill Coltern, grunting with the effort as he got to his feet.

'No,' she replied, shaking her head. 'I can't remember seeing him before. Anyway I only caught a glimpse of him, and it *was* dark.'

Bill, his arms folded, paused for a moment, looking down at

his scuffed shoes, as he took in the implications of what she had just told him. He raised his eyebrows and looked her in the eyes, there was a serious expression on his face.

'Rose, I reckon you should call the police,' he advised her.

She thought about his suggestion momentarily, then came to a decision.

'If I see him or anyone else for that matter, looking at me suspiciously again, I will.'

Marjory, who had been listening to her attentively, butted in

'Rose, do you think it could be someone your husband has hired to keep an eye on you?'

'I don't know why he'd do that,' she countered, her hair falling over her eyes as she shook her head from side to side.

'Unless he's trying to catch me with another man, to give him a reason for a divorce.' She gave a wry smile. 'Not much chance of that,' she sniffed, adding. 'I'm not interested.'

She looked at her wrist watch, it was nearly ten-o-clock. 'Time to pack up,' she muttered to herself, as she turned and walked into a small closet at the back of the bar; reaching out, she took her coat off a hook.

'I'll be getting off now, Bill,' she called out, as she pulled on the coat.

'Okay, Rose,' said Bill, a worried frown on his brow, as he pulled a pint for a customer. 'Don't forget what I've told you. If you have any more trouble, let me know,' he reminded her concernedly.

She smiled her thanks. 'It's gratifying to know that someone's bothered about me,' she told herself. Then after pulling her coat collar up round her ears, she went out through the large glass doors and into the dark night.

She shuddered as a blast of cold air buffeted her as she stepped out on to the sidewalk, the strong blustery wind almost taking her off her feet as she crossed the well lit road that ran parallel with the sea front. She bent into the cold blast as she entered the park gates. The wind howled through the trees, as Rose made her way along the winding path that led through the ornamental gardens, that throughout the summer were a sight to gladden the heart. But this was the last week in October and the leaves were still falling; swirling and twisting in the cold wind. Shadows from the creaking branches of the gnarled old trees danced and swayed in the flickering light from the lamps that lined the footpath.

Rose at just five feet in height, was a small woman in her early fifties; still holding on to her looks despite the worry lines on her face. She shivered as the wind whipped up ripples on the pond to her right. Casting her mind back, she thought about the stranger that Marjory had told her had been making enquiries about her. Could it be the same man who she'd seen in the car?

'Why would he be interested in me?' she muttered under her breath.

She shook her head worryingly as she snuggled her chin into her chest, and pulled her coat collar up further around her ears. She quickened her step. Suddenly something in the darkness ahead of her, caught her eye.

'Is that the glow of a cigarette that I can see in the shadows of one of the tall trees that line the path?' she asked herself.

'Who's there?' she called timidly; squinting her brown eyes, as she stopped for a second and peered into the gloom.

Only the creaking of the tree branches as they swayed in the wind, and the rippling of the stream as it ran into the pond, could be heard in reply. A nervous smile played on her lips as she hunched her shoulders and carried on hesitantly, a shiver going down her spine. She thought about her estranged husband Jimmy. Was it possible that he could have hired someone to keep an eye on her? Maybe he was checking on her to see if she had a lover, giving him the opportunity to get the divorce he'd been demanding from her.

'Fat chance of that,' she told herself.

She'd had enough of men after her experience with him. And there was that anonymous letter she'd received, telling her that her husband had taken out insurance for a large sum on her. Her forehead wrinkled into a deep frown, as she cast her mind back to those early years of her marriage. In all the years they'd been together her husband hadn't shown any interest in life insurance. On the contrary, he'd always been against it.

'The only way we gain anything out of you people,' he'd

told the insurance agent who knocked on the door, 'is to drop dead a couple of weeks after we've signed up.' Then he slammed the door in his face. Anyone who came to the door selling insurance got an earful.

It had been almost a year since she'd left Jimmy; she'd had enough of his cruel ways. Quite a few times she'd gone to bed crying, nursing the bruises that he'd inflicted on her in one of his many drunken bouts. What a contrast he was, to the young man she'd met and fallen in love with, she told herself wistfully.

Rose had been born in Long Eaton in Nottinghamshire. Her parents had both worked at Grangers, a nearby lace factory. Dad had worked on one of the many machines; her mum had been a brass bobbin filler; so it was only natural that Rose should follow them into the firm. She worked for them until it was closed in the late fifties. It was on one of the firm's trips to Skurness that she had met Jimmy Drawell, a twenty year old, gangly, freckled-faced young man. He told her he lived at Grimsby; and that he had a job working on the trawlers as a deck hand. After their first meeting she arranged to meet him in Nottingham; then they took to meeting for weekends in Skurness. Six months later as they were walking along the sands at the seaside resort during one of their weekend visits, he asked her tentatively, 'Rose, how much do you think about me?'

She raised an eyebrow and glanced up at him out of the corner of her eye, her head inclined to one side, as she gave him a questioning look.

'I think a lot of you, Jimmy,' she replied, her shyness preventing her from admitting her strong feelings for him.

He stopped and faced her, his blue eyes intense. 'Enough to marry me?' he whispered, in a voice full of emotion.

She looked up at him, her eyes sparkling; then she threw her arms around his neck and kissed him. He had his answer. They were married three months later and took up residence in a flat in Cleethorpes. All went well until Jimmy lost his job as a deck hand, making life difficult for them.

The first few years of their marriage were hard, having to start with the bare necessities.

But on reflection, she told herself they were good. They had both wanted children, but after three years of trying it hadn't happened. Jimmy's attitude towards her slowly changed; gradually he turned on her, belittling her at every opportunity. Then he started drinking heavily at the local pub and knocking her about when he came home drunk. The love she had for him turned to hate. In one of his drunken rages he told her, 'You're useless you bloody bitch. Get out of my sight.'

One night when he was out at the pub drinking, she decided that she'd had enough; packing her belongings together, she left him. She moved to Skurness where she found a job at the Hotel on the seafront. As for him getting a divorce, 'He will just have to wait until I'm good and ready,' she told herself, as she took a deep breath of the cold night air and carried on towards the park exit.

Lighting a cigarette the man leaned on the railings that surrounded the pond in the middle of the park gardens. A myriad of coloured lights from the seafront illuminations reflected on the ripples, caused by the gusts of wind that sent red and brown leaves scudding across the water's surface like a flotilla of small boats. The occasional quacking of the ducks could be heard over the sound of the small waterfall, that babbled its way through a few rocks that had been placed at the bottom of it. He lifted the cap on his head and ran his fingers through his dark hair as he thought deeply about the deed he was about to perform. Taking a long drag on his cigarette, he let the smoke drift gently through his nostrils; then with a callous half smile, he flicked the butt onto the grass at his feet. Positioning himself behind the trunk of one of the trees at the side of the path, he lit another cigarette and waited. Ten minutes had gone by, when the woman he'd been making discreet enquiries about entered the park on the way to her lodgings. He dropped his fag on the ground, as she drew almost level with the tree that he was using as cover.

The shadowy figure stepped out in front of her, from behind the tree, his cap pulled well down over a thin face. Rose stepped back in shock at his sudden appearance. She was glued to the spot as his hand reached out as if to caress her. There was a look of horror on her face as she quickly drew her head back; the over head lights cast a reflection from the metal object in his hand. She opened her mouth to scream: all that came out was a gurgle, as she crumpled to the ground like a rag doll, blood spurting from the deep wound in her neck. The killer wiped the razor sharp knife on her skirt, with trembling hands. Standing for a moment to catch his breath, he looked down at the blood welling from the wide cut in her neck, her fingers twitching as the life drained out of her prostrate body. His stomach heaved as he quickly glanced furtively both ways along the empty footpath. He could see the glow from the bright lights on the Promenade in the distance. Tinny music could be heard coming from the arcades as he slipped silently away to where he'd parked his car at the rear of the gardens. There was very little traffic on the quiet road as he clambered into the car and slid behind the steering wheel. He sat for a few seconds to settle his churning stomach; then taking out a handkerchief, he wiped the cold sweat from his brow. He ducked his head as a car turned onto the road, its headlights lighting up the line of parked cars as it drove slowly by, searching in vain for a parking space. Sitting up again he checked the road, it was clear. His hand was shaking as he clumsily pushed the key into the ignition. The engine burst into life; engaging the gear, he gave another quick look up and down the road, then drove off.

Patrick Callaghan, a sixty-five year old, five-foot four Irishman had lived in Skurness for over twenty years. He had settled there with his wife and two children after serving twenty-five years in the R.A.F, most of it at the Air force base at Waddington in Lincolnshire, which was the main reason for him settling in the county. He burped as he finished off his sixth pint of Guinness. After wiping the froth from his mouth with the back of his hand, he stood up from the table and stretched his short legs; then, leaning with one hand on the back of his chair to steady himself, he threaded his way ungainly between the tables to one or two bawdy comments from the customers.

'Get stuffed,' he grunted back at them, a wide smile on his

face, as he staggered clumsily towards the exit door of the ex-servicemen's club.

'Goodnight, Johnny, my old pal,' said Pat in a slurred voice, as he gave the man who was sitting at the reception table near the entrance to the club a friendly slap on his back.

'Are you okay, Patrick?' asked John, his voice full of concern as he watched the short well-built stocky Irishman drunkenly swaying from side to side, as he fought the effects of the beer he'd consumed.

'Of course oi'm okay,' replied Pat in a strong Irish accent, his ruddy face creasing into a broad smile, as he pushed open the glass door, his stocky figure colliding with the doorframe as he attempted to pass through the door. John, a knowing smile on his face, shook his head, as he watched the Irishman negotiating, with some difficulty, the sloping concrete footpath outside the club. Pat made his way along the well lit road; then turned off and went through the park garden gate to take the short cut that led to his home in Lumley Avenue. He was waving his cap and in a soft voice, giving quite a good rendition of When Oirish eyes are smiling...'

With the overhead lights reflecting off the top of his shiny bald head, Patrick weaved his way along the winding path that led through the surrounding trees and bushes. Suddenly he stopped singing and came to a halt, as he tried to focus his bleary eyes on what looked like a crumpled heap of clothing on the path in front of him. Placing his cap on his head, he leaned forward, swaying from side to side, to get a closer look: It was a woman, she was lying face down. Bending down... he momentarily staggered and almost lost his balance, as he reached out a hand to her.

'Come on, my darlin,' he mumbled as he bent down and took her arm. 'Let me help you.'

Gripping her by the shoulder with his other hand, he turned her over, causing her head to fall back, revealing the deep wound to her throat. A large pool of blood was spreading out under her body. The Irishman gave a sharp intake of breath, then jumped up and stepped back with shock, as the woman's eyes stared emptily back at him.

'Oh my God!' he exclaimed, a look of horror on his face.

He stood looking down at her helplessly. He'd seen a few dead men during the Second World War in his early days in the forces, but nothing prepared him for this.

'What can I do to help her?' he asked himself.

His befuddled mind told him he had to do something. He reached out with his right hand and checked her pulse, there was no beat; even to someone with his limited knowledge, it was obvious that she was dead. Turning away from the gruesome scene, he ran back along the winding path through the gardens and back out on to the main thoroughfare, swaying from side to side. Climbing the sloping path leading to the club, he burst through the door.

'Quick, John,' he gasped breathlessly as he leaned on the reception table for support. 'Call an ambulance and the police. There's a w-w-woman, sh-she's been attacked...' He could hardly get the words out as he pointed excitedly out of the door.

'Steady on, Pat, steady on,' countered John soberly, as he got to his feet and placed a hand on the stocky little Irishman's shoulder in an attempt to calm him down.

'You're telling me that a woman has been hurt.'

Pat nodded his head vigorously.

'First of all!' exclaimed John, 'where is she?'

Pat took a deep breath, and steadied himself, then went on. 'She's laying on the path in the park gardens, and I think she's dead.'

John a tall gangly grey haired man, looked down at him in disbelief.

'Dead?' he queried.

'Yes, don't just stand there man, get on the phone quick!' Pat exclaimed in his Irish brogue, a note of urgency in his voice.

John, realising Callaghan was deadly serious, left his seat at the entrance and went behind the bar: picking up the phone, he rang up and informed the necessary emergencies. After putting the phone down he turned back to Callaghan.

'The police have told me to tell you not to go away, they'll almost certainly want to interview you when they arrive,' he told him.

'I'll go back to the park and wait until they get there,' replied the, by now a more sober Irishman, as he turned to go back out of the club door.

Chapter Five

Detective Inspector Robert Laxton had just settled down to watch the news on television, with a tot of Southern Comfort and a dash of soda water in his hand when the phone rang. Horatio his cat, who was stretched out on his lap washing himself, was unceremoniously dumped on the floor, as Laxton reached out and picked it up; it was Chief Inspector Wilberton from head office Lincoln.

'Robert, can you get down to the park gardens in Skurness? There's been a homicide,' he said; there was a note of urgency in his voice. 'I'll see you down there.'

'Right,' replied the Inspector, nodding at the phone. 'I'll get down there straight away.'

He glanced at his watch as he jumped to his feet. It was ten forty-five p.m. Switching off his telly, he pulled on his coat and went out to his car. A few seconds later he was guiding it out of his driveway and onto the lane, his headlights lighting up the ruins of Old Bolingbroke Castle as he drove off in the direction of Skurness.

The body was blanked off from public view and the park gates were manned by policemen to prevent the public from wandering through the gardens. The perimeter of the area was taped off as Detective Inspector Laxton arrived at the scene of the crime. Forensics, dressed in white coveralls and equipped with strong lamps, were conducting a thorough investigation. He approached Bernard Howsell, head of forensics, who was supervising the search for clues among the brown and red autumn leaves that were scattered by the wind, on and around the body of the dead woman.

'What have we got then, Bernard? he said grunting, rubbing his cold hands together vigorously in an attempt to bring some warmth into them.

Howsell, a lean wiry man, had a grim expression on his thin face as he looked up at the Inspector through thick rimmed glasses.

'Female, around fifty-five.' He shrugged his shoulders. 'Give or take. Jugular severed by a sharp instrument judging by the neat cut, causing massive loss of blood...'

At that point Laxton butted in. 'How long do you estimate she's been dead?'

Howsell rubbed his chin with the palm of his hand for a few seconds as he thought over what the Inspector had asked him.

'About an hour at the most, I would say,' he replied hesitantly.

Robert Laxton shivered as he buried his chin deep into the upturned collar of his duffle coat; his thick iron-grey hair protecting his head from the cold night air, his grey eyes half closed against the strong wind. Skurness wasn't the warmest place during late autumn. The east wind blowing in from the sea was bitter, and the surrounding grass was beginning to take on a white coat of frost. The scene of the crime seemed surreal under the flickering overhead lights, as he looked down at the small figure of the dead woman, looking pathetically like a doll, broken and cast aside by some petulant child. D. C. Jane Bullyn, a notebook in her hand, approached Laxton. A short stocky man was walking beside her.

'This is Mr Patrick Callaghan, sir,' she told him. 'He found the body and reported it.'

The Inspector turned his attention to Callaghan, who had been waiting patiently to be interviewed. The Inspector could see, by the way he swayed from side to side, that the short, stockily built Irishman had consumed quite a few drinks. He told Bullyn to take notes.

'Now let me see,' she muttered, pen in hand. 'Today is the twenty seventh of October.'

Laxton nodded, then turned to Callaghan. 'What can you tell us?' he asked.

'Well sor,' he said, looking up at the tall detective. 'I was on my way home when I just found her lying on the path. I tried to help her, but she was dead.'

'Did you see anyone else in the vicinity?' asked the Inspector, knowing full well that the stocky Irishman would have difficulty seeing anything in the state he was in.

The little man shrugged his shoulders, and shook his head.

'No, sor, as far as I could see, I was the only one in the park at the time.'

'Have you ever set eyes on this woman before?' enquired the Inspector, smiling to himself at the Irishman's slurred reply.

Callaghan swayed dangerously and almost overbalanced as he leaned over the body and peered at her face; then straightening up, he took his cap off and scratched the back of his head for a few moments. Suddenly his round face lit up.

'I've got it, sor!' he exclaimed triumphantly. 'She's the woman that works behind the bar at the Hotel, across the road. I've seen her there now and again. But I'm sorry,' he mumbled apologetically, shaking his head, 'I'm afraid I don't know her name.'

Laxton grunted his thanks, telling the little Irishman to leave an address where they could get in touch with him, in case they needed to speak to him at a later date. The stocky man nodded to the Inspector and touched the peak of his cap, then turned and went on his way along the path to the park exit. There was a humorous glint in Laxton's eye, as he watched the short Irishman striving valiantly to walk in a straight line.

'What have we got here then, Robert?' a voice enquired.

The Inspector turned round. It was his superior, Chief Inspector Wilberton.

He'd been on his way home from his bridge club, when he got the call over the radio that a woman's body had been discovered. His hands were deep in his overcoat pockets as he walked over to where Laxton was standing over the body of the woman.

The Inspector gave the Chief a brief outline of what had transpired so far.

Wilberton kept nodding his head as he listened intently to what the Inspector had to say.

D. C. Bullyn, who had joined in the search for clues, called out from behind the trunk of one of the large trees.

'There are some footprints here, sir, and a couple of cigarette ends,' she announced, sticking her head out from behind the tree.

The Chief, followed closely by Laxton, walked over to the spot that she was indicating.

'Well done, Constable!' Wilberton exclaimed, bending down and carefully examining the footprints that showed clearly in the soft ground. 'Size eight I would say.' Then he turned to the Inspector. What do you think?'

Laxton, who had bent down and picked up one of the cigarette ends that lay among the leaves with a pair of tweezers and held it up in front of his eyes, was deep in thought as he looked down at the Chief out of the corner of his eye. 'I think they're Lucky Strikes.'

'Lucky Strikes? Have you gone completely barmy, man?' snapped Wilberton, a look of annoyance on his face. 'I asked you about the footprints.'

'Oh err, yes I agree,' rejoined the Inspector. 'I was just saying, these cigarettes are Lucky Strikes, an American brand,' he announced, holding out one of the butts held in the tweezers to give the Chief a closer look.

Wilberton eyed the aforementioned evidence, then looked up at the six-foot-three man and shook his head despairingly as he turned away.

'Stay with it, Laxton, stay with it,' he remarked acidly, adding, 'Take Constable Bullyn with you and keep me informed.' Then after having a word with the head of forensics, he left the scene of the crime.

Unperturbed, Laxton continued with his inquiries. He was used to the Chief's tirades. D.C. Jane Bullyn, a twenty-five-year-old, attractive hazel-eyed brunette, was around five-foot-six tall. She had a ready smile, which she tried out on Laxton, with little response.

'Right, Constable, we'll visit the Seaside Hotel next and see what we can find out there,' he asserted, somewhat authoritatively, as he sunk his chin deeper into his collar.

Bullyn followed close behind the Inspector, as they set off along the winding path through the park gardens, towards the

Seaside Hotel, which was situated on the sea front directly across the road from the park gates. The manager, Bill Coltern, was in the process of locking up as the two detectives arrived. They identified themselves and he invited them inside the hotel with the comment, 'Before we bloody freeze to death.'

Laxton, after establishing that the murdered woman's name was Rose Drawell, went on to ask him one or two questions about the dead woman. Bullyn, a pen and paper in her gloved hands, took notes.

'What's this all about then?' Bill Coltern asked, raising his eyebrows questioningly. He was visibly shocked when the Inspector explained to him what had happened, shaking his head in disbelief at the thought that the little woman who had just left the Seaside Hotel, was dead.

'I should have gone with her,' he muttered feelingly shaking his head from side to side as he looked down at the floor. 'She told me she was worried. I should have taken her more seriously.'

'You weren't to know what was going to happen to her,' Constable Bullyn told him consolingly.

After ascertaining the address of the murdered woman, the Inspector questioned him in an attempt to throw some light on the murder.

'Did you see anything happen which you considered a threat to her, before tonight?'

Bill scratched his stubbly chin as he thought carefully. Laxton screwed up one of his eyes imperceptibly at the irritating, rasping noise.

'There was some mention by one of the waitresses, of a stranger asking one or two questions about her,' he volunteered.

'When would that be?' queried the Inspector.

Coltern paused, squinting with his right eye as he thought back.

'I would say it was three nights ago.' he rejoined.

'What kind of questions was he asking?' queried Bullyn.

Coltern, a deep frown on his forehead, shook his head slowly from side to side.

'You'd best have a word with Marjory,' he advised, nodding

his head towards one of the staff before going on to tell her…

'She and Rose were good friends, and she was the one that told Rose that someone had been asking questions about her.'

Laxton approached Marjory Banes as she was putting her coat on preparing to leave. She was a tall, gaunt forty-five-year-old; her long, bleached, blonde hair was tied in a bun at the back of her head, the mousy brown roots clearly showing. She was almost inconsolable when he explained to her what had happened to her friend; tears rolled down her thin, high cheek-boned face. Dabbing her eyes, she took a deep breath and prepared herself to answer the Inspector's questions.

'Did you notice anyone acting in a suspicious manner?' he asked her, in a comforting tone of voice.

'There was one man. He asked me to point out Rose,' she told him tearfully.

'When did this happen?' asked D.C. Bullyn, as she took down notes.

'Let me see now,' Marjory murmured, half closing her eyes and plucking at her bottom lip, as she cast her mind back. 'It would be two nights ago. Rose did say that she saw a man who seemed as though he was watching her as she was on her way back to her lodgings.'

When she was asked to describe the man, she could only give a vague description.

'I would say he was about five-foot-nine or ten, of slim build, and had brown hair.' She stopped to blow her nose; after dabbing it with her handkerchief, she carried on, her voice quavering with emotion. 'I couldn't see the colour of his eyes, he wore a flat cap pulled well down over his face, as if he were covering it up.'

'Have you seen him here before?' queried Bullyn.

'No, he was a complete stranger,' the distraught woman mumbled through her handkerchief. She paused for a moment to gather herself, then went on…

'I did tell her that I didn't like the look of him. Bill offered to take her home.'

'What did she say to that?' continued Bullyn, still probing.

Marjory brushed back a tendril of hair that had fallen over

her eyes; then shrugged her shoulders with a sigh.

'She declined the offer, saying she would be okay,' she murmured tearfully.

'Did Rose say that she knew the man?' persisted Bullyn.

'Well,' replied Marjory, 'although she didn't really get a good look at him, she did say that he was a complete stranger to her.'

The Inspector thanked them for their help, telling them that he may want to question them at a later date; then, accompanied by Bullyn, he walked out of the hotel into the cold night air. Giving a shudder, he pulled his coat collar up round his ears and pushed his hands deep into his pockets; glancing at the tower clock, he saw that it was eleven-thirty. Taking a deep breath of the freezing air, he looked up at the myriad of stars in the clear night sky, then turned to D.C. Bullyn.

'That will do for tonight Constable,' he said wearily as he was about to go to his car. Then he stopped, turned towards her and asked her, 'Would you like a lift home?'

'Yes please,' she replied, nodding her head.

His face broke into a smile, as he opened the passenger door.

'Jump in,' he told her.

They climbed into his car. Leaning back in the car seat; he took a deep breath, then exhaled slowly, as he relaxed before starting the car and driving off.

The stars were twinkling in a clear sky, but there was no moon to light the way, as they drove the five or so miles to where Bullyn lived with her mother, the cars headlights reflecting off the tarmac as he drove carefully along the icy deserted road. As he was dropping Jane Bullyn off at her home in Burgh, a village just outside Skurness, he asked her if she had a car.

'Well,' she replied, 'actually it's Mum's car. If she isn't going out anywhere, then I use it. If she goes to Lincoln, she drops me off at the police station, then goes off shopping.'

He leaned towards her across the passenger seat as she opened the car door in readiness to climb out.

'I'll tell you what,' he paused for a moment as she turned to listen, then went on, 'it isn't all that much out of my way. I'll pick you up in the morning and give you a lift.'

'Thank you. That would be a great help,' she told him, a wide smile on her face as she accepted his offer.

Then with a wave of his hand, and a, 'See you tomorrow,' he continued his journey home.

Standing at the gate for a few seconds, she followed the car with her eyes until its rear lights disappeared into the darkness.

'He's a strange man,' she told herself. 'One minute it seems as though he doesn't like me, the next minute he's offering to give me a lift to the station.'

She shrugged her shoulders as she opened the front door. Her mother Nancy, who was busy filling the electric kettle with water, noticed the frown on her daughter's forehead, as she walked into the well lit modern kitchen.

'You're quiet tonight, Jane,' she hinted as she switched the kettle on. 'Is something troubling you?'

'Yes, Mum,' she muttered in a low voice, almost as if she were talking to herself. 'I've just been offered a lift by the Inspector.'

'That was good of him,' rejoined Nancy, spooning the tea into the pot as she turned to look at her daughter. 'What's wrong with that?'

'Nothing, Mum,' she replied as she took off her warm coat. After hanging it on a hook in the hallway, she pulled a chair up to the kitchen table and sat down, adding, 'It's just that he gave me the impression that he didn't take kindly to my company. In fact I've been on the verge of asking to be given another duty.'

'I don't think you should go that far, Jane,' Nancy advised her.

She paused for a moment as she poured out two cups of tea.

'He's probably a confirmed bachelor, they're usually a bit stand offish when it comes to dealing with women. He's obviously a man's man,' she commented as she raised the cup to her lips and took a sip of her tea.

'I would have a word with him if I were you, if of course, he doesn't change his attitude towards you,' her mum advised her.

'Anyway,' she added, after pausing for a second to take a sip of her tea. 'What was the trouble tonight?'

Jane didn't answer straight away, as she thought over whether she should tell her mother of the tragic event in the park in Skurness. She looked across the table at her, a serious expression on her face. After a couple of seconds she came to a decision.

'A woman was murdered in the park in Skurness,' she told her sombrely.

There was a sharp intake of breath from Nancy.

'Poor woman,' she said feelingly. 'Do they know who did it?'

'No,' replied Jane with a shake of her head. 'But we do have one or two small clues.'

It was midnight when Robert Laxton arrived at his cottage in Old Bolingbroke, a quiet little village around fifteen miles from Skurness; entering the lounge, he switched on his record player. The strains of The Blue Danube drifted around the cottage, as he ate his way through a plate full of sandwiches that his housekeeper Annie had made up for him earlier in the day. After washing the sandwiches down with a mug of coffee laced with brandy, he leaned back in his easy chair. Horatio his cat, leapt on to his lap and snuggled down purring contentedly. Robert Laxton, a half smile on his face, stroked him affectionately, then closed his eyes and relaxed as he listened to the haunting music of Johann Strauss. After half an hour or so, he got up and placed the cat in his basket, had a hot shower and went to his bed, where he flopped down and instantly fell fast asleep. It was one a.m.

He was awakened the next morning by the sound of the postman delivering letters. They hit the floor with a resounding thump. He clambered out of bed and yawned loudly as he stretched his arms out wide; then he took ten deep breaths, filling his lungs each time and breathing out slowly, as he looked out of the window at the morning mist that hung over the Bolingbroke Castle ruins. Scratching his head, he staggered sleepily down the stairs and into the hallway, Horatio almost tripping him up as he pushed against his ankles, purring. He picked up the usual pile of junk mail, skimmed through them quickly, then unceremoniously dropped them straight in the waste paper basket unopened.

After having a wash and a shave, he dressed and made himself a bowl full of cereal. This was followed by a coffee and a couple of slices of toast. He looked through the mirror and ran a comb through his wiry hair. Giving a nod of satisfaction he put the comb away. He was feeling better already. He looked down at the black and white cat, fussing around him and meowing loudly.

'Okay, Horatio.' He laughed as he went to the fridge and took out a carton of milk and a tin of pilchards, Horatio's favourite. 'I've got the message.'

The cat followed him, purring his appreciation.

He filled a saucer with milk, and placed it on the kitchen floor together with the plate of fish with Horatio pushing his hand out of the way to get at the fish.

'All right! All right!' he exclaimed laughingly, before turning to go out of the door and making his way to the garage. Annie, his cleaner, cook and general dogsbody, was just arriving on her bike, as he manoeuvred his car out of the driveway. He chuckled to himself when he saw the wide smile on her round face as he waved his hand and blew her a kiss. A few minutes later he was setting off in his car and driving through the winding country lanes on his way to Burgh to pick up D.C. Bullyn. The sun was just appearing over the horizon and was beginning to show through the cold morning mist, which was clearing as he drove through the hilly countryside of the Wolds, to Burgh. Pulling up outside the neat bungalow, he tooted the horn to let Jane Bullyn know that he'd arrived; much to the annoyance of an elderly man who was walking by. A few seconds later she came running down the garden path, a big smile on her face as she wished him…

'Good morning, sir,' as she climbed in the car

He nodded his head and smiled back, telling her as she fastened her seat belt, 'You can drop the sir.'

Her face reddened slightly at his unexpected familiarity as he put the car into gear and drove off.

Chapter Six

Three quarters of an hour later the Inspector and Constable Bullyn arrived at headquarters; Sergeant Bellows, a bluff heavily built man, was at the incident desk as they walked through the door.

'The Chief wants a word with you,' he told Laxton.

Nodding his acknowledgement, the Inspector, accompanied by D.C. Bullyn, walked through to where Wilberton was waiting for them in his office. Bullyn waited outside the open door as Laxton entered the office and pulled up a chair, leaning his elbow on the desk as they went through the evidence together. The Chief leaned back in his chair, his hands clasped in front of him; his brow was creased as he addressed the Inspector.

'You don't seem to have a very good description of the man who was asking questions about the dead woman in the Hotel!' he exclaimed disappointedly, as the chair balanced precariously on its back legs.

'I'll be making more enquiries today,' replied Laxton testily, in reply to the Chief's comments.

'Robert, I'm putting you in charge of this case,' Wilberton told the Inspector, ignoring the sharp response to his comments. 'Drop everything else. I want you to find what and who is behind this murder, I'm assigning D C. Bullyn to work with you.'

'Do you have to?' asked Laxton, in a low voice, the expression on his face showing his discomfort. 'I'd much prefer to work on my own.'

'Maybe the Inspector doesn't like the opposite sex, sir,' a sharp female voice snapped.

Laxton looked over his shoulder on hearing Jane Bullyn's comments as she entered the office. He coughed into his hand in an attempt to hide his embarrassment.

'That will do, Constable. I don't want any friction between you two, I'm sure the Inspector didn't intend to demean you,' Wilberton told her, waving his hand soothingly, as he attempted to calm her.

Jane Bullyn had just been transferred to the plainclothes branch of the Lincolnshire police force, after spending four years in uniform. She could sense that the Inspector wasn't keen on the idea of her being his partner. Her mum had got it right when she said he was a man's man. Maybe he really didn't like women around him.

'Well,' she told herself, 'he can bloody well lump it.'

She'd had her orders and that was that. Born in Derbyshire, she'd moved to Lincolnshire with her parents when her father had been transferred from the Derbyshire Constabulary. He had been a member of the police force until he'd been taken ill with a massive stroke three years ago. A lump formed in her throat, as she pictured the proud man made so helpless by the dreadful affliction. Within six months he was gone out of their lives forever. Her mother had never got over the loss of her husband. She could often be heard to say, every time something untoward happened,

'If only your dad were here now.'

She sighed as she pulled herself together, discreetly half closing her eyes as she swallowed hard. She didn't want the Inspector to think she was soft. Laxton turned and strode purposefully out of the office, his long legs eating up the ground. Bullyn had to break into a run to keep up with him. After climbing into his car, he leaned over, and pushed the car door open for his new partner, then waited until she'd settled down. He sat for a minute without uttering a word. Finally he turned to her, there was a serious expression on his face.

'I'm sorry if I offended you Constable, it wasn't intentional. It's just that I like to work alone, and I'm certain you won't enjoy my company.'

He paused for a moment, then added bluntly, 'The truth is, I'm not too keen on having women around me for any length of time.'

She looked down, gazing at her shaped finger nails, for a few seconds, as if checking them to see if they were clean. Then she arched her eyebrows and looked up at him.

'Inspector Laxton, I've been assigned to work with you, not marry you,' she replied softly, looking him straight in the eyes. 'Just tell me what to do and I'll do it,' adding as an afterthought, 'Anyway you're too old for me.'

Laxton returned her look for a few seconds, his grey eyes unfathomable. Then suddenly the frown that creased his brow disappeared; his face softened as his lips curled into a cheeky lopsided grin. He switched on the ignition, and the engine burst into life.

'Okay, partner,' he grunted, in acceptance of the situation. 'Let's go!'

With this he put the car into gear, then, putting his foot down on the accelerator, he pulled out on to the road to join the traffic.

An hour later he stopped the car and they climbed out. They approached the guest house in Algar Road Skurness, where Rose Drawell had lodged. The name on the door, 'Seldom In' caused them some amusement. As D.C. Bullyn rang the bell, a dog barked in the background as a plump woman in her late fifties answered the door. The two detectives introduced themselves and showed her their identities. The woman nodded her head and told them her name was Mrs Janner.

'Mrs Janner, I'm making inquiries about the murder of Rose Drawell. I believe she was one of your lodgers?" said the Inspector, trying to make himself heard above the incessant yapping of the Jack Russell terrier at her feet, which Nellie Janner was struggling to hold back by its collar.

'Yes she was. Won't you come in?' she said, standing back from the doorway. 'Stop it, Lady,' she snapped at the terrier in a sharp voice. The dog, cringing at her stern order, was reduced to muted growls.

'Who is it, Nell?' a man's gruff voice called from the kitchen.

'It's the police, they're making enquiries about Rosie,' she shouted back to him.

'That's my husband, Ron,' she said, over her shoulder, as she led them along the hallway. 'Nosey old sod, he doesn't like to miss anything.'

Laxton smiled inwardly at her comments.

The curlers in the woman's greying hair bounced up and down as she shuffled along in front of them: the two detectives exchanged glances as they followed her into the large comfortable lounge. The dog spread herself out on the well worn carpet, having grudgingly allowed them in. She cocked one wary eye up at Laxton. There was a strong smell of stale cigarette smoke pervading the air as he sat down on the settee, his knees jutting above the coffee table in front of him. Bullyn sat beside him. A couple of dirty mugs were on the table by the side of a cracked glass ashtray half full of cigarette stubs. They declined the offer of a cup of tea, as Mrs Janner positioned herself opposite them, her frock riding above her knees, exposing the elastic round her silk stocking tops and about three inches of blotchy white skin.

Ron walked into the lounge, one hand in his trouser pocket, pulling down on his braces, a chipped mug of tea in the other. He gave them a curt nod as he clumsily lowered himself down into an easy chair. After giving the back of his sparsely covered head a good scratch, and adjusting his crotch, he reached out for his morning paper and put on his glasses, ignoring them as he took a noisy sip of his tea. His wife gave him a hard look as the Inspector started the questioning. The dog gave a low growl and cocked an ear at the sound of his voice, then moved strategically into a corner of the room, as Ron took a swipe at her with the rolled up newspaper.

'Mrs Janner, can you give us any information about Rose Drawell, which could help us to apprehend her killer?" he asked her, doing his best to ignore the distraction.

She raised an eyebrow, giving him a questioning look.

'What I mean is,' explained the Inspector, after waiting for a moment and seeing that she didn't quite grasp what he meant, 'do you know if she had any men friends?'

The grey haired woman crinkled her eyes as she gave his

question a few seconds thought, lightly tapping her pursed lips with her forefinger as she did so. Then spoke up.

'Well, she was married you know,' she began, pausing for a few seconds as Constable Bullyn took notes, then carrying on.

'Rose has lived on her own ever since she separated from her husband. She told me he'd tried to get a divorce, but she wouldn't give him any satisfaction.'

'Why was that?' asked Laxton.

'Well, she couldn't stand the sight of him,' she declared with a shrug of her shoulders.

'As for men friends. I must say, I haven't seen her with anyone. She never showed any interest. She always told me she wouldn't touch another man with a barge pole.'

'Do you know why she left her husband?' asked Bullyn, a pen hovering over the note book in her hand.

The landlady, a well-endowed woman, leaned forward, lowering her voice secretively, her breasts jutting out. Laxton, averting his eyes from the large cleavage confronting him, exchanged glances with his companion.

'Jimmy was a swine to her, and he liked his drink,' she answered in a low voice, placing her finger and thumb to her mouth and tipping her head back, then she told them...

'She did say that he often came home at night blind drunk, and er, forced himself on her.'

She pulled her face in distaste at the thought.

'He often knocked her about,' declared her husband Ron, from across the room, adding, 'When she first came here she was covered in bruises.'

'Did he ever threaten her while she was staying here?' queried Bullyn.

Ron Janner, paused for a moment, his round glasses balanced precariously on the tip of his nose as he tipped his head back and finished off his tea noisily. Placing the empty mug on the top of the tiled fireplace, he wiped his mouth with the back of his hand.

'He didn't have to, did he?' he rejoined, his hand muffling his words. 'The beatings she'd already had were enough.'

Laxton just kept nodding imperceptibly as Bullyn wrote

down the details. After half an hour he knew almost everything he wanted to know about James Drawell, including his address in Hanton Avenue, Grimsby.

'Before we leave you Mrs Janner,' he said. 'If it's not too inconvenient. Could you show us Rose Drawell's room, I'd like to have a look round it.'

'That's no problem,' she replied, getting up from her chair. 'Follow me.'

The Jack Russell growled as Laxton's big feet passed close to her.

The landlady led the way upstairs to a self-contained room. Opening the door, she let them in and left them alone. Laxton cast an experienced eye around him, as he wandered around the room, noticing the tidiness and comfort that only a woman can provide. The lodgings were a bit basic, he thought. A single bed stood in the corner. An en suite toilet and shower room completed the amenities. He opened the top drawer of the one unit provided, and rifled through a few papers.

'Nothing much in here,' he grunted, an exasperated expression on his face as he replaced them back in the drawer.

Reaching down, he opened the second drawer. It was empty except for a folded up sheet of paper with writing on it. He took it out.

'Mmm, this is interesting,' he muttered in a low voice, as he unfolded the paper.

It was a typed letter addressed to Mrs Rose Drawell. The letter contained a warning for her to be careful, as her husband had taken out an insurance policy on her, for one hundred thousand pounds. There was no signature on the letter. He searched in vain through the drawer, as he tried to find the envelope so that he could check the post mark.

'Have you found something?' asked Bullyn, as she saw him studiously reading.

'Yes this letter!' he exclaimed, a thoughtful expression on his face as he handed it to her.

'What does it mean?' she queried, after reading it carefully, adding…

'Do you think that someone may be warning her that she

may be in some sort of danger.'

'I don't know for sure,' answered, Laxton, shaking his head. 'But it does look as though, James Drawell, her husband, could have a motive.'

'I don't think that amount of money would be enough to make him kill her or even want her out of the way,' she told him, with a shake of her head.

He was quiet for a few seconds, as he chewed on his bottom lip, then went on…

'Stranger things have happened. Anyway, I think we'll pay him a visit.'

'Did you find anything?' asked Mrs Janner as they descended the stairs.

'Mrs Janner,' rejoined the Inspector, pausing for a moment as he attempted to formulate an answer that didn't give too much away…

'Let's just say it was helpful.'

After thanking the couple for their co-operation, the two officers left.

'Well, Jane!' exclaimed Laxton to his partner as they climbed into the car. 'We may have something to go on.'

'Do you think the letter is significant?' queried Bullyn. 'After all it isn't unknown for husbands or wives for that matter, to take out insurance on their spouse.'

Laxton thought for a moment as he turned on the ignition and started the engine.

'I agree,' he grunted. 'But it does seem a little unusual to take an insurance out *after* they've split up.'

Putting the car into gear, he accelerated and set off on the journey to Grimsby.

Chapter Seven

Heavy clouds were gathering overhead, as the two detectives approached Grimsby, which was roughly a forty-mile journey from Skurness. A rumble of thunder could be heard in the distance as Laxton changed gear and negotiated a roundabout on the outskirts of the town. It was some time since he'd had the dubious pleasure of visiting the area. He sniffed the air and was pleasantly surprised at the changes there'd been. There was a time when you could smell when you were nearing Grimsby Docks. A natural smell if you take into account that it was one of the main fishing ports in the country. They drew up outside a smart semi-detached house in Hanton Avenue; climbing out of the car they opened the wrought iron gate and walked up the crazy-paved foot path. Bullyn rang the doorbell, there was no answer; she rang it again. A lean angular man came from around the side of the house dressed in overalls and carrying a trowel in his right hand. His jaw was stuck out belligerently as he approached them.

'Yes,' he remarked somewhat sharply. 'What do you want?' It was obvious by the expression on his face that he wasn't very pleased at being interrupted.

'Mr James Drawell?' Laxton asked the man.

'Yes,' he replied, a questioning frown creasing his forehead. 'How can I help you?'

After showing him their credentials, they were asked to follow him to the rear of the house, to where he had been building a low wall around the garden. Throwing the trowel into a bucket of water, he pulled off the garden gloves he was wearing and ran his fingers through his receding hairline as he sat down on an old wooden garden seat and kicked his Wellington boots off, replaced them with his slippers, then invited them into the kitchen.

Turning his attention to the tall Detective and his partner, he asked them…

'What is it you want?' albeit, in a more approachable tone of voice.

Laxton decided to leave it to Bullyn to break the news to him of his wife's death. He turned and gave a nod towards her.

'Would you like to sit down, Mr Drawell, I'm afraid we have some bad news for you.'

She paused for a moment as she waited for him to take a seat, then told him, a note of solemnity in her voice.

'Mr Drawell,' she hesitated for a second, then went on, 'I'm afraid your wife is dead.'

His face blanched visibly as he took a deep breath and let it out slowly. He was obviously shocked as he reached out for a packet of cigarettes and a lighter, that were on the kitchen table. He took one out and placed it between his lips, then offered the two officers one. They declined his offer with a shake of their heads. His hand shook as he flicked the lighter with his thumb and lit up, then he took a deep drag to steady his nerves. The two detectives watched as he let the cigarette smoke drifted slowly out of his nostrils.

James Drawell, a thin raw-boned man around five-foot-ten, with a slight stoop, and sporting the large plaster on his forehead, didn't look too well. He had a frown on his forehead, and his watery blue eyes seemed troubled. Since his wife Rose had left him a year earlier, he'd lived alone. He was born in Lincolnshire, in Algarkirk, a village situated about fifteen miles from Boston. He wasn't very intelligent, having missed out on his schooling. He'd been in trouble with the police as a juvenile, just petty stuff. His headmaster had written on his school report, 'Lazy at his lessons. Showed no interest.' He moved to Grimsby in his teens and got work as a deck hand on the trawlers.

'How was she killed? Did she suffer?' he questioned nervously, a slight tremor in his voice

'She didn't say she was killed, Mr Drawell. She said she was dead. Actually she was murdered,' stated the Inspector pointedly, keeping his unblinking eyes trained on the man in front of him, waiting for some sort of response. He wasn't disappointed.

James Drawell turned away and gazed through the window, deliberately avoiding eye contact with the Inspector. He looked uncomfortable. Taking another deep drag on the cigarette, he got up out of his chair and walked over to a cabinet where he took out a decanter of whisky.

'Would you like a drink?' he asked the two police officers, as he held out the decanter.

'No thank you,' they both told him in unison, shaking their heads. He poured himself a large whisky and tossed it straight back, screwing his eyes up as the amber liquid went down his throat. Something was clearly troubling him.

'Where were you last night, between ten and ten-thirty?' queried Laxton, as James Drawell walked back to his chair with the decanter still in his hand. The Inspector waited patiently for an answer to his question; Jane Bullyn was taking notes. Drawell kept his head lowered as he topped up his drink. Raising the glass halfway to his lips, he paused and lifted an eyebrow as he turned his head and looked at the Inspector out of the corner of his eyes.

'Why do you want to know?' he questioned, taking a good swig of the drink.

'Okay, let's put it this way,' Laxton said bluntly, 'where were you around ten-o-clock last night?'

'I was at the hospital having treatment,' he told them as he sat down. 'I had an accident at about seven p.m. I slipped on the stairs and banged my head on the banister. I went to A and E. They kept me in overnight. You can check with the hospital, they'll verify it.' He touched the plaster on his head gingerly, telling them that the wound needed six stitches.

'If what you say is true Mr Drawell, you've got an alibi,' Laxton told him; a touch of disappointment could be detected in his voice as he turned to his partner and told her to make a note of the hospital that Drawell attended.

'What's this got to do with the death of my wife?' Drawell asked, a puzzled look on his face, as he took another swig of his drink. 'Her death has got nothing to do with me. I didn't murder her, if that's what you're insinuating.'

The Inspector ignored his protestations and pressed on with his questioning.

'Is it true that you wanted a divorce?' he put to him, still probing.

He looked Drawell straight in the eyes as he asked the question.

James Drawell dropped his chin into his chest, there was a thoughtful look on his face as he looked down and gazed into his glass. He swilled the remainder of his drink round and round for a few seconds as he mulled over the question. Then tilting his head, he tossed it back before answering.

'Yes it's true, I did ask her for a divorce, but she wouldn't give me one, damn her,' he replied acidly, as he placed the glass on the table. 'Anyway I'm asking you again, Inspector. What has her death got to do with me?'

'Well, at the moment, Mr Drawell... Nothing,' Laxton snapped. There was a touch of contempt in his voice, as he and Bullyn prepared to leave.

'By the way, it's come to our notice that you took out a life insurance on your wife?' remarked the Inspector, turning round, his hand on the door handle.

'Yes I did,' returned Drawell. 'What's wrong with that? It isn't against the law is it?'

'No it isn't against the law. It just seems a strange thing to do. Specially to someone you weren't living with and wanted to divorce,' Laxton countered, as he walked out of the door, followed by Bullyn.

'You were a bit hard on him in there weren't you?' commented Bullyn as they climbed into the car. Laxton turned to his partner as he fastened his seat belt. He had a confused expression on his face.

'That man knows more about the circumstances of his wife's death than he's telling us,' he replied. 'I can sense it.'

During the drive back home the Inspector had plenty to think about. One thing he was certain of, James Drawell had insured his wife for a considerable sum of money. Although this gave him a reason to have done the murder, his alibi proved that he could not have killed his wife; but somebody had. And it had turned out to be very convenient for James Drawell. A little too convenient thought the Inspector.

The sun was just disappearing over the tree tops, leaving everything in a misty semi-darkness, as he dropped Jane Bullyn off at her home; he switched the car's headlights on as he turned off towards Old Bolingbroke and his cottage. Except for having to brake suddenly to avoid a stoat as it shot out of the hedgerow in front of the car, the journey home was uneventful. Annie, his daily help was just leaving as he turned the car into the driveway and climbed out.

'Your dinner's in the oven, sir,' she told him, a wide smile on her face as she greeted him. 'Oh and I've fed the cat.'

'You're a darling, Annie," he said grinning, looking down at her and reaching out to give her a friendly hug.

'Get away with you,' she chuckled, as she ducked under his arm and slipped passed him, her ample breasts bouncing up and down as she quickly went to her bicycle, which was leaned against the wall of the cottage; then making her way down the path to the gate, she hopped on to the bike and rode off. Laxton smiled to himself, shaking his head, as her large rump went up and down as she pedalled along the lane and disappeared round the bend.

'What would I do without her?' he asked himself with a sigh.

Annie, a fifty-six-year-old spinster lived with her elderly mother in the village. She was what you might call, a self-employed home help. She had looked after Robert Laxton for over five years and had become very attached to him.

Chapter Eight

Robert Laxton, a fifty-two-year-old Yorkshireman whose rugged good looks often turned the ladies' heads, was a confirmed bachelor, preferring to live alone. His thick, wiry iron-grey hair and strong jaw gave him a pugnacious look. He had a military bearing and when he walked, he strode out with a purpose. When he looked people in the eye, he saw right into their soul. You couldn't fool Robert Laxton. He gave people the impression that he was hard, but they could not be more wrong. He was a compassionate man, with the occasional tear in the corner of his eye. In nineteen-thirty-nine, at the beginning of the Second World War, he and his sister Rosanne had been evacuated from Heeley in Sheffield, and sent to live at a farm in Norfolk, for the duration of the war. The farm was owned by John and May Holcorn. It had been a hard life for the two children at first; they took quite some time to settle down, but over the five years that they were there, they became used to it, often helping the farmer. For the first two years Mum and Dad kept in touch, writing to them regularly, then the letters stopped coming. Uncle John and his wife, Auntie May, as they became known to them, wouldn't tell them what the reason was. It was very upsetting for the children, who had come to the conclusion that their parents had forgotten them.

'You'll find out in due course,' was the repeated answer to their questioning.

Auntie May was very strict with them, always telling them off for the slightest thing, but Uncle John made up for her, taking them out in the fields with him whenever they weren't at the local school, which was a two mile walk along the country lanes, in a lazy little village called Pentney. He was a jolly man and always had an apple for each of them. It was the beginning of nineteen forty-four, and the war was going well for the allies.

Robert, at the age of fourteen, had grown into a strapping lad. It was at that time that they were informed that they had lost both their parents during the Sheffield blitz just over two years earlier. A direct hit by a land mine had reduced the row of four terraced houses in which they lived, to a pile of rubble, killing them both instantly. The war was drawing to its close, when they were told that they would soon to be leaving the farm; they were to be sent to live with their Aunt Lizzie. May broke down in tears, as the time drew near for them to return back home.

'I don't want them to leave us,' she sobbed when she heard the news that they were to go back to Sheffield to live.

'We've got no choice, luv,' asserted John. 'They have to go to their nearest relatives.'

They did attempt to adopt them, but to no avail. John had got it right. They were told the children would be going to live with their Aunt after the war.

In nineteen-forty-five Aunt Lizzie took the two children under her care. He was fifteen years old. Rosanne was two years older. At the age of eighteen he was called up to do his National Service, and went in the R.A.F. After finishing his square bashing at West Kirby near Liverpool, he chose as his trade the R.A.F police, and was posted to Halton, where he passed his police training course. Then it was on to Scampton in Lincolnshire, where he stayed until the end of his National Service. After a few months in civvy street, he found it difficult to settle and signed on for another five years with the R.A.F police, most of which he spent at Waddington in Lincolnshire After reaching the rank of Sergeant, he decided he'd had enough and was demobbed in nineteen fifty-six. From then on it was a natural progression to the Lincolnshire police force in his late twenties.

He well remembered his National Service: there was a faraway look in his eyes as he cast his mind back and dipped into the reservoir of his memories; thoughts of the girls he and his mates used to meet in the Arboretum, a park in Lincoln, went through his mind. He smiled to himself as he remembered Rita and the Bandstand. That was where he'd lost his innocence.

'Ah well,' he told himself, giving a long sigh. 'That was a

long time ago, and I haven't met a woman yet that could tie me down.'

The truth was, he wasn't the marrying kind. He had his loves, poetry, the beautiful Wolds, of which he often waxed lyrical. Horatio his cat, and his music. His favourite was Johann Strauss. After taking a shower and a meal, he stretched his long frame on the settee, and stroked Horatio, who had leapt onto his lap, then with a whisky and soda in his hand, and to the strains of Tales from the Vienna Woods in the background, he contemplated the day's events.

It was a typical November day and there was a smell of premature fireworks in the misty morning air as the Inspector picked up his partner Jane Bullyn at her home in Burgh. He smiled to himself as he saw the curtain move slightly when he tooted the car horn to let her know that he'd arrived. Jane came running to the car still fastening her warm coat.

The journey across the Wolds was uneventful as they made their way over the undulating country lanes. When they arrived back at headquarters in Lincoln, Bellows asked them if they wanted a coffee, they both said yes. The Sergeant called out to Constable Edwin Dibbling, a twenty-one-year-old new addition to the local force.

'Put the kettle on, Eddie.'

He leaned over to the two detectives and told them.

'I'll bring you a drink in later.'

Laxton gave a brief smile and nodded his thanks; then followed by his partner he went into the Chief's office.

Wilberton, who was sitting behind his desk poring over a document, raised his eyebrows as they opened the door and entered; he greeted them and pointed to a couple of seats opposite him. They walked over to the two seats and sat down. Laxton went on to tell of the day's events. Folding his arms the Chief leaned back in his chair and listened intently to the Inspector discussing his conclusions, including the letter he'd found in the murdered woman's room.

'Mmm, so you don't think James Drawell had any reason to kill his wife?' he said thoughtfully, as he made a pyramid with his fingers.

'I didn't say that he didn't have any reason to kill his wife,' countered Laxton, leaning forward and placing his hand on the desk. 'On the contrary, he had a very good reason. In fact according to the letter that we found in her drawer, he had one hundred thousand reasons. The point is that he has an alibi that proves he couldn't have done the deed.'

Wilberton held his hand up and interrupted him, handing him the typewritten letter that he had been reading as they entered the office.

'I think you'd better read that.'

The Inspector ran his eyes swiftly over the letter, which had been posted a day earlier. It was almost a replica of the letter that he'd found in Rose Drawell's flat. It was clearly meant as a warning.

The letter was unsigned, informing them of an insurance taken out on Rose Drawell by her husband, for the sum of one hundred thousand pounds, three months earlier. He lifted an eyebrow as he looked at the Chief. There was an 'I told you so' look in his grey eyes as he handed the letter back to Wilberton.

'Do you think both letters could have been written by the same person?' he queried as Constable Dibbling came in carrying a tray with three mugs of coffee on it. After placing the tray on the desk, the Chief nodded his thanks as the young Constable gave a nervous glance at the three officers, then quickly retreated back out of the office.

'It does seem to look that way, we'll have to wait and see,' said the Chief as he reached out and took one of the mugs of coffee from the tray, with the two detectives following suit.

Taking out a pair of spectacles, he carefully placed them on his nose and looked at the letter again.

'They were certainly written on the same typewriter,' he concluded, adding, 'There's a fault in the letter 'O', almost making it look like a six. Just the same as the other one, which proves the point.'

He tugged at his left ear for a moment, as he continued to study the letter, then looked up at the Inspector, who was taking a drink of coffee.

'What do *you* think?'

Laxton placed his mug back on the tray and nodded his head.

'I would say they were from the same source,' he muttered as he finished his drink and placed the empty mug back on the tray; he waited for a moment for Jane to finish hers, then, pushing the chair back, he got to his feet.

Wilberton, his glasses still on the end of his nose, leaned back in his chair and clasped his hands in front of him. He chewed on his bottom lip for a moment as he weighed up the situation. Then spoke to the tall detective.

'I'm going to leave it with you, Robert,' he declared, raising his eyebrows and looking him in the eyes over the rim of his glasses.

The Inspector took a deep breath and stretched his arms out wide, almost as if he was about to yawn, as his partner placed her empty mug on the tray and got to her feet. He breathed out slowly, then, giving a farewell nod to the Chief he turned to leave.

'I think we'll follow up on this information first, regarding the insurance that James Drawell has taken out on his wife,' declared Laxton, turning to his partner, as they left the office and walked across the small police car park to his car. He looked at his watch as Jane Bullyn quickened her step to keep up with him; it was ten a.m.

The Inspector pushed his hands deep into his coat pockets. It was a typically cold, November morning. The weak sun was just beginning to appear over the roof tops, doing its best to break through the morning mist, as the Inspector stopped the car outside the Lincoln office of Trenter and Sloe Insurance Agents and Solicitors. There was a strong smell of furniture polish mixed with cigar smoke as the two detectives entered the neat and tidy office. A very tall man was just about to take a seat behind a highly polished desk as they entered; a cigar butt was smouldering in an ashtray as Laxton introduced himself and his colleague to him. The tall man took two long strides as he walked out from behind the desk and shook hands with them. After inviting them to take a seat he went back behind his desk.

The two detectives nodded their thanks and sat down.

'And what can I do for you?' enquired the solicitor politely as the two made themselves comfortable.

'We're making inquiries into an insurance that has been taken out by James Drawell, we believe he is one of your clients.' The Inspector told him in a low voice.

The statement was directed at the six-foot-five, smartly dressed bespectacled grey-haired man, who introduced himself as a Mr Andrew Sloe. His secretary, Miss Audrey Branden, a forty-two-year-old spinster, who was working at a typewriter; raised an eyebrow as she looked over her thick horn rimmed glasses and cast a sidelong glance at the Inspector as he spoke to the solicitor, then quickly looked away, running her fingers nervously over her short brown hair self consciously as he looked down at her, his brow furrowed. There was a questioning look in his eyes.

'I don't know where you got that information from, it's supposed to be confidential,' returned Sloe, stroking his angular chin thoughtfully as he raised an eyebrow and looked at the Inspector.

Laxton leaned forward and placed his elbows on the desk.

'The fact that it's confidential doesn't really matter, now that James Drawell has admitted that he's taken it out,' replied the Inspector, conversationally.

'I'm not saying it isn't true,' replied the solicitor, raising a hand and shaking his head. 'It's just that any information regarding such matters, will have to wait until there's been an official inquiry into the death of Mrs Drawell.'

'Do you know if Rose Drawell and her estranged husband were amicable after they split up?' enquired Bullyn, chewing the end of her pencil as she looked across the desk at the thin, gaunt man. She saw that Andrew Sloe had a pronounced stoop to his shoulders.

'It was as if he were trying to give the impression that he was shorter,' she thought to herself as he replied to her question.

Sloe picked up the cigar, which by now had a good half inch of ash on it, from the ashtray, gave it a tap with his finger and placed it between his lips. Taking a deep drag he blew a stream of smoke towards the ceiling, before answering her.

'All I can say about the matter, is that Mr Drawell enquired six months ago about a divorce. We agreed to act on his behalf. Our advice to him was that it would cost him a substantial sum of money if his wife didn't agree to the divorce, as the law would come down heavily on her side,' confided the solicitor.

'What would be the reason for that?' asked Laxton, a questioning frown on his forehead as he leaned forward and looked the solicitor in the eyes, his hands clasped in front of him. D.C. Bullyn, concentrating her eyes on her writing pad that was laid on the desk, was busy taking notes.

Andrew Sloe raised his eyebrows and looked straight at the Inspector in return, his eyes looking like two large blue marbles through the thick lenses of the rimless glasses that were perched on the end of his long thin nose.

'She was very badly treated by him,' he confided in a low voice. 'She came to see us about a year ago, requesting us to act on her behalf, with a view to taking him to court for injuring her in one of his violent attacks.' The solicitor paused for a couple of seconds, deep in thought, then carried on,

'She was badly bruised about the face at the time. We told her we couldn't do anything to help her, as her husband had already engaged us. We suggested another reputable firm of solicitors.'

He rolled his cigar between his thumb and forefinger and shrugged his shoulders, adding…

'As far as I know she didn't go through with it. I'm afraid we didn't see her again.'

Thanking Mr Sloe for his help, Laxton got to his feet, then, closely followed by Bullyn, he walked out of the office. They were just about to get in the car when Miss Branden the secretary, a rather plump middle-aged woman, came out of the solicitor's office, her feet tripping quickly across the paved pathway to catch up with the two detectives as they went to the car.

'Can I have a word with you, Inspector?' she asked in a low secretive voice. Laxton stopped and turned as she approached him.

'Please do,' he said, a knowing look on his face, as he looked down at her.

She hesitated for a moment, nervously biting her bottom lip before addressing him.

'I don't know how to tell you,' she started agitatedly, her face taking on a high colour, as she looked up at him over the rims of her glasses. 'I... I...' Laxton butted in.

'It was you who wrote the two warning letters, wasn't it?' he told her kindly, as he saw the flustered state she was in.

She nodded and shuffled her feet uncomfortably, as she looked down at the floor, a guilty expression on her face.

'I felt sorry for her. I knew Rose quite well, and I knew what a nasty piece of work her husband was,' she replied, going on to tell him. 'I felt she was in danger of being hurt, so I thought I'd warn her. After I heard that she'd been killed, I sent that letter to the police.'

The Inspector thanked her for her help, telling her that she had done the right thing in informing them.

'I hope this won't cost me my job,' she remarked, a worried frown wrinkling her brow.

'Don't worry, Miss Branden, it will be our secret,' he assured her, with a gentle pat on her shoulder. Thanking him, she quickly made her way back to the office, as he walked round the car to the driver's side, opened the door and climbed in. Leaning over, he opened the passenger door to let Bullyn in, then, after starting the engine, he pulled the car out into the traffic. He glanced across at Bullyn out of the corner of his eye.

'What time is it?' he asked her.

She checked her watch. 'Quarter to twelve,' she replied. 'Why do you want to know?'

'I'm feeling hungry,' he grunted. 'I thought we might stop for a pub meal before we go back to the station.'

'Well it's a bit early for lunch,' she said, laughing. 'But I don't mind if you're paying.'

'Just like a woman.' He grinned back at her. 'Always on the make.'

He made his way to a pub he was familiar with on the outskirts of Lincoln, where he knew they could get a decent bar meal. Pulling into the pub yard, they clambered out of the car and made their way to the heavy glass door that led into the bar room. There was a strong smell of cigarette smoke as he elbowed his way up to the bar; he ordered two portions of pie and chips and two glasses of lager. A juke box on the far side of the room was blasting out a rendition of an old Jim Reeves record as he picked up the lagers and made their way to a table and sat down, a few minutes later the meal arrived. After thanking the waitress, they tucked in.

'Do you think the murder of Rose Drawell could be a random killing?' Jane Bullyn asked him, after clearing her throat with a drink of lager.

Laxton looked at the fork full of chips in his hand for a few seconds as he thought over her question; then popped them in his mouth and chewed on them.

'Although I don't have a clue as to who may have been responsible for the murder,.' he mumbled as he swallowed the chips, 'I'm almost certain that it wasn't a random killing. James Drawell knows more about it than he's telling us.'

He tipped his glass and took a long swig at his lager, then dabbed his mouth with the paper napkin that had been provided. After finishing the meal, he paid the waitress who had come to clear the table. Robert Laxton looked round at the olde worlde décor; a row of pewter mugs were lined up on a shelf in front of him. He smiled to himself at the humorous figures they portrayed; he turned his gaze and glanced at the ceiling which was stained the usual yellowy brown with nicotine.

'The place could do with a good cleaning,' he told himself with a shake of his head.

Jane Bullyn excused herself and went to the ladies' room to tidy up. He twitched his nose with distaste as cigarette smoke drifted towards him from the next table; his face registered relief as he saw his partner emerge from the ladies' room. He swiftly got up from his seat and joined her, and they went out to the car. Starting the engine, he engaged the gear, then, driving the car out of the pub car park, they made their way steadily through the busy city traffic back to headquarters. As they walked into the outer office Laxton noticed that young Dibbling was mashing a pot of tea. Bellows, seeing the look on his face, leaned over towards him and winked as he walked past.

'I'll send you a cup in,' he grunted.

The Inspector gave him an appreciative smile as they went through into the Chief's office, where he went through the day's events.

'It seems to me,' exclaimed Wilberton, after having gone through the evidence in some detail, 'that, although we know he did not kill his wife, there is a distinct suspicion that James Drawell may be involved in his wife's murder in some way.' He was pacing backward and forward with his hands clasped behind his back, looking at the floor studiously as he was speaking. He stopped as Constable Dibbling came in with a tray carrying three cups of tea.

'Put them there, Constable,' he told the young officer, indicating his desk, then after thanking him he carried on.

'As I was saying. Taking into account the fact that he has recently taken out an insurance policy on his wife, it has all seemed to be a little too timely.' There was a deep frown on his forehead as he stopped and picked up one of the cups; looking up at Laxton, who was nodding his head in agreement, he repeated in a low voice. 'Just a little too timely for Mr Drawell.'

'We could bring him in for questioning, sir,' suggested Bullyn after taking a sip of her tea. 'We might get more out of him once we get him here.'

Laxton shook his head. 'That wouldn't work,' he interjected as he reached out for the remaining cup. 'We haven't enough on him, except for the insurance that he's taken out on his wife, and that isn't a crime.'

'Anyway,' grunted Wilberton, 'we'll keep our eye on him, he might just slip up.'

With this he closed the discussion, after the two detectives finished drinking their tea and were just leaving the building to go to the car there was a shout of,

'Constable Dibbling, clear these away will you?'

Jane Bullyn looked out of the corner of her eye at Laxton, as they drove back to Burgh. She liked what she saw. Clean cut rugged features, with a strong pugnacious jaw line. She took in the 'crow's feet' in the corner of his eye. His face was creased, in a lived in, mature sort of way and there was a touch of grey in his sideburns. All in all, she concluded, quite handsome. He looks about the same age as my Dad would have been, she told herself.

'Is there a woman in your life?' she asked him tentatively.

He turned the steering wheel, pulling out to overtake a bicycle, then gave her a quick sideways glance, a quizzical look in his grey eyes. He didn't answer for a few moments, chewing on his bottom lip, as he digested her rather personal question. Then he spoke.

'Actually there are two women in my life,' he told her. 'Why do you ask?'

'Just curious,' she replied. 'You don't seem to me, the marrying kind.'

'I'm not,' was his surprising response, a smile playing on his lips.

'Do they mean a lot to you?' she asked, still probing. 'The two women I mean.'

'Yes, of course they do,' was his reply. 'I'm quite fond of them.'

He went quiet for a moment as he wondered where the conversation was going; then went on to explain.

'One of them is my older sister, Rosanne. Although I must admit I haven't seen her for a couple of years.'

'I suppose the other one is your mother,' she put to him, although strangely enough she'd never heard him mention his parents.

His face softened. 'I'm afraid both my parents are dead,' he replied feelingly.

'Oh I *am* sorry,' she said in a low voice. 'I didn't…'

He butted in. 'It's okay. I lost them a long time ago, during the war to be exact. They were killed during the blitz on Sheffield.'

'You said there were two,' she persisted. 'Who is the other one?'

He looked at her again, out of the corner of his eye, a half smile on his face.

'She looks after me well, and she's a good cook. I don't know what I'd do without her,' he enthused. He was finding it difficult to hide his humour as she went quiet. Suddenly he burst out laughing.

'She's my housekeeper, Annie,' he said chuckling.

'Oh you're incorrigible,' she said, giving him a gentle punch on his arm, as they approached Jane Bullyn's home.

Still smiling, he stopped the car to let her out. He leaned across the passenger seat as she disembarked, telling her in a low voice.

'Anyway I'm too old for you. Remember?'

'You are,' she answered mysteriously as she eased herself out of the car, closing the car door; then with a wave of her hand, she turned away from the car and set off up the garden path, towards the warmth of the bungalow.

Robert Laxton watched as she walked quickly along the path that led to the door, with its windows lit up invitingly. He sighed, then with a slight shake of his head, he engaged the gears and went on his way. Jane Bullyn stopped in the doorway for a couple of seconds, looked over her shoulder and watched the rear lights of the car disappear into the murky November evening. She looked up at the darkening sky to see two rockets exploding into a myriad of coloured stars then fading away. She suddenly remembered it was November the fifth. Bonfire night.

Chapter Nine

'Come on, Toby,' shouted Rebecca Moristone, as she approached the rickety old garden gate at the bottom of the back garden, and set off along the path through the fields. She took the same route every morning that she and her husband had taken for years. They had always enjoyed a brisk walk before breakfast.

'Tunes up the body,' her husband Harold always used to say.

Rebecca Moristone stopped for a few seconds and breathed in the fresh smell of dewy green grass; she looked up at the grey November sky. Heavy clouds hung over the hills on the horizon.

'Looks like we're going to get some rain,' she muttered to herself. Her black Labrador Toby, was jumping about excitedly, his tail wagging; he was eager to get going.

'All right! All right! she exclaimed irritably, as she opened the gate. 'Off you go.'

The old lady turned and followed him as she walked with some difficulty, away from the big rambling farmhouse, with Toby sniffing under the bushes ahead of her. She and her husband Harold had lived all their married years at Brambles Farm, having taken it over from Harold's father after his death over twenty years ago.

'They had been good years,' Rebecca told herself as she set off down the valley. 'Well, that was until Harry had been diagnosed with lung cancer. I told him time and time again to stop smoking, but he wouldn't take any notice.'

Sighing deeply, she shook her grey, almost white head as she cast her mind back over those eventful years to when she and Harold used to take these walks.

'Harry was his own man, nobody was going to tell him how to live his life,' she mumbled to herself, as she strode out as energetically as she could, the painful twinges from her arthritic hip making her catch her breath every so often.

'If fags were bad for you the good Lord wouldn't have provided them,' was his usual comment. Anyway, she told herself, that was his excuse.

'Where have all those years gone,' she asked herself. Was it *really* ten years since he'd passed away?'

She stopped for a moment as she rested her weight on her walking stick. Her face screwed up as she winced at another sharp jabbing pain from her hip; she massaged it for a few seconds, then she pressed on, as the morning sun filtered through the November mist that hung over the fields in the hollows. The cows were bunched closely together as they lazily munched the long grass. 'A sure sign of bad weather,' she muttered to herself as the cattle looked up at her disinterestedly as she hobbled by, then went back to their munching. Reaching the bottom of the meadow she followed a narrow length of beaten track that led over a small stone bridge that spanned a stream. She stood for a couple of minutes and looked down into the water as it babbled its way over the pebbly bottom of the stream; then she turned and followed another path that lead through the wooded area and back to the farmhouse, with Toby snuffling under the bushes, leading the way.

She recalled the many times Harold had taken their only son Roger to the stream. She could see him now, proudly holding up his jam jar with three or four small fish swimming around in it. A smile played on her lips when she recalled how he used to proudly say, 'Look what me and Dad have caught mum, three sticklebacks.' She sighed, tears forming in her eyes. She rubbed them angrily with the back of her hand.

'Why did the good Lord have to take Roger and his wife Amy, in the prime of their lives in that horrific car accident?' she muttered to herself.

They'd only had one child, a son who they named Richard, after Harold's brother. They'd left him at home to stay with her and Harold, his grandparents, while they went on holiday.

'We are going on a special vacation, Mum. It's our anniversary. If you would just look after Richard for us?' he'd asked, hopefully.

'If it's all right with your dad, it'll be all right with me,' she'd told him.

Richard was six years old at the time.

The tragic accident happened as they were on their way home. They were involved in a pile up on the motorway. It was shown on television. As Harold said when he saw the mangled wreckage, 'They didn't stand a chance.' There were tears in her eyes, as her mind drifted back to that terrible day.

She screwed her face up and shook her head at the thought of her grandson, Richard. He was nothing like his dad. Oh, he hadn't been a bad boy when he was young, but he'd grown up to be, what Harold would describe if he were here today as a, 'complete waster.' But then he was her only grandson, and her only living relative. He hadn't liked it when she'd refused to help him to pay off his gambling debts.

'Well,' she told herself out loud, 'he had to realise that he must work for a living like his father and grandfather had to do. I'm not going to encourage idleness.'

She shuddered at the thought of what he would do with the farm, when she was no longer here. She was of a mind to leave him out of her will, she told herself. Breaking out of the shadows of the trees, and back on to the driveway, which led back to the farmhouse she had stopped and leaned on her stick for a moment to catch her breath when she saw a heavy-set man with a walking stick, standing at the gate at the end of the long drive, waving to her. 'Now what does *he* want?' she muttered as she limped down the drive to meet him. Toby growled, the hair on his shoulders standing up, as they approached the man.

'Can I help you?' she enquired, holding on to Toby by his collar.

'Mrs Rebecca Moristone?' the man asked, his eyes cold despite his polite expression, as he opened the gate and approached her.

'Yes,' she replied. 'What can I...' She didn't finish the sentence. The stranger took one step towards her. Without another word, he swung the heavy walking stick, aiming a savage blow to her head. She screamed as she fell to the ground, vainly holding her stick above her body for protection. The stick was knocked out of her hand, as he continued to rain blow after blow on her head. Blood splattered on his trouser bottoms. Toby, his hackles up, bared his fangs as he growled menacingly, then went for the man, closing his jaws round his forearm, which he'd raised to protect himself. He kicked out at the dog and broke free, but not before Toby had ripped a strip of cloth out of his jacket sleeve. The man quickly closed the gate behind him, rubbing his sore arm. He hurriedly clambered into his car, with the snarling Labrador jumping up at the window. Taking out a handkerchief he wiped the sweat from his fat jowls, then, turning on the ignition, he put the car into gear and quickly drove off up the country lane and out on to the main road that led to Birchwood.

Roger Barsant, a tall skinny man in his thirties, stopped his post office van in front of the gates, at the end of the drive leading to Bramble Farm. He wasn't in a very good mood, being late after struggling to start the engine. He cursed at the thought of the long walk he always had to make, to deliver the mail to the farmhouse. He cast his eyes at the two letters in his hand. They both looked like junk mail, he told himself. And there was that damned dog to contend with.

'It's about time they allowed me to bloody well drive up there, or put a mail box at the end of the drive,' he muttered out loud, a scowl on his face. Rain was starting to fall as he unfolded his long legs. Tugging his hat well down over his eyes and pulling up his coat collar, he raised his eyebrows and glanced at the low, heavy black clouds, that were being driven across the stormy sky. He climbed out of the van and approached the side gate. Toby, as usual, was growling at him. Damned dog, he thought. Why the hell didn't they keep it fastened up?

'Good dog, good dog,' he coaxed soothingly, as he pushed the gate open. Suddenly he gasped; there was a look of horror on his face as he saw the stricken old lady lying on the ground, her grey hair covered in blood, her sightless eyes wide open. He gave a sharp intake of breath at the shock of the bloody scene that confronted him. He stood transfixed for a moment, not quite knowing what to do, then pulling himself together, he rushed back to the van and switched on the intercom. A tinny voice asked him what did he require.

'Get on to the police and ambulance service. Mrs Moristone of Bramble Farm has been attacked. I think she's dead,' he said hoarsely.

Robert Laxton stopped to pick up his partner Jane Bullyn at her home. She was carrying a small case, which she placed in the back of the car before climbing in. He glanced at the case and gave her a questioning look as he started the car and moved off.

'Sandwiches and a flask of tea,' she told him, as he accelerated and picked up speed.

They were on their way to headquarters when the message came through telling them of the killing of the old lady. They exchanged meaningful glances.

'It looks as though we've got another murder on our hands,' breathed Bullyn.

Laxton nodded his head in agreement. Then asked, 'Where did they say it was?'

'Brambles Farm,' she replied, adding, 'It's near Birchwood, just off the A46 , I reckon it's about four or five miles away.'

'We'll get straight over there.' Laxton told her, as she read out the directions.

The two arrived at the large, imposing farmhouse on the outskirts of the village of Birchwood which was situated about four miles from Lincoln. They approached the scene where the attack on the woman had occurred. The area was taped off and a screen had been placed around the dead woman. The place was swarming with members of the forensic team dressed in white coveralls. As the two detectives looked down at the crumpled body of the elderly grey haired woman, the head of forensics, Bernard Howsell, approached them.

'What have you got for us, Bernard?' asked Laxton, hunching his shoulders and massaging his cold knuckles vigorously as Bullyn stood by, her hands thrust deep in her pockets.

Howsell stroked his bald head with the palm of his hand as the spots of cold rain fell on it.

'The postman found her at eight-thirty this morning. As far as we can deduce, she's been badly beaten about the head. The extent of the damage suggests a thick piece of wood or a heavy walking stick. As there aren't any splinters, I favour the walking stick,' he said with a grunt. 'To my reckoning, she's been dead for about two hours.'

'What evidence have you found so far?' enquired the Inspector, his face registering his consternation, as he surveyed the gory scene.

'The postman tells us her name is Rebecca Moristone, she's a widow. She apparently lives alone at the farmhouse. We found this on the path.' Howsell held up a clear plastic bag. It contained a strip of blue cloth with a stripe in it.

'Whoever did this,' growled Howsell, 'must have blood on their clothing. It's splattered all over the place.'

'Could the dog have ripped the strip of cloth out of his clothing?' Bullyn questioned.

Laxton nodded in agreement as he thoughtfully tried to conjure up a picture in his mind of what may have happened. There was a grim look on his face as he looked down at the small beaten body of the frail old woman.

'She didn't stand a chance,' he growled, telling her...

'Whoever did this, really came here with the sole intention of taking her life. The dog obviously attempted to defend his mistress. There's also every chance that he may have bitten the attacker.' He turned to Howsell. 'Have you been up to the farmhouse yet?'

The head of forensics, who was kneeling down to get a closer look at the ground around the old lady's body, raised his eyebrows and looked up at him, shaking his head.

'No not yet,' he grunted as he got to his feet. 'I thought we'd wait until you arrived.'

'Have you any idea what the motive might have been?' queried Bullyn as the three of them walked up the path towards the farmhouse, their heads bent into the strong wind and by now, heavy rain.

Howsell raised his eyebrows and looked at her, then back at the Inspector, a questioning expression in his watery blue eyes.

'This is Detective Constable Bullyn,' Laxton confided to him in a low voice. 'She's my new partner.'

'Well it's a bit too early to say yet. Until we've given the house a good going over we won't really know,' replied Howsell as he lifted the large brass doorknocker and hammered hard on what looked like a heavy barn door with an old iron door catch. The sound echoed through the house. Laxton gave him a questioning look. Howsell shrugged his rounded shoulders.

'You never know, there may be someone in the house.'

The Inspector took out a handkerchief and covered the iron door catch before pressing down on the lever. The heavy door creaked as he swung it open to reveal a typical farm kitchen. A fire in the grate still glowed invitingly in the old black leaded Yorkshire range set in stone, as they walked in. A photograph of a young couple and a boy stood on one side of the stone fireplace, another one depicting a middle-aged smiling couple on the other side. Above the fire place hung an oil painting of a country scene. Glancing round the homely kitchen, he noticed that the table had been set for one.

'It looks as though the old girl lived alone, and had just gone out for a pre-breakfast stroll through the grounds,' he announced.

They carried on through into a spacious lounge, where an antique, black, horse hair three-piece took centre stage. A large Georgian window with two or three bottle end panes in it looked out over open fields.

Bullyn carefully opened the drawer of an old sideboard, with her gloved hand. There was around one hundred and fifty pounds in twenty and ten pound notes in the drawer, together with a pension book.

'It certainly doesn't look as though robbery was the motive,' she declared.

Laxton joined her and looked in the drawer, then stood looking around the tidy lounge. He scratched the back of his neck.

'Do you want to know what my conclusions are?' he said studiously.

His two companions turned to him.

'I don't believe whoever killed her has been in here. In fact I don't reckon the murderer had any intentions of coming to the farmhouse after he'd killed the old lady.'

'You don't think robbery was the reason why he killed her then,' offered Howsell.

Laxton shook his head negatively, his eyes half closed as his brain worked overtime weighing up the circumstances confronting him.

'Then why the hell did he beat her so brutally?' demanded Howsell. A note of anger could be detected in his voice.

'For some reason, he obviously wanted to make sure she was dead,' suggested the Inspector, adding. 'He must have had a very strong motive to attack her so savagely.'

After making further enquiries, they learned from the postman, (who seemed to know quite a lot about the family's affairs), that the murdered woman had only one relative, a grandson, Richard. Her son and his wife, Richard's parents, had been killed in an accident. Rebecca Moristone employed a daily help, Mavis Wath, her housekeeper, in whom she'd often confided. They were told that she lived a little further along the lane in a small cottage which went with the job of housekeeper to the residents of the farmhouse. Howsell went back to where his team were busily gathering evidence. Laxton looked up at the sky. The rain had stopped and there was a break in the clouds, showing the black of the, by now almost bare branches of the trees, devoid of their leaves. They stood out starkly against the steely blue late autumn sky, as the two detectives walked up the paved path and approached the door. Bullyn lifted the heavy iron knocker with a lion's head on it, and gave two sharp raps. A short skinny man, wearing a thick cotton shirt with the sleeves rolled up to his elbows, opened the door, rubbing his sparsely covered head self-consciously. He looked at the two officers through his spectacles, which resembled two jam jar bottoms, magnifying his faded blue eyes.

'What can I do for you?' he asked in a gruff, unfriendly voice.

Jane Bullyn pushed herself forward and explained to him who they were. Telling him that their elderly neighbour Mrs Moristone had been attacked and murdered.

'We're looking for information which may help in the arrest of the person who attacked her,' she explained to him, in a friendly tone.

The little man, taken aback by the news, scratched his unshaven chin. He looked them both up and down, as if making sure they both passed muster, before speaking.

'You'd best come in then,' he said gruffly, leading the way along the narrow hallway.

Laxton at six-foot-three, ducked his head to avoid the low door frame that all these country cottages seemed to have, as they were invited into the quaint kitchen.

'And what would your name be, sir?' Bullyn enquired as she followed the Inspector.

'Isaac Wath,' he rasped throatily. 'But it isn't me you want, it's my wife Mavis, she's the one that knows all the old girl's business.'

After offering them a chair, he went out into the garden where his wife was pegging out the washing.

'Mavis,' he shouted. 'The police are here. They want to ask you some questions.'

A short stout woman came in with an empty basket in her hands.

'Let's hope the rain keeps off for a while,' she muttered to herself as she walked through into the kitchen wiping her hands on her apron.

She looked at the two officers questioningly, as she placed the basket on the floor and elevated her eyes to look up at them. Laxton left it to Bullyn to inform her of what had happened to Mrs Moristone.

'I'm afraid I have some distressing news for you,' she told her softly. 'Your neighbour, Mrs Moristone has been attacked and killed.'

'Oh my god!' gasped Mavis, holding her hands to her face.

She swayed imperceptibly.

The Inspector grasped her gently by the shoulders to steady her; after helping the somewhat ample, down to earth woman to a chair, he then proceeded to question her.

'Can you tell us if Mrs Moristone has any relatives, other than her grandson?' he asked her in a quiet voice.

'Well no,' she exclaimed, tears still running down her cheek. 'As far as I know she only had one grandson. His name is Richard. She said that when she passed on, she was leaving everything to him. She told me he was her only relative.'

Her round face was streaked with tears, Bullyn gave her a handkerchief to dab her eyes. The woman blew her nose into it then held it out to give it back, Bullyn shook his head, and she carried on with her narrative.

'She didn't really trust him you know, but as she said, he's all she's got,' she declared, dabbing her eyes and face with the handkerchief. 'It broke her heart when she lost her son and his wife you know.'

Laxton nodded his head sympathetically as he paced backward and forward, his hands clasped behind his back.

'You say that her only relative was her grandson,' interjected Bullyn. 'What happened to her son and his wife?'

'They were both killed in a terrible car accident over twenty years ago,' replied Mrs Wath, shaking her head and looking up at the two detectives. 'She never really got over it.'

'You say she didn't trust her grandson,' the Inspector put to her, softening his tone of voice. 'Do you know why?'

'Well, when he lost his parents he came into a lot of money from the insurance.' She paused to wipe her nose, then, after giving it another good blow, she continued, 'She told me that he'd squandered it on drink and gambling, then he recently had the cheek to ask her for a large sum of money to help him out of serious trouble.'

'Did she give it to him?' enquired the Inspector.

The short stout woman shook her head.

'I couldn't say,' she replied, telling them,

'I'm not one for prying into other people's affairs you see.'

Laxton looked down at his feet and smiled to himself. Then

asked her.

'You say he asked her recently for the loan, Mrs Wath. How recently?'

She wrinkled her brow for a moment and tugged at her ear reflectively, as she attempted to recall when the old lady had told her it was.

'I would say it was nearly two weeks ago,' she confided.

'Did she tell you how much he was asking her for?'

'Ten thousand pounds,' was her quick reply.

'Mmm,' he thought to himself. 'A tidy sum.' Then he turned to the little woman.

'Thank you, Mrs Wath, you've been a great help,' he told her. Then as an afterthought. 'Can you tell us Richard Moristone's address?'

She hesitated for a moment. 'Well I can't tell you offhand,' she replied.

Going to an old oak sideboard in the small lounge, she shuffled through some odd bits of paper, picking them up one after the other and discarding them.

'I don't know,' she said irritably. 'I'm sure it was in here somewhere.'

Laxton waited patiently as she rummaged among the drawer full of bric-a-brac.

'Ahh here it is,' she said triumphantly, holding up a slip of paper in her hand. Written on it was an address and a phone number.

'He gave me this phone number,' she told them, holding out the slip of paper.

'He said I was to get in touch with him if anything should happen to his grandma.'

Jane Bullyn took out a pen and wrote the number and the address down in her note book, as Mavis read it out. She explained to them that it was a flat on Anlaby Road in Hull. After thanking the couple again for their help, they left. The blue sky had given way to a blanket of cold mist as they made their way to the car.

Laxton was quiet as he drove through the patches of thick fog that had descended on the countryside around them. Bullyn turned and looked across at him, she could see he was deep in thought.

'What do you think then?' she asked him.

The Inspector, keeping his eyes on the road, slowed down almost to a stop as they met a thick patch of fog, then he spoke.

'What I would like to know is, why would someone attack her with the obvious intention of killing her, without robbing her? Where is the motive?'

He shook his head, a baffled expression on his face, as he went up through the gears and quickened up.

'It just doesn't make sense,' he declared.

They arrived back at headquarters at mid-day. Wilberton called them into his office. After they had taken a seat, he listened attentively, as the two detectives laid out all the facts. Holding a black marker in his hand, the Chief Inspector wrote all the relevant details on a sheet of white paper that was pinned to a large board that had been fixed on the wall of his office, then stood back holding his chin with his thumb and forefinger. After studying the information he'd written for a few moments, he turned to Laxton.

'As I see it the only person who may have a motive, taking into account the information we've received up to now, is the grandson, he's the only one who would have anything to gain by her death,' he suggested, then he went on…

'I want you to go to Hull and interview Richard Moristone as soon as possible. See if you can find out where he was on the day of the murder of his grandmother. I'll get on to the headquarters there and clear the way for you.'

'We'll get on to it right away,' said the Inspector, getting to his feet, as Wilberton picked up the phone and spoke into it; then followed by Bullyn, they walked out of the office and made their way to the car.

'That's the second murder we've had within a few days,' announced a perplexed Laxton as he manoeuvred the car out of the station car park and set off on their journey to Hull. He turned his head and glanced at Bullyn.

'What do you reckon is going on?' he asked her, giving her a chance to have some input.

Jane Bullyn was quiet for a moment as she mulled over the present situation.

'In both cases they were women, and more to the point they both seem to be motiveless. In my opinion that connects them,' she answered as the Humber Bridge came into view in the distance. They could just make it out through the mist.

'It could be that there's a serial killer on the loose,' she said. 'The two women seem to have been murdered for no apparent reason.'

'I still don't buy that theory,' replied Laxton, giving her a meaningful look.

'Even serial killers leave something to show why they are doing it,' he added.

'I still think the killer is out of his mind,' insisted Bullyn.

Laxton shook his head, before telling her…

'There's got to be a reason. Unless of course it's as you say and we *do have* a maniac on our hands,' he rejoined.

It was a typical November day as they travelled along the approach road that led to the bridge. The heavy mist hung over the Humber like a shroud as they drove across its wide span. Laxton showed his identity at the toll and was waved through.

'I don't know about you,' he muttered, 'but I'm beginning to feel hungry.'

She smiled and reached over into the back seat and lifted the case onto her lap.

'I told you I'd got some sandwiches and a flask of coffee.'

'I don't want to take your sandwiches, there won't be enough for the two of us,' he told her, a look of embarrassment on his face as he pulled the car into a lay by.

'Don't be silly,' she replied as she opened the case. 'Mum's put some in for you as well.'

'Mmm,' he muttered. 'I must thank her when I drop you off tonight.'

She handed him a pack of four ham sandwiches and a piece of homemade fruit cake.

He tucked into them hungrily. After washing them down with the coffee, he sighed.

'I really enjoyed that snack, your mum really knows how to

make fruit cake.'

Starting the car they continued on their journey.

Twenty minutes later they arrived at the police headquarters in Hull; Chief Inspector Landworthy was waiting for them in his office. After the introductions they were asked to take a seat. Landworthy shuffled through some forms for a second or two, then looked up at the two officers in front of him over the rim of his glasses. The Inspector waited patiently as the Chief twiddled a pen in his fingers, his pale blue eyes inscrutable; suddenly he placed the pen on the desk and clasped his hands in front of him.

'Let's see,' he paused for a moment before continuing. 'It's D.I. Larkton isn't it,' he said, dropping his eyes and looking down at one of the sheets of paper in front of him.

'Laxton,' corrected the Inspector, emphasising the 'x'.

'Hrumph,' muttered Landworthy, a frown on his forehead. 'What is it exactly you want?'

Laxton laid out in detail what had happened to Rebecca Moristone and that they needed to interview her grandson. The Chief studied the situation as he took off his glasses and ran one of his fingers up and down the Napoleon-like bridge of his nose. Then, coming to what seemed a sudden decision, he reached out and pressed a button on his desk. The door opened and a constable came in.

'Yes, sir,' he said sharply.

'Get me Sergeant Melner will you?' the Chief snapped.

The constable went out. A couple of minutes later a uniformed Sergeant Melner walked into the office and stood in front of the Chief. He turned and nodded at them, a slight smile on his face.

Laxton was impressed; the Sergeant was a big man. He was almost six feet tall; not as tall as him, but a good two stone heavier. He had a jovial look about his full face and bulbous nose; the end of which was riddled with blue veins, a testimony to his liking for the odd glass of scotch. He reminded Laxton of the laughing policeman at the fun fair. He smiled inwardly; he wouldn't like to be the one to tell the big man that, he told himself.

Landworthy looked up at the big uniformed policeman in

front of him.

'I want you to accompany Detective Inspector Laxton and his partner to this address in Anlaby Road,' he ordered, handing him a slip of paper.

'Give them every assistance.'

Melner, a friendly smile on his chunky face, turned to the two officers and acknowledged them with a nod. Laxton nodded back at the big man in appreciation. Then after thanking Landworthy for his co-operation the three of them left and made their way to the car. Melner eased his big frame into the passenger seat and Bullyn seated herself in the rear.

Melner directed the Inspector through the heavy traffic in Hull city centre, to Anlaby Road, where he told him to stop the car.

'There it is,' announced the Sergeant in a bluff Yorkshire accent, pointing up at the elevated second floor flat. They climbed out of the car and went to an outer door that opened on to a flight of concrete steps which led up to the flat.

Bullyn rang the door bell. A man who looked to be in his thirties opened the door, a nervous look on his face. He visibly relaxed when he saw the uniform of Melner. It was as if he'd expected someone else.

'Richard Moristone?' enquired Laxton.

'That's me,' he replied, asking, a little brazenly, 'And what can I do for you?'

After identifying themselves, they were invited into the cosy flat. They were met by the smell of perfume and stale cigarette smoke as they walked into the comfortable lounge.

'Hi there!' a woman drawled in an American accent, waving her hand as they entered.

She was stretched out on the settee, her legs crossed, exposing her thighs. Melner, taking it all in, smiled, showing his appreciation. 'Quite a looker,' thought Laxton as he acknowledged the attractive brunette with a nod of his head. Jane Bullyn ignored her, as the dark haired woman lifted her legs to sit up, exposing more of her thighs. She told them her name was Monica. The Inspector turned to address Richard Moristone.

'I'm afraid I have some distressing news for you, Mr Moristone,' he began, then waited a couple of seconds before carrying on…

'I have to inform you that your Grandmother is…' Moristone held up his hand, stopping him halfway through the sentence, telling him that he'd already been informed of his grandmother's death and that she had been murdered.

'How did you find out?' the Inspector put to him, a questioning expression on his face.

'Mrs Janner, my grandmother's er, housekeeper, phoned me about half an hour ago and told me about the murder of my gran.'

'Please accept our condolences, I'm sure it must have been quite a shock,' Laxton told him, adding…

'I'd like to ask you a few questions regarding the death of your grandmother.'

Moristone, a slim, athletic five foot nine, looked up at the tall man.

'There isn't anything I can say about her murder,' he replied uncomfortably. 'But if you must ask questions, fire away!'

'Well,' the Inspector began. 'First of all, do you know of anyone who would bear a grudge against her. Let's say enough to want to kill her?'

Moristone's face went slightly pale. His hand shook slightly as he took out a cigarette from his silver case, and placed it between his lips. Laxton waited patiently as he lit it, took a deep drag as he put the case back in his pocket, held it for a few seconds, then blew a perfectly formed smoke ring, which drifted past the Inspector's ear before fading away. Then recovering his composure, he looked the Inspector in the eyes.

'I didn't know my gran all that well, so it wouldn't be likely that I would know her acquaintances would it?' he countered somewhat sharply.

Laxton's eyes hardened as he pressed on.

'When did you last see her?' he queried.

Moristone took another deep drag, blowing the smoke directly at the Inspector, then stubbed the cigarette out in the ashtray. Laxton's eyes narrowed, showing his annoyance.

'The last time I saw her was about ten days ago,' he replied, telling the Inspector…

'And I can account for my movements this morning. I was seeing my bank manager, at nine a.m. trying to negotiate a loan.'

At that moment there was a clatter behind Laxton, as an ashtray hit the floor. He turned round in exasperation. Bullyn was on her knees, trying to clear up the mess she had caused by knocking over the ashtray.

'Don't worry, honey, I'll get the vacuum cleaner. I'll soon clear it up,' an American accent assured her.

Bullyn, appearing flustered, thanked her, as Monica went to a closet and returned with the vacuum cleaner. Laxton frowned at his partner as he concluded his questioning. After asking Moristone to contact them if he came up with any information that might help with the investigation into his grandmother's death, the two detectives accompanied by Sergeant Melner, left the flat, to the sound of the vacuum cleaner being used.

'You were a bit clumsy in there weren't you?' he exclaimed as the three of them negotiated the concrete steps outside the flat. The statement was more an admonishment.

Bullyn smiled as she looked up at him secretively, through her long eye lashes.

'That wasn't clumsy,' she told him in a low voice. 'It was deliberate.'

Laxton frowned questioningly. She put her hand in her pocket. Then held it out palm up. There were two cigarette stubs. One had lipstick on it. Written on them was the word 'Lucky'. The rest of the name was missing. She read it out loud.

'Very clever, but that doesn't prove anything,' said Laxton, shaking his head as he opened the car door and sat behind the steering wheel.

'No, but you never know,' she confided as she climbed into the passenger seat.

She paused for a moment as she fastened her seat belt, then went on…

'It could be an opening. Don't forget, the person who murdered Rose Drawell smoked Lucky Strikes. '

The Inspector looked across at Bullyn, pausing for a few seconds, as he waited for Melner to squeeze his bulk into the rear seat. Then told her...

'Lots of people smoke Lucky Strikes. Anyway, why would Moristone want to kill her. He probably hasn't even heard of her. Except possibly on the telly.'

He was about to start the engine when another car pulled up behind them. Two men got out of the car and went to the door which led to the second floor flats. They stopped at Richard Moristone's door and rang the bell.

'Hold on, sir!' exclaimed Sergeant Melner, twisting round in his seat and looking through the rear window of the car at the two men, as they seemed to push their way into Moristone's flat when the door opened.

'What is it, Sergeant?' enquired Laxton, following Melner's gaze.

'Those two men that have just got out of the car behind us, I know them. They're a couple of local villains, and they've got form. We've had dealings with them a few times,' he explained. 'It looks as though they're going into Moristone's flat.'

'What do you think?' he added concernedly.

'I think we should check to see what they're up to,' rejoined Laxton, taking the key out of the ignition and opening the car door again.

They quickly climbed out of the car and went back to Moristone's flat. They were just climbing the concrete steps, when they heard a scream. They looked at each other, then they made a rush to the door of the flat.

Chapter Ten

Gregory Mendois blew out a thick stream of tobacco smoke as he reached out for the internal phone to speak to his financial manager; he wanted to find out if Richard Moristone had contacted them with regard to the money he owed. He was informed that Moristone hadn't been in touch for over two weeks. There was an inscrutable look on his face as he tapped the desk in front of him with his forefinger. He chewed on his cigar for a few seconds, as he decided what to do about it. Picking up the phone again, he contacted the floor manager, speaking sharply into the mouth piece.

'Arnie, I want you to pay a visit to Richard Moristone. The three weeks he was given to pay his debts are up,' he told him 'Take Carl with you and find out what he's doing about the ten grand he owes. Shake him up a little, but I don't want you to overdo it. I don't want any marks on him that he can take to the police.'

Arnie nodded into his mobile, a cold smile playing on his thick lips. He went over to Carl, who was doing a bit of work on the roulette wheel and whispered a few words in his ear. He nodded his head in return and followed the big man out of the casino.

Arnie slowed the car down as they approached Moristone's flat, pulling into the kerb behind another car that was just about to draw away. They disembarked and went through the outer door to the flat and rang the door bell.

Richard Moristone answered the door. There was a look of resignation on his face as he opened it.

'What now, Inspector?' he snapped, his voice fading as he saw Arnie and Carl standing in the doorway. There was fear in his eyes as he quickly tried to close the door, just as Carl slammed his shoulder against it knocking him backwards into the room. Arnie reached out with his hand and pushed him in the chest, causing him to lose his balance and stagger back; falling over a small coffee table, he went crashing to the floor. Carl slammed the door shut behind him. Monica screamed out.

'What do you want?' she gasped, a terrified expression on her face as she backed away from the two big men.

'Him, darlin', that's what we want,' jibed Carl, pointing his finger at the fallen man, and leering at her. He turned his attention to Moristone, who was still on the floor rubbing his knee vigorously, where it had come into contact with the coffee table.

Arnie looked down at him, his eyes narrowed.

'We've come for the money you owe the casino,' he growled. 'The three weeks is up.'

'I haven't got it yet,' mumbled Moristone, as he got up from the floor. 'You'll have to tell Mendois he'll have to wait a little longer for it. I'm having difficulty finding such a large amount.'

'You've already had seven days extra to find the money,' growled Arnie menacingly. 'Now we've come to collect it.'

Richard Moristone, raised his eyebrows and looked up at the cruel face; plucking up courage he told them.

'Now look here, I'm trying my hardest to find the cash. I do have ongoing plans to get hold of it. You'll just have to wait a little longer.'

There was a mirthless smile on Arnie's face as he reached out and grabbed him by the throat, smashing his fist into the terrified man's face. He drew his fist back to hit him again. Monica grabbed hold of his arm with both her hands to stop him. He shook her off and backhanded her across the face, knocking her to the floor. She screamed as he lashed out at Moristone again.

'Stop it,' she cried, beating the big man on the back with her small fists. 'You'll kill him.'

Reaching out, Carl grabbed her by the arms and held her back. Moristone's face was a bloody mess as he lay on the carpet moaning with pain. Arnie, a maniacal look in his eyes, bent down, reaching for the beaten man again, his orders not to mark him forgotten in the heat of the moment. Suddenly the flat door burst open, as the Inspector and Melner dashed in, closely followed by Bullyn.

'Oh no you don't,' bellowed Melner, grabbing Arnie's uplifted arm in his big strong hands, just as he was about to deliver another blow. He gave a grunt as he exerted himself and twisted Arnie's arm up his back, holding the big man in a Half Nelson.

Arnie partly suppressed a scream of pain, as he felt his elbow being almost dislocated. 'Aghh, you're breaking my arm,' he yelled, as Melner, a grim smile on his face, gave it another jerk for good measure. Carl stepped back, a look of apprehension on his face when he saw how Melner was holding Arnie. He made a quick move towards the door.

'What's this all about then?' demanded Laxton; addressing the stricken man on the floor, as he stood in front of the door to prevent Carl making a run for it.

Moristone groaned loudly as he struggled to get to his feet. He held a handkerchief to his mouth as the blood ran down his chin. He looked up at the Inspector, a pained expression in his eyes.

'It's nothing,' he told him, shaking his head, his voice muffled by the handkerchief.

'Do you want to press charges?' asked Melner, pushing Arnie's arm further up his back and giving a smile of satisfaction as he saw the big man wince with pain.

Moristone looked at his two attackers with hatred; but there was also fear in his eyes as he remembered their warning not to involve the police. He lifted an eyebrow to the well built Sergeant and shook his head, giving an emphatic, 'No.'

Laxton turned his attention to the two subdued heavies.

'And your names are?' he demanded.

They paused for a moment and looked at each other, then reluctantly gave their names, but they adamantly refused to tell him why they were there. The Inspector's brow furrowed as he studied the pair for a few seconds, his eyes like two chips of ice. Then he turned to Melner.

'Place these two under arrest,' he ordered. 'We'll take them in and question them later.'

Melner took out a pair of handcuffs that were hooked on his belt and secured the two villains, who by this time were looking extremely worried. He got on his mobile phone and asked for another car to take the two men to the police station.

'On what charge?' asked Carl.

'G. B.H. and breaking and entering. That will do for a start,' snapped Melner.

'Moristone isn't pressing charges,' growled Arnie, a pained expression on his face.

'No,' replied Melner, his eyes hardening as he looked at the two heavies. 'But I am.'

'And so am I,' a female voice spoke up. It was Monica. She was still on the floor nursing a badly bruised arm. At that moment a police car pulled up outside the flat. A couple of burly police constables took the two handcuffed miscreants, (who were sullenly looking down at the floor), away for questioning.

'Thank goodness you came back,' declared Monica, who was holding a handkerchief to another bruise on the side of her face, as she struggled to get up.

'Why were they here?' Bullyn asked her, as she helped her up from the floor.

'Richard owed them a large sum of money for gambling, he...' She suddenly stopped, realising she was speaking out of turn, as she caught the slight shake of the head, and the black look that Moristone was giving her.

'She's got it wrong...' he blustered. 'It was nothing to do with money.'

Laxton raised a questioning eyebrow as he looked from one to the other, a calculating glint in his eyes.

'I think you'd better come along to the station,' he advised Monica, fearing for her safety.

She shook her head negatively. 'No Inspector,' she said sharply. 'I don't want anything more to do with it.' Then added, after a pause. 'Or him.' There was a note of finality in her reply, as she looked across at Moristone distastefully; then picking up her coat, she marched angrily out of the flat. This was followed by Sergeant Melner informing Moristone that he may be required to give evidence at a later date. A few minutes later the three police officers left.

After dropping Melner off at the Hull police station, Laxton had a word with the Chief.

'I think it would be a good idea to check on the two attackers we've arrested and find out who they are working for,' he said, running his long fingers through his wiry hair, adding…

'Moristone was obviously covering up, when he refused to admit what it was all about,' he asserted, as he and Jane Bullyn prepared to leave and return to headquarters in Lincoln.

'We already have some idea what they're up to,' the Chief told him. 'We've received information that there's an illegal gambling syndicate operating in the city. We are told it is being run by a man called Gregory Mendois.'

The two men were questioned as to their involvement with Mendois. After being told that they would also be charged as accessories, they opened up. They admitted that they were employed by him, but that they had no share in the illegal gambling casino. The Chief Inspector turned to Laxton.

'I'm going to strike while the iron's hot,' he told him grimly, declaring…

'We'll set up a raid on the casino for tonight. I'll contact your office in Lincoln and let you know how we get on.'

Laxton, a grim expression on his face, thanked him, telling him…

'I wish we could stay and help, but we must get on with trying to catch the killer or killers of the two women.'

Chapter Eleven

Gregory Mendois looked out of his office window overlooking the empty casino. There were three hours to go before it opened. Staff were busy making sure everything was ship-shape. The phone rang, he picked it up. A man's voice on the other end told him that Arnie and Carl had been arrested. They were being held for questioning. Deep lines creased his brow as he thought over what he had been told.

'What have they been charged with?' he asked disconcertedly.

'From what I can gather, G.B.H.,' was the reply.

'G.B.H.,' Mendois repeated. 'How come?'

'They were caught in the act of beating up a Richard Moristone and his girlfriend.'

'The bloody idiots,' he spat. 'I told them distinctly not to be too rough.'

He plucked at his lip, his mind was in turmoil as he thought over what he had just heard.

'Are they likely to talk?' he asked his informant nervously, fearing the consequences.

'They already have,' replied the voice grimly. 'They know everything, including the fact that you are running an illegal gambling casino. You can expect a visit from them any time.'

Mendois thanked him for the information and the tip off, then he slowly replaced the phone in its cradle. There was a deep frown on his forehead as he turned away.

Pacing backward and forward nervously, he thought over what he should do next; then he made a decision. Pulling his sleeve back, he checked his watch. It showed three-thirty p.m. The casino was due to open at six p.m. Stroking his chin slowly, he tried to think calmly. There wouldn't be any point in the police coming before he opened. That meant that there wouldn't be a raid until at least six p.m. He looked at his watch again nervously. He had two and a half hours to clear everything out. He went down to the bar and gave out instructions to the staff, telling them that it was urgent. He ordered all the equipment that had any connection to the gambling side of his business, to be removed and taken down to the cellars and locked away. The next two hours was a flurry of activity as the room was transformed. There was a smile of relief on his countenance, as he cast his eyes over the large room, which now resembled a night club. To all intents and purposes he was running a respectable establishment.

It was six p.m. as Chief Inspector Landworthy accompanied by Sergeant Melner and two police constables stopped their cars outside the premises which they had been informed was being used as a casino. They burst through the doors. The Chief's eyes scanned the room. There was around half a dozen couples sat at the tables drinking; a few more customers were leaning on the long bar. A four piece band were giving a pleasant rendition of 'Solitaire'. He turned and spoke to Melner.

'It looks as though they've been tipped off,' he informed him. Melner nodded his head in agreement as Gregory Mendois approached them, a cigar in his mouth and a knowing smirk on his face.

'Can I help you, gentlemen?' he drawled, taking a long drag on the cigar.

'We have reason to believe that you are running an illegal gambling establishment,' Landworthy announced, ignoring the club owner's disdainful posture.

'I'm sorry to disappoint you, Inspector, but as you can see this is not a gambling casino,' he declared, blowing a stream of smoke over the Inspector's shoulder, as he gave a sweep of his hand to emphasise the fact, then asked him, 'Whatever gave you that idea?'

'The two men you sent to beat up Richard Moristone,' snapped Melner, butting in, annoyed at the fact that Mendois had been tipped off.

'They told us that he owed you a ten thousand pounds gambling debt, and they were there to collect on your behalf.'

'I didn't send them to hurt him, Sergeant,' he explained, with a shrug of his shoulders. 'They were only to talk to him about a debt he owed me for services rendered.'

Landworthy eyes hardened. 'So you admit that you sent them?' he intoned.

Mendois shrugged his shoulders nonchalantly as he took a long drag on his cigar.

'It's on their own heads if they went too far,' he drawled, as he leaned his head back and blew a stream of cigar smoke towards the ceiling.

'Right,' snapped Landworthy, taking offence at Mendois's superior attitude. Turning to his officers, he ordered them to search the premises.

'You can't do that,' protested Mendois, his face contorted with anger. 'You don't have the authority.'

The Chief Inspector reached into his pocket, took out a sheet of paper and showed it to the angry club owner.

'This is a search warrant,' he snapped. 'That gives me the authority.' Then he turned to Melner.' Take the two constables and search his office.'

Melner led the way, pushing the club owner unceremoniously to one side.

Ten minutes later the Sergeant came down the stairs from the office, and went to his superior. 'We've found this,' he said in a low voice. There was a glint of satisfaction in his eyes as he handed over a cheque signed by Richard Moristone for ten thousand pounds. Landworthy read it, then looked up, a grim expression on his face. He ordered Melner and the other men to go through all the rooms including the cellars. Half an hour later a voice called out from the vicinity of the cellars.

'Here, sir.'

The Chief Inspector followed the direction of the voice as he descended the steps to the cellars. Large barrels of beer lined one side of the large, dank, dungeon-like basement room, there was a musty smell of sour beer and dry rot. A long wine rack stood back against a whitewashed wall. It had been slid back to reveal an alcove. Melner was nowhere to be seen, as Landworthy strained his eyes as he attempted to locate Melner in the darkness.

'Where are you, Sergeant?' he called out.

'In here, sir,' called Melner. His voice came from inside the damp smelling alcove.

Heavy cobwebs spanned the corners as Landworthy peered through the gloom of the poorly lit cellar, and carefully made his way to where the gruff voice was coming from. The Sergeant, bending to avoid the low ceiling, was shining a torch on a roulette table, half a dozen folded card tables and a pile of neatly stacked gambling equipment. The Chief gave a satisfied grunt. Brushing a spider from his face and dusting the cobwebs from his uniform, he returned to the bar room, where he approached an apprehensive Mendois and told him what they had discovered in the cellars. The casino boss's face fell as he realised the game was up. His hand shook as he stubbed his cigar out in the ashtray, then the Chief Inspector read him his rights, and told him in a grave voice, 'Gregory Mendois, I'm arresting you on a charge of extortion and running an illegal gambling establishment. There may be other charges later. 'Take him away,' he ordered the two constables, who took up a position on each side of Mendois and held him by his arms. He shook them off angrily.

'Okay,' he snapped. 'I can manage.'

The Chief gave a nod, and he was allowed to walk out of the club to the police car.

After a trouble free, but boring journey, Laxton and Bullyn duly arrived back at the Lincoln headquarters. Bellows greeted them as they went through into the Chief's office, where the Inspector went over the day's events with him.

'Mmm, all in all a very satisfactory result,' muttered the Chief, poking his little finger in his ear to scratch it. 'It seems that our Mr Moristone does seem to have a strong motive for wanting his grandmother out of the way after all. Ten thousand pounds worth.'

Laxton leaned back in his chair and folded his arms. 'Don't forget he also has a cast iron alibi,' he reminded him. 'He couldn't have killed her.'

Wilberton nodded his head.

'That may be so, but he could have got someone else to do the job for him,' he rejoined just as Bellows came in with a tray carrying the obligatory coffees, then swiftly left.

Jane Bullyn reached out for one of the steaming mugs as she asked the Chief, 'Wouldn't that take a lot of money?' Then she went on... 'If he couldn't get the money to save him from Mendois, how would he get the far larger amount that would be needed to hire someone to do something like that?'

'Well thought out, Constable,' said Wilberton, taking a drink of his coffee and looking at her approvingly. 'You're dead right of course.'

'That doesn't get us any nearer to finding out who committed the two murders', Laxton, put to them, leaning forward in his chair and placing his empty mug on the tray.

'Let's just hope that we haven't a serial killer on our hands,' he added.

Wilberton chewed on his bottom lip as he nodded his head slowly in agreement.

Laxton checked his watch, it was seven p.m.

'It's getting late,' he told Bullyn, as he got to his feet and went to the door, he stopped and turned as the phone rang, Wilberton picked it up and put it to his ear.

'Yes, yes I've got that,' he said into the mouth piece, then after thanking the speaker he put the phone down. He looked at the two detectives, a serious expression on his face.

'That was Chief Inspector Landworthy at Hull.' He paused for effect. 'Gregory Mendois has been remanded in custody awaiting trial.'

'Bloody good show,' enthused Laxton as he and his partner went through the door.

Chapter Twelve

Gloria Basser walked into the large well furnished lounge, running a comb through her long blonde hair. She had just taken a shower, and was fastening her negligee round her shapely body. Her husband, John, leaned back and looked at her in admiration. He'd met Gloria while on holiday abroad. She'd been a budding actress until an illness had curtailed her career. Now in her late forties, she had a haunting beauty. He gave a deep sigh. Her green eyes were still lovely and sexy. They'd been married for over twenty years, and his love for her was as strong as ever. They didn't have any children. Gloria had suffered from cancer of the womb, which resulted in her having to have an hysterectomy, an operation that had rendered her incapable of having them. Reaching out, he took her by the hand, gently pulling her onto the settee. She feigned resistance as he wrapped his arms around her still slim waist. He felt a stirring in his loins as he pressed his lips to hers, when the phone rang. With a look of disappointment on his face, he reached out to pick it up.

'Let it ring,' Gloria whispered huskily, her eyes half closed with desire, as she reached out and grabbed his hand before it reached the phone.

John paused for a second as he looked into her smouldering eyes, then gave a throaty laugh as he ignored her plea and picked up the receiver, placing it against his ear.

'Oh, hello, Charles, yes, I see. What kind of trouble?' He paused, his brow creasing, as he listened for a couple of minutes, intermittently nodding his head.

'Okay we'll sort it out tomorrow,' he declared

He turned to his wife, still holding on to the phone.

'Will you need the car tomorrow, darling?' he asked her.

'Yes,' she told him with a nod of her head. 'I've got an

appointment with the hairdresser at eleven.'

'Okay,' he told her. 'No problem.'

He turned back to the phone.

'I'll catch the nine a.m. train. I should be there around eleven-thirty. Goodbye.' There was a troubled look on his lived in, maturely handsome face as he slowly replaced the phone.

'Who was that, dear?' asked Gloria, her long blonde hair falling over her face as she leaned over towards him. She ran her fingers affectionately through his slightly greying hair.

'It was my partner Charles Insten, he wants me to go to London. It seems he's in some sort of trouble, which may affect the business. Anyway, darling, we'll leave that until tomorrow,' he told her, taking her into his arms again, and pulling her close.

'Now where were we?' he murmured, embracing her as their lips met.

John Basser had felt uncomfortable about Charles Insten, his junior partner, for some time, after discovering he was gambling too much. He'd already warned him about his conduct, and had threatened to dissolve their partnership if he didn't mend his ways. Insten had promised he would give up gambling and concentrate on the business.

It was a typical, cold, dank, November morning and it was just beginning to spit with rain as the woman sat waiting patiently in the red car, parked fifty yards from the detached house of John Basser. She'd been following him on and off for two days, but the opportunity that she was waiting for hadn't presented itself. Last night she had received a phone call, informing her that Basser would be catching the nine a.m. train for London the next day.

'Maybe today will be the day when I shall be able to fulfil my mission,' she told herself.

A silver Rover pulled out of the driveway and onto the street, then drove off. The red car started up and followed at a discreet distance. Ten minutes later the Rover stopped outside Lincoln railway station. John Basser climbed out of the car. After a few words with his wife, he gave her a kiss, and walked into the station as she drove away. He had told her he would be back that evening. After buying a ticket, he waited on the platform with the other commuters, for the train to Grantham, where he would pick up the one for London.

Pulling into the station car park, the woman got out of the red car and walked into the reception area of the station, where she watched as Basser purchased his ticket, then followed him on to the appropriate railway platform. The train could clearly be seen in the distance as it approached the station. The commuters crowded up to the edge of the platform as they waited for it to pull in. John Basser was at the front. She positioned herself behind him, her heart pounding, as she waited for the right moment. The train rattled towards them. It was about thirty feet away, when Basser felt a hand in the middle of his back. His eyes widened with sheer terror, as he teetered for a couple of seconds, trying to keep his balance; the hand pushed harder, propelling him on to the track in front of the train. He screamed, as the engine rattled unfeelingly over him. Then everything went quiet except for the sound of the train's brakes screeching as they fought to stop. The woman, her long blonde hair falling over her shoulders, backed away furtively to mingle with the shocked commuters, then quietly slipped away. She was shaking as she staggered into the car park, her stomach churning. Leaning against the bonnet of the car she fought against the nausea that swept over her. Then she was physically sick. Wiping her mouth with a handkerchief, she clumsily unlocked the car door and collapsed into the driver's seat. She held her head in her hands for a few seconds, then burst into tears, as the thought of what she had done overwhelmed her.

After a few minutes she dried her eyes and composed herself, put the key shakily into the ignition, started the car, and drove away.

It was nine-thirty a.m. as Laxton and Bullyn were making their way to headquarters. He was just negotiating a large roundabout on the outskirts of Lincoln, when the message came over the intercom that there had been another possible killing at Lincoln railway station.

'If this is another murder. That'll be three in the last two weeks,' said Bullyn. 'It's almost unbelievable.'

'These things happen,' rejoined Laxton philosophically. 'Anyway, we don't know yet. It may be accidental,' he added as he stopped the car in the police station car park. Although he had to agree things were beginning to hot up.

'By the way,' he said, laughing as he was about to disembark, you questioned me yesterday about my private life. What about you?'

'What about me?' she queried, looking across the car at him.

'Well,' he quipped, 'what about your love life? I haven't heard you mention any serious boy friend.'

'That's because I haven't got one,' she replied.

'What about your parents?' he enquired 'You don't talk about them either.'

She went quiet for a moment, then spoke in a soft voice.

'My Dad's dead.'

'I'm sorry to hear that,' he told her, a little chastened.

'Oh that's okay,' she replied. 'It's been quite a few years now since we lost him.'

'We?' he queried, looking at her out of the corner of his eye, as they walked out of the police station car park

'Me and Mum,' she sighed, reaching down into her shoulder bag. She pulled out a photograph and held it in front of him. He took the photograph from her hand and studied it closely. The photograph was of Jane, her mother and her dad. He was struck by her mother's deep beauty and the sadness in her eyes. She was clinging to a tall dark haired man who looked to be in his forties. He looked down at Jane then back at the photograph.

'It's easy to see where you get your looks from,' he remarked.

Blushing slightly at the compliment, she looked at the picture again; she'd never quite looked at it like that, yet it was true, her mother was an attractive woman.

'How come your mother hasn't married again?' he asked, as they approached the entrance to the police station.

'It's probably because she hasn't met the right man yet,' she answered. Then she cocked her head on one side, raising an eyebrow and looking up at him. 'I'll introduce you to her.'

He smiled down at her.

'She wouldn't be interested in an old dog like me,' he said and chuckled.

Bellows greeted them with a gruff, 'Good morning.' Laxton nodded his head in reply.

Wilberton was waiting for them as they walked into his office.

'Have you heard the news?' he asked them.

'Do you mean about the man who has been killed at the railway station?' replied the Inspector, a questioning frown on his forehead.

'Yes, I want you to go to the scene of the accident straight away and look into it. According to what the Station master had to say over the phone, it doesn't look straight forward,' the Chief told them.

'We'll get down there right away,' Laxton assured him, as he turned to go back out of the door, with Bullyn close behind.

Ten minutes later they arrived at Lincoln Railway Station. Laxton checked his watch; it was ten forty-five a.m. as they approached the area that had been cleared and taped off. Paramedics were in the process of removing the body from under the train as the two detectives arrived on the scene. A crowd of onlookers were milling around the perimeter. Forensics dressed in white coveralls were waiting to go over the scene of the incident, after the paramedics had removed the gory mess. Laxton and Bullyn spent the next hour and a half questioning the people who had been waiting for the train, which had been delayed for over an hour. Of the ones who were still waiting to continue their journey, some were too traumatised to give an opinion, others said they thought he'd slipped. One man said that the dead man had shot out as though he had been pushed.

'Mind you,' he'd said, not wanting to get too involved, 'I'm not saying that's what actually happened.'

Laxton was disappointed at the response from the commuters. The fact that there were so many around when the incident happened, he was surprised that no one had seen anything of note. He cast a trained eye on the amenities, notably two surveillance cameras, one at each end of the platform.

The Inspector had a word with the harassed Stationmaster, as Bullyn went for two coffees.

'Can you tell me what you know about the incident?' Laxton asked him.

'Well, as far as I could ascertain, after talking to the engine driver. The fellow just seemed to jump out in front of the train.'

'Do you think he took his own life?' the Inspector put to him.

The Stationmaster tugged at his ear for a moment, as he thought over Laxton's query.

'I can't say that, but what I will say, is that from the comments that I've heard, he certainly didn't just fall under the train,' he replied with a slight shake of his head.

'I've noticed that you have surveillance cameras installed,' said the Inspector, raising his eyebrows and looking at him. 'Are they all working?'

'Yes,' was the reply. 'In fact they were recently overhauled and new tapes fitted. I'll just check when they can be made available.'

Laxton thanked him as he went off at a half run, leaving him to sip the coffee that Bullyn had brought him. The hot drink warmed him up. He'd just finished the drink, when the Stationmaster returned.

'The tapes should be ready some time tomorrow morning. I'll give your office a ring when they've been developed,' he informed them.

The Inspector, his hands pushed deep into his overcoat pockets, acknowledged the Stationmaster with a nod of his head as he stood on the edge of the concrete platform, just about where the dead man had stood, and looked down at the shining steel rail track, his face impassive as he thought deeply about the tragic event. Bullyn walked up and stood beside him. She glanced up at his troubled face.

'Do you reckon he jumped?' she asked him.

Laxton, his eyes on the dark blood stains on the sleepers in the four foot, turned his head slowly and grunted an emphatic, 'No I don't.'

'How can you be so sure?'

'If he had planned it, he wouldn't have screamed as he went down.' He took a deep breath.

'No, Jane, it wasn't suicide. It was either accidental, which is quite possible, or it was murder,' he said with a confident note of certainty in his voice, as he finished his coffee and handed her the empty cup. She took them away. He waited for her to return, then turned away from the murder scene and checked his watch as they walked back to the car. It was just turned twelve forty-five and he was beginning to feel hungry.

She was a little surprised at the mention of her first name. It was only the second time he'd used it. It made her feel strangely closer to him, she felt, as they climbed into the car and drove off. Laxton pulled into the pub car park. It was the one that they had frequented before. Bullyn opened her shoulder bag and fumbled about in it.

'What are you looking for?' he asked.

'It's my turn to pay,' she replied.

He shook his head and held up his hand.

'It's my treat,' he told her, one side of his mouth lifting in a half smile.

'I'll pay for the drinks then,' she insisted.

He shrugged his shoulders as they got out of the car.

'Okay you win.'

They walked up to the bar and ordered scampi and chips and two lagers.

After the meal they sat for a while discussing the horrific incident that had occurred that morning. Then thanking the waitress they left and made their way to the car and climbed in. They arrived at police headquarters in Lincoln fifteen minutes later at two p.m.

'I'll put the kettle on,' Bellows told the Inspector in a low voice, as they walked past him.

Laxton nodded his thanks and continued on, into the Chief's office.

'Ah, Robert,' said the Chief, looking up from his desk as the tall detective walked through the door followed by his partner. He indicated with his hand for them to take a seat before carrying on...

'What have you got to report?'

Laxton sat down and crossed his long legs, clasping his knee cap with both hands; he then went on at some length, to tell him all about the horrific incident.

'It's quite difficult to ascertain whether it was an accident, a suicide or whether he'd been pushed,' he told Wilberton.

'Weren't there any witnesses?' asked the Chief, a look of incredulity in his eyes.

'Oh, there were plenty of witnesses that saw him fall under the train,' Laxton rejoined 'But none would commit themselves. That is with the exception of one who said that it looked almost as if he'd been pushed.'

'Did he tell you why he came to that conclusion?' queried Wilberton.

'It was just his opinion,' replied the Inspector with a shrug of his shoulders, adding... 'Nothing concrete.'

'Were there any surveillance cameras installed?'

'Yes, we should be getting the results from them tomorrow morning,' Laxton told him. 'Hopefully we'll be able to make out what happened.'

Wilberton got to his feet and walked across the office, a cane and a piece of chalk in his hand. Pulling down a rolled up chart that was hanging on the wall, he reached up and started writing. After a couple of minutes he stood back and turned to the two detectives, who were sat watching with interest.

'Regarding the two murders that are under investigation,' he said, pointing with the cane. 'First we had the killing of Rose Drawell in the park gardens in Skurness. The only one to profit from her death is her estranged husband, James Drawell. We've checked his alibi. He was in the hospital at the time of her murder. Result... She was killed by a person or persons unknown.'

'He paused and looked down at his highly polished shoes for a few seconds, as Sergeant Bellows brought in three cups of tea on a tray and placed it on the desk. Wilberton raised his eyebrows and directed his gaze at them.

'Any questions?'

Laxton shrugged his shoulders noncommittally as he reached out for one of the cups; Bullyn shook her head and took a sip of her tea.

The Chief picked up a cup, took a drink and carried on.

'Next we had Rebecca Moristone found brutally murdered outside her home; again the only person with a motive is her grandson, he also has a perfect alibi. Which means she was also killed by persons unknown, and what have we got to show?'

He slammed the cane down on the desk in frustration.

'Nothing,' he growled.

Bullyn spoke up.

'We do have the cigarette ends and the footprints that were found at the scene of the Rose Drawell murder,' she said, then added, 'there's also the strip of cloth that the dog ripped out of the clothing of the person that killed Rebecca Moristone.'

'That's true,' the Chief replied grudgingly. 'What I mean is, we haven't got a suspect in the frame yet.'

Laxton stroked his chin thoughtfully.

'This case is going to be a tough one to crack,' he muttered. 'Whoever has committed these murders, they have thought them out well. All we can hope for is a break.'

Finishing off his tea he got to his feet and looked at his watch, it was three forty-five.

Wilberton rolled the chart back up.

'Let's hope we have a bit more luck tomorrow,' he muttered as Laxton and Bullyn left the office and walked out to the car.

The late afternoon autumn sun was low in the sky, as they negotiated the twists and bends of the narrow roads that wound their way through the Lincolnshire countryside. The bare trees cast twisted shadows that distorted the Inspector's vision as he drove carefully along the undulating highway. Turning off the main road, he drove the car along a narrow country lane, finally stopping outside a wrought iron gate that opened on to a crazy paved path that wound its way to the front door of the neat bungalow in the village named Dalesworth, where Jane lived. The village consisted of one main street, which took in four shops, a mixture of old cottages and newly built bungalows. A short lane led to a two hundred year old church; its steeple standing out above the surrounding properties. Laxton sat for a moment as he ran his eyes over the seemingly quiet, homely parish. He gave a slight nod of approval as they climbed out of the car and went through the gate. Red and brown leaves from the bushes that fronted the property, tumbled along in front of them as her mother, who was walking up the path to meet her, greeted her with an affectionate hug and a peck on the cheek. Jane introduced them. Nancy raised her eyebrows and caught the eye of the Inspector as she reached out with her small hand and smiled at him.

'I'm very pleased to meet you, Mr Laxton,' she purred, adding, 'Jane has told me so much about you.'

'Not all bad I hope,' he replied in a low voice.

He looked down into her green eyes, holding her gaze for a second. A warm feeling went through him as he returned her smile with a lop-sided boyish grin. Then, turning away, he gave a wave of his hand, got back into the car and started the engine. He sat for a few seconds, gazing at Nancy. He felt a strange stirring in his breast as he watched her walking up the path with her arm round Jane. Sighing deeply, engaged the gear and slowly drove off. Jane Bullyn noticed that her mother was strangely quiet as they went indoors.

'Your Mr Laxton is quite a handsome man, Jane,' she confided. There was a slight flush to her cheeks and a faraway look in her eyes as she spoke.

Robert Laxton arrived back at his cottage in Old Bolingbroke. Annie's bicycle was leaning against the cottage wall as he disembarked from the car and opened the door.

Annie was just placing a hot plate full of mouth watering homemade steak and kidney pie on the table. He smacked his lips as the aroma hit his nostrils.

'Annie,' he whispered in her ear as she straightened up. 'You're an angel.'

She looked up at him over her shoulder, her cheeks turning slightly red at his compliment.

'Go away with you,' she said giggling as she dodged the embrace he was about to give her.

He smiled and rubbed his hands together as he sat down and reached for the knife and fork. Annie stopped and looked at him for second, as she was about to leave. If only he could meet a nice woman she told herself as she watched him tucking in to his meal.

'Goodnight, Mr Laxton,' she called to him as she left.

He raised his fork and mumbled his reply through a mouthful of pie. He topped this off with a glass of Dom Perignon, then, with Horatio purring contentedly in his lap, he placed a record on his record player and relaxed for the rest of the evening as he listened to the haunting rendition of the music by Strauss.

The next morning Laxton and Bullyn arrived at the Lincoln headquarters. Wilberton looked up from behind his desk. The Inspector went over the facts with him again.

'The Stationmaster did say that the tapes would be ready today.'

Bullyn butted in. 'Probably sometime this morning.'

Laxton nodded his head in agreement, then, just as he and Bullyn turned to leave, the phone rang. The Chief picked it up.

'Yes, yes,' he said, nodding his head. 'I've got that.'

He raised an eyebrow as he looked up at Laxton. The Inspector saw that there was a look of satisfaction on the Chief's face.

'That was the Stationmaster. The film is ready,' he told him. 'He says there are some interesting developments.'

He sat back in his chair and rubbed the palms of his hands together in anticipation. He'd been getting some stick from the Superintendent, because of the lack of progress so far in the recent cases.

'We may be finally getting a break,' he enthused, adding…

'I want you to go there and see if there is anything that will help in the investigation.'

'Okay,' replied Laxton. 'But I'd like to call at the coroner's office first to see if they have anything for us.'

Ten minutes later they arrived at the Lincoln coroner's office. Laxton was informed that they were about to perform an autopsy on the dead man. He asked to see the body and was led to the theatre, where Bernard Howsell the head of forensics and a pathologist were looking at the body.

'Which part do you want?' the pathologist asked them, a grim smile on his face as they followed him into the theatre where they performed the autopsies. The torso was covered by a sheet, only the head was showing. There wasn't a mark on it. John Basser looked as if he could open his eyes any moment, thought the Inspector, as the pathologist prepared to shave the greying hair from the head, in preparation for the examination of his brain to determine whether natural causes could have contributed to his fall.

Laxton looked down at his partner, who hadn't found the pathologist's remark very funny. She wasn't looking too well.

'Did he have any identification on him?' Laxton asked Howsell.

'Yes. We found his driving licence. His name is John Basser,' he replied. The sound of the electric razor almost drowning out his words.

'Has his next of kin been informed?' enquired Bullyn, screwing her eyes up at the sight of John Basser changing to a skinhead.

'Yes, they were informed yesterday.'

'Anything else?' asked Laxton.

'Well, we found these items in his pockets,' the man replied, indicating with his free hand.

Spread out on the table in plastic bags were a driving license, pen, cigarette lighter and a half pack of Lucky Strike cigarettes and a wallet which contained seventy five pounds in notes. Bullyn looked at the license and wrote down an address that was written on the back of it. Thanking him, Laxton decided to leave and continue with their inquiries, before the pathologist started the examination. Their next stop was Lincoln Railway station, where they sought out the Stationmaster and enquired about the film.

'Ah yes, follow me. We do have some very interesting

footage,' he informed them mysteriously, as he lead them to a room equipped with a television monitor. Pushing a tape into the monitor's recorder, he pressed play. After a little manipulation he set it at the position required. It showed the early morning commuters waiting for the train to Grantham.

'Watch closely now, it's coming up to the incident,' he whispered. They leaned forward.

The film showed the train approaching the crowded platform, suddenly a man shot out of the crowd, his arms outstretched as if he was trying to stop himself from falling. He landed on the track in front of the engine. Bullyn turned and looked at the Inspector, a look of horror in her eyes.

'That was no accident," she gasped

Laxton, holding his chin in his hand as he watched the incident unfold, concurred. He instructed the Stationmaster.

'Take it back to where they were waiting for the train.'

The tape was replayed. It showed the man in question, waiting patiently as the train drew in the station. There was a woman standing directly behind him. She was wearing a light grey coat with a high collar pulled up, a woolly hat and a thick scarf half covering her face. She was obviously intent on not being identified.

'Slow the tape down now,' asked the Inspector. 'There!'

Jane Bullyn and the Stationmaster gave a gasp of disbelief as it showed the man teetering on the edge of the platform. It was obvious that he was struggling to keep his balance. A hand could be clearly seen in the middle of the man's back. The two detectives looked at each other, then Laxton spoke up.

'It looks as though we've got another murder on our hands,' he declared. 'He was pushed.'

The murderous act was played over and over again. The scarf dropped as the woman reached out, tendrils of her long blonde hair falling down across her forehead.

'Can you get the face of the woman enlarged?' Laxton requested, adding. 'It looks as though we've finally got something to go on.'

The Stationmaster nodded his head in assent.

'I'll get it ready as soon as I can,' he told them as he

carefully took the tape out of the recorder.

Thanking him for his help, they left and made their way to the car.

'We'll get the address and have a word with Mrs Basser,' Laxton told his partner as he turned the steering wheel and joined the traffic.

Bullyn read out the address from her writing pad.

'When did you get that?'

'When we were at the autopsy. It was on the driving licence,' she told him.

The two police officers arrived at the home of the late John Basser, a large detached house standing well back from the road, in Wardingham, about ten miles outside Lincoln. They walked up the long drive which was lined with evergreens, and approached the large ornate front door. Bullyn reached up and pressed the door bell. A slim attractive blonde, in her late forties answered the door; her mascara was smudged and there were black lines where the tears had run down her face.

'Mrs Basser?' enquired Laxton, looking into her tear filled blue eyes.

The woman nodded, giving him a questioning look. After identifying themselves, they were invited into the spacious hallway, and were led through a large archway, lined with carved wood, into a massive lounge. The walls were hung with expensive paintings. It was obvious the Bassers were loaded, thought Laxton as they took a seat. Another plain, severe looking woman was present, whom she introduced as her elder sister Caroline. She had just arrived to stay with her for a few days to provide some comfort to Gloria Basser, who was overcome with grief. Directing them to two easy chairs, she sat beside her sister opposite them, on the plush comfortable settee.

'The first thing I have to ask you, Mrs Basser. Do you know if your husband had any enemies?' enquired the Inspector, leaning forward, his elbows on his knees.

'None that I know of.' She wept, shaking her head and dabbing her eyes with her handkerchief 'As far as I know he was well liked. Why do you ask?'

'We have reason to believe he may have been murdered,'

replied Laxton in a quiet, assured voice, as he answered her query.

'Murdered,' she gasped, shaking her head slowly from side to side in disbelief. 'Who would want to murder John?'

'That, Mrs Basser, is what we're trying to find out,' declared the Inspector.

'Has he ever been involved with any women?' asked Bullyn pointedly, a note book in her hand.

The distraught woman looked at her in horror. 'My John, involved with other women. Never.' She protested vehemently. 'We were very close.'

At that moment Caroline, who sensed that her sister was becoming overwrought, intervened, asking them if they would like a coffee. They all said 'Yes', to the offer. The Inspector continued, telling her, 'We have evidence that a woman with long blonde hair may have pushed him in front of the train.' Laxton's eyes narrowed, as he watched her expression carefully to gauge her reaction.

'Why would she do that?' she questioned. Then she saw the look in his eyes.

'You don't think… Oh no you can't think I …'

Laxton butted in.

'I'm sorry Mrs Basser. You must understand; until we find the perpetrator of this crime, everyone is under suspicion,' he paused and looked at her, a serious expression on his face. 'Even you I'm afraid.'

'I loved my husband dearly, Inspector,' she sobbed. 'I'd rather die myself than harm him.'

Laxton nodded, a look of understanding in his eyes. He believed her.

Caroline brought the four cups of coffee on a tray and placed it on the small veneered table in front of them. After thanking her, the Inspector went on with his questioning.

'Where were you at the time of his er ...' He looked down at his hands self consciously, as he struggled to find the right word. Then raising his head he looked her in the eyes.

'Murder you mean, don't you?' she whispered, almost inaudibly.

'I'm afraid I can't come to that conclusion without further investigation,' he told her as he picked up one of the cups of coffee.

'But you have already said it was murder,' she pointed out to him.

He shook his head. 'I said it *may* have been murder. It's still quite possible someone could have fallen against him and pushed him accidently,' he explained in a quiet voice as he raised the cup to his lips and took a sip.

He could see, with the look of disdain on her face, that she didn't believe that one.

'To answer your query about my whereabouts, I had just taken him to the railway station to catch the train to London,' she explained, adding, 'if I had only stopped to wave him off this might not have happened.'

'Can you tell me why he would be going to London?' he asked.

'He was going to meet his partner Charles Insten. John spoke to him on the phone yesterday evening,' she explained, pausing for a moment as she tried to recall the conversation. 'He said something about him having trouble with the business. They run a joint investment service. It's based in Lincoln, but they have a small office in London. He'd had a few arguments with Charles about his debts in the past, but nothing serious as far as I know.' She sobbed into her handkerchief. 'I hope the swine that did this rots in hell.'

The Inspector comforted her saying, 'We'll do our best to get to the bottom of what happened to your husband, Mrs Basser.'

'Would you like me to get a policewoman to stay with you?' D.S. Bullyn enquired.

'No, I'll be all right thank you,' she murmured, brushing aside a few loose blonde hairs that had fallen over her eyes. 'My sister will be staying with me for a few days.'

After further questioning, they bid goodbye to the heartbroken woman and her sister, and made their way to the car.

'You don't really think it could have been an accident do

you?' asked Bullyn, as she fastened her seat belt.

He smiled grimly. 'No I don't,' was his short reply. 'I was just trying to ease the pressure.'

Laxton was silent as he started the car and pulled out of the drive. He had a perplexed look on his face.

Jane Bullyn shook her head from side to side in frustration, muttering, 'What's going on?'

'First of all,' Laxton paused, as he overtook a slow vehicle, then continued... 'James Drawell has a good alibi. That rules him out of his wife's murder, even though he has a strong motive.' He paused and took a deep breath before continuing.

'Moristone also has a strong motive; his grandmother's money giving him a good reason for wanting her out of the way. He also has a cast iron alibi.' He paused then told her... 'I'm sure Basser's wife had nothing to do with her husband's death. So we now have three murders committed by persons unknown, for no obvious reason.'

There was a look of incredulity in his eyes as he concentrated on his driving.

Wilberton was waiting for them as they arrived back at Lincoln. After listening carefully to Laxton's summary of events, he made a decision.

'Robert I want you and DC Bullyn to go to London this afternoon and question Charles Insten, to see if we can make some sense out of the murder of his partner.'

He picked up the phone and paused for a second, rubbing the receiver against his chin as he studied the situation; he raised his eyebrows as he spoke to Laxton.

'I'll get in touch with New Scotland Yard in London and clear the way for you to contact Insten and interview him.'

With this he dialled the number. They were just leaving when the Chief told them, 'Oh, by the way. Hull have been in touch. Gregory Mendois has been charged with fraud and running an illegal gambling hall. Officers from Hull found gambling equipment hidden in the cellar.'

Laxton gave a smile of satisfaction as he went to the door to leave.

'I reckon that little lot should be worth a few years!' he

exclaimed.

He looked at his watch as they went to the car; it was twelve fifteen. Turning to Jane Bullyn, he asked her, 'Do you fancy a pub meal?'

She cocked her head on one side. 'Are you paying?' An impish grin played on her face. He grinned back at her.

'It depends on how much you eat,' he retorted, looking her up and down before adding...

'By the size of you, I'd say you don't come cheap.'

She aimed a playful slap at him.

'You cheeky sod.' She laughed as he swayed out of the way and climbed into the car.

Chapter Thirteen

The long drive to London took over two hours. Laxton checked the clock in the car as they turned off the A1. It was three-forty. After contacting New Scotland Yard, the pair made their way over Waterloo Bridge, passing through the run down area around Waterloo Station to the office of Basser and Insten. He hadn't realised how drab it was in his younger days. 'But then,' he told himself, 'everything looks good when you're nineteen.'

Laxton breathed a sigh of nostalgia as they passed the old Union Jack club, where he'd spent many a weekend leave when he was in the R.A.F. A single room, and a large mug of soup when you came in after a night out, and all for four and sixpence. He smiled inwardly at the thought, as he manoeuvred the car through the heavy London traffic. Parking the car they made their way through the crowded shopping area to a tall building that was given over to offices. Laxton looked up at the high rise building, before entering through two heavy glass doors. They approached the lift. Bullyn selected the eighth floor, where Insten's office was located. It turned out to be a small area sectioned off by metal cupboards in a very large room, full of the sounds of telephones and printers. A pall of blue cigarette smoke hung in the air as they wandered in and out of the sections. A young dark haired woman wearing a pair of thick rimmed glasses, seeing that they looked lost, approached them, a questioning frown on her forehead.

'Can I help you?' she asked, dipping her chin and looking at them over the rims of her glasses.

'We're looking for a Mr Charles Insten,' Bullyn told her.

'I'm afraid he's away at the moment. He did say he wouldn't be long,' a female voice called out from an adjacent section, as they stood waiting for a reply.

Laxton looked over the top of the metal cupboards to an

adjoining area, from where a pretty blonde haired young woman was addressing them.

'That's okay,' he told her. 'We'll wait.'

Charles Insten, carrying a briefcase, entered the lift and pressed the button for the eighth floor where his office was situated. He was in trouble and he knew it. Being the junior partner in Basser and Insten Financial consultants, he'd been investing heavily in the stock market to build up his portfolio. The problem was that the F.T.S.E. had gone down rapidly in the last six months, taking his shares down with it. He was on the verge of bankruptcy. The lift stopped as it reached the eighth floor and the door slid open. His double chin wobbled as he stepped out of the lift. In the last month he'd taken to gambling heavily on the horses as he attempted to recoup some of his losses. An acquaintance who had connections with the racing fraternity, had provided him with inside information. He'd borrowed money from the petty cash and had bet heavily. The money went quickly, unfortunately the horses didn't, sending him deeper into trouble. He shook his head in despair. If his partner John Basser discovered that he was in such a precarious financial position, he would be finished.

'Why does everything that I touch have to go wrong,' he muttered, as he shuffled along the corridor. 'Then again if events pan out well...' he told himself, his eyes narrowing at the thought, as he entered the large room where his office area was situated.

He hadn't had a very good start in life. An only son, his mother had brought him up on her own. He never knew his father. She'd had to work hard to give him a decent education. Being clever with figures, he eventually made it to university, coming through his degrees successfully. After leaving university he was accepted by a firm of consultants. He was made a junior partner after the death of John Basser's father who had been the founder of the company. Living alone, (he never was a ladies' man.) To put it bluntly, he was no Errol Flynn, on the contrary. His short obese figure, thick cherubic lips and gimlet-like eyes weren't exactly an attraction to the women. This didn't stop him having a strong sexual appetite, which he assuaged by making use of the many women posing in their short dresses up and down Soho. The only problem was, they were expensive. Gone were the days when you could walk through Hyde Park and be offered, 'Ten bob short time.' Which meant ten minutes behind one of the large trees, then on your way.

He shook himself out of his reverie, as he approached his office area. A tall man and a woman were talking to the secretary who was in the adjoining section. He called out to the young woman.

'Hello, Judith, are there any calls for me?'

'No, but there are two people here asking for you,' she replied in a loud voice as he neared his allotted area.

'Can I help you?' he asked them, a little breathlessly, on his arrival, as he placed his brief case on his desk.

'Are you Charles Insten?' queried the tall man.

Insten looked up him and nodded. 'Yes,' he replied, then quickly looked away, avoiding eye contact. Laxton made a mental note of the shifty look on his face.

'I'm Inspector Laxton and this is my partner Detective Constable Bullyn.' He had a serious expression on his face as he looked at the 'Oliver Hardy' figure in front of him. 'I'm afraid I've some distressing news for you.'

Insten, with fumbling fingers, adjusted his tie under his double chin nervously. His florid face was taught, as if he half expected what was coming.

'Oh,' he said. 'And what news would that be?'

'Your partner John Basser is dead,' declared Laxton bluntly.

Charles Insten leaned heavily against a large metal locker. Although he'd somehow seemed to expect it, the news obviously, still came as a shock. Bullyn helped him to a chair, where he sat for a few moments with his head in his hands, sweating profusely; he pulled out a handkerchief and dabbed his forehead and neck.

'Did he suffer from his injuries?' he muttered, without looking up, adding...

'How was he killed?'

'I didn't say he had been killed Mr Insten,' replied the Inspector, the words dripping from his lips like acid.

'He fell in front of a train. It all happened so quickly. I doubt if he knew much about it,' Laxton told him solemnly, then he asked him...

'Do you know why he would be coming to London?'

'Yes I asked him to come. I was having problems which I wanted him to help me sort out,' replied Insten, as he nervously reached first in one pocket, and then the other.

Pulling out a packet of cigarettes; he took one out and placed it between his lips. He held the packet out and offered them one. They both declined as he cupped his hands and lit up, taking a deep drag.

'What kind of problems?' queried the Inspector.

Insten shrugged his shoulders. 'You know,' he muttered, in a low voice as smoke drifted down his nostrils, 'business matters.'

Laxton looked at him out of the corner of his eye for a moment, then let it go.

'Did you and John Basser ever fall out?' asked Bullyn, a note book and pen in her hand.

Insten shrugged his shoulders again, took another puff at his cigarette, paused for a couple of seconds before cocking his head back and blowing out a thick cloud of smoke towards the ceiling. His small beady eyes were half closed as he answered the question.

'We had a few minor tiffs,' he admitted, reaching out and tapping the ash from the end of his cigarette in an ashtray that was on the desk. 'But nothing serious.'

The Inspector studied him for a few seconds as he tried to weigh him up. He wasn't impressed. There was something about the man that didn't ring true.

'Where were you yesterday, on the day of his death?' Laxton asked him pointedly, adding, 'Say about twelve noon.'

Insten's head swivelled round as he looked at the Inspector.

'I was here,' he returned sharply. Then he stood up and shouted over the top of the metal cupboards.

'Judy, what time was I here till yesterday?'

The young woman popped her head up, her forehead wrinkled as she paused to think, then replied,

'Well, you were here till lunch time. I would say round about twelve-thirty.'

Charles Insten sat down and turned to the detective.

'There you are!' he exclaimed, holding both the palms of his hands out. 'I was here.'

Laxton nodded, accepting that he couldn't have been physically involved in the murder.

'Tell me, Mr Insten,' he intoned. 'What happens to the business now that John Basser is no longer with us?'

Insten, took another drag at his cigarette, shuffled his feet uncomfortably, then stubbed the cigarette out in the ashtray, before answering the Inspector.

'I suppose I will have to take over the running of the business myself,' he acknowledged with a shrug of his rounded shoulders.

'What about Mrs Basser, won't she have something to say about that?'

Charles Insten looked up at him and snapped.

'She doesn't have anything to do with it. John and I have a written agreement that if one of us left the business, the remaining partner would take over.'

Laxton tugged at his earlobe as he digested the information.

'That's very convenient for you,' he drawled.

Insten's head shot up. His small eyes like chips of ice, were fixed on the Inspector.

'What do you mean by that remark?' he retorted it was obvious that he didn't like the inference.

The Inspector shrugged his shoulders.

'It means that you had a very good reason to want him removed,' he retorted bluntly.

Charles Insten looked away quickly, breaking the eye contact.

'I had nothing to do with the death of my partner,' he blustered.

Laxton chewed on the corner of his mouth for a few seconds as he absorbed the sweating Insten's reply.

After a few more routine questions they turned to leave.

'We'll be off now,' said Laxton. Then as if a thought had suddenly occurred to him, he stopped and turned.

'Do you know of any reason why anyone would want to *murder* John Basser?'

He emphasised the word 'murder' for effect. He wasn't disappointed.

Charles Insten's face blanched, his double chin wobbling as he vigorously shook his head from side to side.

'As far as I know, he didn't have any enemies,' he mumbled unconvincingly as he pulled out his large handkerchief and wiped his brow.

Laxton, unimpressed by Insten's reply, studied him for a few moments through narrowed eyes, then, after thanking him for his co-operation the two detectives turned and left, making their way towards the lift.

'Well what do you think of that?' Laxton asked his companion as he pressed the button indicating the ground floor.

'He reacted very strangely,' she replied as the lift descended smoothly. 'I wouldn't swear to it, but it looked as though he knew more than he was prepared to admit.'

The Inspector nodded his head in agreement, as the lift door slid open. The darkness was closing in as they stepped outside the office block into the cold windy night; she gave a shudder as she pulled her coat collar up and went to where they had parked the car.

'What I can't understand is, why did he ask if his partner John Basser had suffered from his injuries?' she queried as she climbed into the car.

Laxton, thinking her comments over as he fastened his seat belt, and glanced sideways at her, his brow furrowed.

'What are you trying to say?' he grunted as he started the engine and pulled out, with some difficulty, into the stream of traffic. Rows of blinding headlights approached them on the opposite side of the highway.

'Well!' she exclaimed. 'He knew Basser wasn't ill, he'd spoken to him only the night before he was killed. Why would he ask about his injuries.'

'Mm... I see what you mean.' He paused for a few seconds, as he slowed down to allow an elderly lady who had just stepped on to the pedestrian crossing, to pass in front of the car, then continued...

'It does seem a strange comment to make,' he told her, adding in a somewhat measured tone... 'specially when he said it before he knew the cause of John Basser's death.'

The Inspector went quiet for a couple of minutes; he was deep in thought as he immersed himself in the seemingly intangible problems facing them. He turned to his partner.

'What are the motives for the three murders?' he put to her.

'If we could find out *why* they had been killed, then we would be well on our way to solving the murders.'

He gave a shake of his head, as he put the insoluble problem to the back of his mind and concentrated on his driving.

It was just going dark and beginning to rain heavily as they moved out of the suburbs of London. He switched on the wipers as he joined the A1 and accelerated, then turning his head, he gave a quick glance at Jane Bullyn out of the corner of his eye.

'We've got three murders and no obvious suspects,' he emphasised turning his eyes back to the busy traffic in front of him, adding...

'The ones who would normally be under suspicion, all seem to have solid alibis.'

It was six-thirty and dark when Laxton and Bullyn arrived back at Lincoln. The heavy rain had made it hard going. Wilberton, who had waited for them to return, leaned back in his chair his arms folded as he listened intently to the Inspector as he gave him the details of his interview with Insten.

'So we still haven't got anyone in the frame for any of the murders,' he intoned, rubbing his chin ruefully.

'Anyway,' he told them as he got to his feet. 'Leave it for now. We'll see what we can come up with tomorrow.'

'There's something I can't quite put my finger on,' confided Laxton to his partner, as they walked to the car. 'Insten and Drawell were far too uptight. They know something.'

'Better let it rest for now,' Bullyn advised him as she

fastened her seatbelt. Then added…

'Why don't you come home with me and have a meal?'

'You're a good cook are you?' he countered, a half smile on his face.

'No not really, but my mum is,' she informed him.

'I don't want to intrude,' he told her as he manoeuvred the car out of the car park and on to the road.

She leaned across towards him and whispered, 'I'll let you into a secret. Mum asked me to invite you.'

Robert Laxton gave her a sideways glance out of the corner of his eye. Her face was impassive as she gazed straight ahead.

'That was good of her,' he drawled as the car picked up speed.

'Here we are,' said Jane, some forty-five minutes later, as they approached the rather small compact bungalow.

Leading the way up the path, she invited him in. He followed her into the kitchen, where she introduced him again to her mother.

'I hope you've got a good appetite,' she told him, looking up into his eyes as she held out a well-manicured hand.

'I'm starving,' he rejoined, as he clumsily shook her small hand.

He looked at her for a few moments, then suddenly realised he was still holding her hand. He quickly let go and looked away, an embarrassed expression on his face. One of her eyebrows arched as she looked up at him, a wry smile playing on her lips.

She was a very attractive woman, he told himself. She had a sprinkling of grey in her brown hair, and a twinkle in her green eyes. As he had told Jane, it was easy to see where she had got her looks from, Laxton was instantly attracted to her. A warm glow went through him. It was the same feeling that he had experienced at their first meeting, only stronger.

'Call me Robert,' he told her, a broad smile lighting up his face.

'And I'm Nancy,' she replied, her warm smile revealing her perfect pearl like teeth as she led him to a seat at the table in the dining room, where she poured him a drink of wine. Jane was busy dishing out the meal.

He picked up his glass and drank her health, as Jane brought in the meal.

Robert Laxton tucked into the braised steak that she had placed in front of him, with gusto. After the meal, he leaned back in his chair and patted his stomach contentedly.

'Nancy, that was great,' he sighed, as he finished his glass of wine.

Jane reached over the table and topped his glass up. He looked across at Nancy as he raised his glass to his lips. He raised his eyebrows and looked at her over the rim of the glass as he took a sip.

'Jane has been telling me all about of the loss of her dad, just three years ago,' he told her in a low voice.

There was a serious look on Nancy's face as her eyes met his.

'Yes,' she replied, a sombre expression on her face. 'He would have been fifty two this week.'

'About the same age as me then,' he confided.

There was a pause in the conversation. Then Nancy spoke,

'Have you ever been married, Robert?' she asked, her eyes looking down at her well manicured fingers as she carefully folded her napkin.

Robert Laxton picked his glass up slowly and took another sip at his wine before answering her.

'No, I'm afraid I've never met the right woman,' he confessed. 'Or should I say I've never been the right one for them.'

A smile flitted across Nancy's face as she looked up at him.

'You underestimate yourself, Robert,' she told him.

An hour or so of exchanging likes and dislikes went by. Laxton decided it was time for him to leave. After thanking them for a very pleasant evening, he bid them goodnight, promising them, this wouldn't be the last time he would visit.

'What a nice man, Jane,' Nancy declared, trying to hide her flushed cheeks, as the door closed behind him. Jane laughed as she noticed the sparkle in her mum's eyes. She hadn't seen her look so happy for years.

The rain had stopped and the moon was beginning to show itself over the bank of heavy clouds, lighting up the countryside as Robert Laxton drove back through the winding lanes on his way back to his cottage in Old Bolinbrocke. There was a warm glow in his breast, and it wasn't the drink that was the cause of it; Nancy had made a great impression on him. He smiled to himself contentedly as he turned the car into his drive and climbed out. Horatio ran to meet him as he approached the door, purring happily as he rubbed his head against his master's leg, almost tripping him up.

'All right, all right, Horatio,' he whispered affectionately into the cat's ear as he bent down and picked him up.

Then, carrying him on his arm and stroking him, he opened the door and entered the cottage. A note from Annie was on the kitchen table, informing him that his dinner was in the oven. He smiled to himself as he read it. He hadn't much of an appetite after the large meal Nancy had given him, he told himself, but he'd better eat as much as he could before he went to bed. Annie wouldn't be pleased if he left it. He looked down at the cat who was circling him, purring in anticipation. Well, he thought, as he scraped half of it on to another plate and placed it on the floor, Horatio could help him out. After finishing his meal, he took a hot shower, then spent the rest of the evening relaxing to the haunting sound of Johann Strauss and his, 'Tales from the Vienna woods.'

Chapter Fourteen

It was a cold and typically foggy November morning when he stopped to pick up Jane Bullyn at her home. He could just make out Nancy at the lounge window, waving her hand at him as Jane climbed into the car. He returned the wave, then set off, carefully driving through the thick patches of fog, on their journey to the police headquarters in Lincoln. Arriving just under an hour later, they walked through to Wilberton's office to find out if there had been any developments since yesterday. They were told they would find him in the gymnasium working out. There was a strong smell of rubbing oils and sweat pervading the air as they approached the Chief, who was stretched out on the floor doing press-ups. He looked up at them as they approached, his face dripping with sweat from his exertions.

'Well,' he wheezed, 'what have you come up with?' He was breathing heavily as he got to his feet and placed his hands on his hips as he faced them.

Laxton, looking at Wilberton in his black tights, was hard pressed to hold back a smile. Bullyn, her shoulders shaking, turned away, trying to hide her face. Wilberton, oblivious to their reactions towelled himself vigorously, listening intently to the Inspector, as he went through his conclusions so far.

'So you think Basser's wife can be left out of the equation?' he put to Laxton, as he wiped the sweat from his face with a towel. 'I don't agree. In my opinion she could be involved. I think you should interview her again and see what you can come up with.'

Then, turning away he stretched out his arms and waved them slowly as he walked in a circle, taking long, slow deliberate steps. The two onlookers were mesmerised.

'Tai Chi,' he told them controlling his breathing. 'You

should try it. It's very relaxing.'

Bullyn looked up at Laxton. 'I can just see you in black tights,' she joked.

Laxton gave a wry grin as he eyed the chief floating over the floor like a ballet dancer.

'I can't,' he whispered in her ear as they turned to leave. 'My legs are too long and bony.'

'I want to have a word with you before you go. I'll see you in my office in about ten minutes,' the chief called after them as they walked away.

Chief Inspector Wilberton at five-foot-nine didn't conform to the usual image of a police officer. He was more the dapper type, very intelligent and shrewd. He was a fitness fanatic, having a black belt in judo, which came in useful when in trouble. To him keeping fit was a necessity, he took his exercises very seriously. The youngest of six children, his parents found it difficult to afford him a good education. Having passed the eleven plus he went on to grammar school where his keen attitude prompted his headmaster to help him gain a place in university, where he met his Spanish wife Maria. They had four children, a son and three daughters. He was born and brought up in Lincolnshire, where he took up a career in the police force, rising rapidly through the ranks to his present position as Chief Inspector at the age of forty-five, seven years younger than Robert Laxton.

Leaning forward, Wilberton pored over the stack of papers on his desk, showing the progress that had been made so far on the three recent homicides. He looked up as the two plain clothed detectives entered his office. He motioned for them to take a seat. Sitting back, his hands clasped in front of him, he looked across the desk at them, a troubled look in his keen blue eyes.

'Now then,' he began, leaning forward and placing his elbows on the desk as Laxton crossed his legs. 'We've got three seemingly motiveless murders. We know for certain they were perpetrated by more than one person. Up to now there isn't one clue that points to who the killers are, or if there's any connection between them. We don't seem to be making much progress,' he said pointedly, a thoughtful expression on his face as he addressed the two opposite him. 'Have you anything more to add?'

Laxton, deep in thought, sucked at his bottom lip for a few moments as he listened to what the chief had to say, then spoke up...

'In my opinion, the fact that the three murders appear to be motiveless, links them together. For instance,' he put to them, counting on his fingers, 'they weren't robbed. Their deaths were obviously planned and as far as we know, the attackers were all unknown to their victims. As for motive, the only people we know who have one and would have anything to gain by their demise, also have a good alibi...'

'Excuse me, sir,' Bullyn butted in.

'Yes, Constable,' remarked Wilberton. 'If you've anything to add, let's hear it.'

'Well, sir, is it possible that they could be hired killers?'

'It's a thought.' He turned to the Inspector. 'What do you think?'

'I can't see that occurring,' returned Laxton, shaking his head slightly. 'For one thing it would take a massive sum of money to hire a hit man or woman. That's if they could get anyone to do it, which I doubt. He paused for a second as he leaned back in his chair, folded his arms and went on...

'For instance, we know a different person was involved in two of the murders. Up to now we've got a man who takes size eight shoes and smokes Lucky Strike cigarettes, and a vague picture of a woman with long blonde hair.'

'A woman could take a size eight shoe, and smoke Lucky Strike cigarettes,' said Wilberton, running his fingers through his hair.

The Inspector nodded in agreement. 'Or a man dressed as a woman.'

'Have you come up with any more information on the murder of Rebecca Moristone?' asked the chief.

Laxton shook his head. 'The only one we've come across up to now with a motive is Richard Moristone, and he couldn't have done it, he was nowhere near the scene at the time of the murder.'

'So… once again we've got someone with a strong motive and an equally strong alibi,' the chief commented.

Laxton uncrossed his long legs and stretched them out in front of him; he was just beginning to get cramp. He reached down and massaged his calves.

Wilberton plucked at his right ear lobe thoughtfully, as he studied the facts so far.

'We haven't made any progress on the female suspect in the Lincoln railway station killing,' he declared. 'The Lincoln Stationmaster has sent us an enlarged close up of her, but it's pretty vague.'

After a few more exchanges they closed the discussion. Then, after a few instructions from Wilberton, they walked out of the office to the car park.

'Okay, you drive, I want to do some thinking,' Laxton told Bullyn, throwing her the car keys. She deftly caught them and slid into the driver's seat.

'By the way,' she said, glancing at him out of the corner of her eye, as she simultaneously kept one eye on the traffic in front of her, 'Mum's been asking me about you.'

He raised an eyebrow as he looked across at her. 'What's she been saying?'

'Well, she's been asking, when you might be calling again?'

'Mmm…' he muttered, a pleasurable feeling going through him at the thought that Nancy was showing some interest in him. 'I'll have a few words with her when I take you home.'

Jane Bullyn stopped the car at the gate of her home and walked to the door. The tall Inspector followed her in.

'Hello, Robert!' exclaimed Nancy, delight in her eyes as she greeted him with a warm smile. 'It's lovely to see you again.'

'The pleasure's all mine,' he replied huskily.

Then, full of feeling, he took her hands in his, and looked down at her with warmness in his grey eyes. She returned his look with affection. His legs turned to water. The strong feelings he had towards her were alien to him. 'What has happened?' he asked himself. The answer was all too obvious, he was falling in love with her.

'I've made you a nice meal,' she told him as she led him into the kitchen where she had set the table.

'Come on, you two, let's eat, I'm hungry,' commented Jane, her sharply spoken request breaking the magical spell.

Robert Laxton was lost for words as he took a seat at the table. Jane, tucking into her meal, looked up from her plate and saw that they'd hardly touched a thing.

'Aren't you going to eat anything?' she remarked. 'Anybody would think that you were in love...'

Her voice tailed off when she saw how they were looking at each other. Then she laughed, looking down at her plate self-consciously.

'Okay I can take a hint,' she said, a knowing smile on her face as she finished her meal, then left them alone at the table.

After picking at the food in front of them, they went to the settee and sat together. Robert Laxton turned to her, his heart pounding as he looked into her green eyes. He placed his hand on her arm.

'Nancy I think I'm in love with you,' he confessed, fearing her response.

'Robert, I *know* I'm in love with you,' she whispered feelingly, as she took his strong hands in hers and squeezed them gently.

He took her in his arms and looked deep into her eyes, and clumsily kissed her on the lips.

'I can see you've got a lot to learn,' she told him, looking up into his burning grey eyes, then reaching up, she put her arms around his neck, giving him a long, gentle kiss.

After an hour of exchanging endearments, Laxton reluctantly bid her goodnight. He was feeling great as he drove home. He could clearly see what the future held for him.

Nancy went into the lounge, a dreamy look in her eyes. She picked up a photograph of herself and her late husband William. She gazed down at the picture of the handsome, tall young man in his army uniform that looked back at her. She sighed as her mind went back. After a whirlwind courtship, they'd married. It was just after he'd finished his National Service. He was twenty years old. Then he joined the Derbyshire police force. They decided to delay having a family until they were secure. Eight years later after a rapid rise through the ranks, he became an Inspector, then Jane was born. The following years were idyllic. That was until William was taken down with a massive stroke. It was heartbreaking to see such a fine specimen of manhood brought down so quickly. She'd done her best to make him as comfortable as she could. Jane had been a big help, taking her dad for walks. He had two more strokes and never recovered. He was forty-nine years old when he passed away. The shock almost killed Nancy. It was Jane again that helped her through the trauma. That was three years ago, the aching and the hurt were fading away now, but the memories were still there. She looked through the window at the tall figure of Robert Laxton, watching the heavy mist swallowing him up, as he strode down the garden path to his car. He turned momentarily and waved as he opened the car door and climbed in. She gave a deep sigh as the car's rear lights disappeared into the misty night. The thought of him sent a warm feeling through her.

The drive back to his cottage in Old Bolingbroke was uneventful except for having to put his foot on the brakes to avoid a hare that had jumped out of the hedgerow and stopped as it became transfixed in his headlights. He switched off the lights for a couple of seconds, then switched them on again. He smiled to himself; the hare had gone. Then putting the car into gear he continued on his journey. His thoughts turned to the three murders. It was as if some weirdo serial killer was on the loose. He had a strange feeling that this wasn't the end of it. Someone, somewhere had planned it all.

Chapter Fifteen

Alfred Hopper, a small case in his hand carrying all his worldly goods, walked towards the gate office of Lincoln prison, on his way out of the imposing building. He was stopped at the office and given a thorough search then allowed to go through.

The lone figure sitting patiently waiting in the parked car, opposite the prison, suddenly straightened up as Hopper walked out of the prison gates, to what he called freedom. The man had made discreet enquiries as to when Hopper would be released. He checked his watch, it was four-thirty p.m. Hopper was late.

'See you again, Alf,' mocked the uniformed officer, as the heavy gate banged shut.

Hopper, a grim look on his face, ignored him. Pulling the flat cap that covered his shaven head, tight down, he hunched his narrow shoulders. Turning his coat collar up, he buried his hands deep in his anorak pockets, to keep out the cold northerly wind that almost took his breath away. The pale sun was just disappearing over the horizon and the light was beginning to fade as he checked his watch; it was four-forty-five p.m. He paused for a moment as he studied which way to go. Then, suddenly making up his mind, he set off walking towards the Cathedral that stood imposingly at the top of the hill. He had been late in getting his release. He should have been allowed out at midday but it seems the lodgings he was booked in at wouldn't be available until six p.m.

He stopped for a moment and turned his head: he looked back at the building that had been his home for the last five years, its twin turrets standing out like some medieval castle from the dark ages. A stone arch framed its heavy doors. Lincoln prison was no holiday hotel. He took a deep breath.

'It's a relief to be breathing free air again, even if it is cold,' he muttered out loud as he stopped and reached into his inside pocket, taking out a small plastic bag in which he kept his tobacco. He turned his back to the wind as he sprinkled the dark shag which was prison issue, onto the rice paper, then, with a dexterity learned while he was inside, he rolled himself a cigarette. Running the tip of his tongue along the edge of the paper he stuck it down with his finger. After placing it between his lips, he struck a match. Holding it in his cupped hands, he lit the cigarette. Taking a deep drag, he continued on his way.

'My stretch in prison may have been at her majesty's pleasure,' he muttered to himself as he shuffled along. 'To me it's been unbearable.'

The year he'd earned for good behaviour had been a god send. His thoughts drifted back, as a picture of his wife Evelyn formed itself in his mind. He couldn't wait to get his hands on her; she'd been the main reason for his incarceration.

'Okay,' he mumbled to himself, as he gave an imperceptible shrug, 'I may have knocked her about a bit, but what had happened to honour and obey? And why did she have to shop me to the 'Bill'?

He stopped for a moment as he took a last drag at the fag end and tossed it into the gutter, before continuing his journey.

'Well, I'll make her pay,' he added. 'But I must tread carefully.'

A heavy mist was beginning to form as Alf trudged laboriously in the direction of the Cathedral that poked out into the darkening sky. He was beginning to feel hungry. If his recollections were right, there was a pub down by Brayford Pool, where he could get himself a decent meal and a drink. He and Evie used to go there regularly, he recalled. It was about half a mile away; it wouldn't take him long to walk there.

The lone figure got out of the car and followed him at a discreet distance.

Twenty minutes later Hopper entered the pub and approached the bar, where he ordered a pint of beer. Then he picked up a menu that was standing on the bar and studied it for a moment. Taking his cap off to scratch the back of his head, he ran his eyes down the list of tasty dishes on offer. The barman brought him his beer and waited patiently for him to order. After taking a drink of his beer, he wiped the froth from his lips, his mind made up.

'I'll have a plate of steak and chips,' Hopper told him. His mouth watered at the thought of a nice big juicy steak. Something he hadn't seen for years.

The barman looked him up and down, taking in the close shaved head and the small case on the floor at Alf's feet. His face broke into a knowing smile, as he took his money for the pint of beer and pointed to a nearby table. He knew an old lag when he saw one.

'If you take a seat the waitress will bring you your meal,' he told him.

Hopper sat down and half closed his eyes as he took a long swig of his beer. 'That was like nectar,' he muttered to himself, as the waitress arrived with his steak and chips.

'That'll be three pound eighty-five,' she announced, placing the heaped plate in front of him. He reached into his pocket.

He was in a generous mood as he threw four pound coins on the table.

'Keep the change,' he told her with a wave of his hand.

Giving him a 'Humph,' and a black look in appreciation of his generosity, she picked the four pound coins up and flounced away.

Knife and fork in hand, he paused for a second as he looked at the large steak in front of him. It looked really inviting. He wasn't disappointed. Mentally rubbing his hands with anticipation, Alf tucked in with relish. This is what he'd missed when he was in the nick, he thought. From now on he was going to make sure he never went back in there. After finishing his meal he leaned back and patted his stomach; he burped loudly, then ordered another drink. There was the semblance of a satisfied smile on his face as he picked up the glass and took a long drink: he was beginning to feel much better as he tipped the glass and emptied it. The alcohol was warming him up. Ordering another pint, he cast his mind back to the time he'd first met Evie in the park. Was it really thirty years ago? He shook his head as he finished off his pint, wiped the froth from his mouth with the back of his hand, and ordered another. His thoughts turned to Evie again. She'd been a real looker in those days, he told himself. Lifting his glass and taking another long drink, he pictured her stripping off that first night in the boarding house where they'd stayed for their honeymoon. He was beginning to feel sexually aroused as he remembered her response. He was twenty at the time and Evie was eighteen. For the first ten years they'd been happy. Oh it had been hard going to start with. After a spell in Grimsby, working in the fish docks, he'd taken a job in Lincoln. Everything was going okay, until he got the sack for punching the foreman, who'd taken a dislike to him from the moment he'd started at the firm. Well the feeling had been mutual. Why should he stand being treated like crap. He smiled to himself at the satisfaction he'd got from that encounter. The first thing he had to do he told himself, was to find a job and settle down with Evie again.

'Are you okay, sir?' the waitress enquired, breaking in on his thoughts. He looked up.

'Yes! Yes!' he exclaimed, then ordered another drink as he drained his glass.

He went back to reminiscing, recalling that the relationship had deteriorated from the moment he told her he couldn't get another job. The situation went from bad to worse as he took to stealing from houses to make ends meet. He was caught in the act and was put away for six months for breaking and entering. Then it was all downhill, finally resulting in him being involved in a bank robbery and grievous bodily harm, for which he'd got six years. He realised now he'd been a fool. On top of all this he'd found out while in prison, Evie was living with another bloke.

'Well woe betide the pair of them when I catch up with them,' he thought as he tipped his glass up to finish off his sixth pint. He checked his watch as he got up to leave, it was five forty-five p.m. It was time for him to get going to his digs. He was feeling a bit wobbly on his legs, as he got to his feet and almost fell over.

'Are you all right, dearie?' the waitress asked him, a worried look on her face.

Swaying from side to side, he lifted his arm and waved her

away. Nodding his head as he grabbed the back of the chair to steady himself, he felt a hand take hold of his arm, supporting him.

'Are you okay, pal?' a concerned voice asked him.

Alf stopped and looked at the stranger through bleary eyes. His head was spinning as he pointed himself towards the exit.

'Yes I'm okay,' he slurred, weaving his way to the door. The man went with him, still holding him by the arm as he went out of the pub and into the dark, misty night.

'Which way are you going?' the man enquired, a note of concern still in his voice.

'To the bus station,' Alf told him, as he staggered sideways.

'I'm going to the bus station, I'll help you to get there,' the man offered, guiding him along the wharf side. Alf thanked him.

It was dark as Alf Hopper, with his helper, walked by the moored boats, only one of which was lit up, showing it was occupied. A heavy mist was hanging low on the water, when Alf suddenly stopped and peered into the mist.

'Hold on a minute, this isn't the way,' he growled.

He hardly felt the long thin knife as it slid under his ribs and entered his heart. He gave a sharp intake of breath as he turned and looked deep into the eyes of his attacker. There was a questioning look on his face, as he shook his head from side to side, then he gave a deep sigh as he slowly exhaled and the life ebbed out of his body. The man caught him as he fell. He wiped the bloodied weapon on Hopper's jacket. After looking nervously up and down the wharf, he callously rolled the body into the water. His hands were shaking as he turned to walk back along the side of Brayford Pool. The heavy mist swirling around him, swallowed him up as he went up the hill to where he had parked the car. Hunching his shoulders, he hid his face behind the upturned collar of his overcoat. He gave a sigh of relief when he reached his car and swiftly climbed in. Once he was safely in the car, he took a deep breath and dropped his head into his hands. He sat in this position for a few seconds, his forehead resting on the steering wheel as he reflected on what he had done. Taking out a handkerchief he wiped the cold sweat from his brow. He felt a strong sense of relief at the fact that except for the waitress, he hadn't been seen throughout the whole operation and she hadn't got a good look at him. After pausing for a moment to recover his composure, he started the car, engaged the gear and drove off into the murky night.

The sun was just beginning to break through the early morning mist, as the seventy-year-old man, leaning on his stick, limped along the wharf side, grumbling out loud to himself as one of his arthritic ankles caused him to wince with pain.

'It's about time I packed this bloody job up,' he told himself angrily as he bent down and rubbed his painful ankle.

He had taken the job of checking the moored boats for mooring fees after he had retired. The extra money it brought him in helped subsidise his meagre pension.

Checking the boats carefully, he hobbled along the waterside, rubbing his rheumy knuckles against the cold breeze. He stopped for a moment and leaned on his stick to take the weight off his feet to ease the pain, when something floating on the surface of the water caught his eye. His eyesight not being too good, he peered closer, then poked at it with his walking stick. The object went under then rolled over as it resurfaced. Its expressionless face devoid of life, lifted out of the water. The old man was taken aback; there was a look of horror on his face, at the macabre sight that confronted him. Then, as if all the devils in hell were after him, he turned, his pain forgotten as he ran in an ungainly gait, as fast as his crippled feet could carry him, back along the pool side, to the Waterways office, which was situated at the side of the wharf. Pushing the door open, he poked his head inside.

'Brian, there's a body in the water,' he gasped breathlessly to a man who was sat at a desk reading a paper. 'Phone the police.'

The man who was dressed in a blue uniform, straightened up and looked at the old man.

'Now come on, Horace,' he said a faint knowing smile on his face. He knew that the elderly man had poor eyesight. 'Are you sure it isn't an old sack that somebody's thrown in the water?'

'I'm telling you it's a dead body, come and look for yourself if you don't believe me.'

Reluctantly Brian got to his feet and followed Horace along the misty pool side to where half a dozen boats were moored.

'There,' said the old man pointing with his stick. 'Under the edge of the wall.'

Brian leaned over and looked down at what looked like an old plastic bag floating in the oily water among the empty bottles and rubbish.

'Give me your stick,' he muttered, shaking his head as he reached down and poked the object. 'There you are what did I...'

There was the sound of indrawn breath as the 'plastic bag', rolled over and two staring eyes looked up at him. His face paled as he turned and ran back to his office; he picked up the phone and rang 999.

Chief Inspector Wilberton took off his reading glasses and looked up from his desk, as Laxton and Bullyn entered his office.

'Ah, Laxton!" exclaimed Wilberton, twiddling his glasses in his fingers. "What progress have you made so far, on the three murders?"

The Inspector shrugged his shoulders. 'At the moment we're stumped, Chief,' he replied. 'We seem to have come up against a brick wall. Although I'm certain there's something sinister going on, I can't break any alibis, they're solid.'

'Now look here, I placed you in charge of these murder cases because I thought you had the experience to solve them. I've been getting some stick from the Super, and I want the killers apprehended, and quick,' Wilberton snapped, sitting back in his chair and stabbing the air with his glasses to emphasise the point. He stopped as the phone rang, he reached out and picked it up. His body stiffened as he listened intently.

'Yes, yes, I've got that. Brayford Pool. Don't remove the body yet. We'll be there straight away.' He looked up at Laxton as he slowly and deliberately put the phone down, a grave look on his face.

'Come on!' he exclaimed, getting up out of his chair. 'It looks as though we may have another murder on our hands.'

Within fifteen minutes Brayford Pool was a hive of activity. Police, forensics and paramedics surrounded the spot where the body was discovered. They worked in unison as they lifted the dead man out of the water, road blocks were set up, and forensics were thoroughly examining the area which had been taped off. A few minutes later Wilberton accompanied by the two detectives arrived at the scene. They looked down at the bedraggled body of the dead man, as they were approached by Bernard Howsell.

'What have you come up with, Bernard?' Wilberton asked the officer in charge of forensics.

'According to information found on the deceased, his name is Alfred Hopper. He was killed around six-fifteen p.m. yesterday. Give or take. We can't confirm exact cause of death yet, but he does have a puncture under his rib cage. These were found on his person.'

He held out a plastic bag.

Laxton held the plastic bag up to eye level, and looked closely at the contents. It contained a couple of five pound notes, some loose change and a small packet of soggy tobacco, which Hopper had used for rolling his own cigarettes. There was also a folded piece of paper confirming his release from Lincoln prison.

'Now let me see. Ah yes, Alfred Hopper! I remember now,' he exclaimed. 'We sent him down for six years for robbery and grievous bodily harm. With good behaviour he must have just got out.' He smiled grimly to himself at the thought that these were the sole possessions and probably total assets of the dead man.

'So much for a life of crime,' he told himself.

He turned to question the old man, who was obviously badly shaken by what he'd seen.

'Now then, sir, can you tell me what you …' he started. The old man butted in as he looked up at the Inspector.

'I… I couldn't do anything for him. He was already dead when I found him," he quavered.

Laxton looked down at the little grey haired man and gave him a pat of reassurance, on the shoulder.

'That's quite all right, sir,' he told him, in a quiet, comforting tone of voice. 'I just want to ask you a couple of questions.'

The old man nodded his head as he leaned on his stick and looked up at Laxton.

'Were any of these boats occupied last night?' the Inspector asked him; indicating with a wave of his hand, as he looked along the row of six cabin cruisers that were moored up.

'Just one. The May Ellen,' the old man replied, his hand shaking, as he pointed to the boat in question, which was moored about fifty yards from where the body was found. A man was pulling his stomach in, as he tucked his grubby striped shirt into his trousers. He had a cigarette in his mouth and was accompanied by a woman; they were sat on the bow of the May Ellen, as Laxton and Bullyn approached to question them. Bullyn, a note book in her hand, asked them their names. The man told her.

'Did you see or hear anything suspicious last night?' queried the Inspector.

The man scratched noisily at his unshaven chin and thought for a moment, his eyes half closed as he took a pull on his cigarette, then gave a nod of his head.

'We didn't go out last night did we May?' he said, turning to his wife. He then told them thoughtfully, cigarette smoke drifting from his nostrils. 'We did hear two men go past, and what sounded like a scuffle. I looked through the window, but it was too dark to see anything clearly. I could just make out a man, on his own, walking back along the moorings. He came past the boat but I couldn't see his face.'

He paused for a moment as he tapped the ash from his cigarette with his forefinger, then he went on...

'All I can tell you is that he was about medium height, I would say he was about five-foot-ten and of slim build.'

'About what time would that be?' queried Bullyn.

His wife butted in. 'It was about six forty-five wasn't it, Alan?'

Alan's brow creased as he studied for a moment; he cast his mind back, trying to remember. He nodded his head and turned to his wife.

'Yes that would be about right. We had been listening to the six-o-clock news.'

The description of the man, given by the two of them, wasn't much to go on. Laxton thanked them both for their help. Wilberton, who'd been busy questioning forensics, approached them, swinging his arms and slapping his hands against his side to bring back the circulation.

'We've had very little information to go on up to now,' his warm breath turning to steam in the cold air, as he spoke. 'You'd better have a word with Alf Hopper's wife and see if she has anything to add,' he told them as they turned to leave.

The two detectives checked the address of Hopper's wife. They arrived at the large terraced house on Station Lane, Louth, which was the home of Evelyn Hopper. A heavily built man in a tatty vest, his paunch, which looked like the result of too many beers, hanging over his belt, answered the door. His tattoos and close-cropped hair gave him a menacing appearance.

'Is Mrs Hopper at home?' enquired Bullyn.

'Evie!' The man called over his shoulder, in a loud voice.

'Yes,' she called from the kitchen, a note of annoyance in her voice. 'What do you want?'

'You've got visitors,' he replied, a contemptuous look on his face. 'It looks like the Bill.'

There was a worried look on the face of the woman, her long blonde hair tied at the back, the dark roots clearly showing, as she came to the door, wiping her hands on her apron.

'I'm Mrs.. er, Evelyn Hopper,' she answered nervously. 'How can I help you?'

Laxton introduced himself and his partner. They were invited into the house and followed her into a grubby lounge. They refused the offer of a cup of tea, as they sat on a settee that smelled strongly of cats. The Inspector addressed Evelyn Hopper who had taken a seat opposite them. She had a cup of tea in her hand.

'I'm afraid we've got some distressing news for you," he

told her sombrely, then after hesitating for a moment, he went on. Evelyn was listening attentively. Her face visibly blanching, when she was told of Alf Hopper's death. Her hand was shaking, as she took a nervous sip of her tea. Her companion placed a protective arm around her shoulder.

'Bloody good riddance!' he sneered callously.

Laxton eyes hardened. The big man quickly looked away.

'He was murdered,' the Inspector snapped, finding difficulty in controlling himself.

There was a loud clatter, as Evelyn Hopper dropped her cup on the floor, spilling tea down her apron: her hand was shaking. Bullyn picked the cup up and calmed her down.

'And your name would be?' asked Laxton, sharply.

The question was aimed at the shaven-headed man.

'Bernard Malson,' he replied, striking a match and lighting a cigarette. He took a deep drag and blew a stream of smoke belligerently towards the Inspector.

Laxton stroked his chin; he was deep in thought for a few moments as he eyed the big, hard looking man in front of him. Malson had a brightly coloured 'diamond back' snake tattooed on his right arm. It started on the back of his wrist and wound its way up his forearm, to finally disappear under his armpit.

'Malson… Malson,' he muttered to himself, half closing his eyes as he cast his mind back. Then it came to him. He looked Bernard Malson straight in the eyes.

'As I recollect, you were sent down a few years ago for grievous bodily harm. You almost killed a man,' he declared.

Malson took another deep drag on his cigarette, held it for a moment, then blew out two streams of smoke down his nostrils before he answered the Inspector.

'That was self defence. There were two of them attacking me. Those bastards will think twice before trying that again,' he countered, sticking his chin out aggressively. Evelyn Hopper reached up and placed her arm around his broad shoulders, in an attempt to calm him down as he stubbed out the cigarette in a saucer that was on the sink top.

'Bernie's my partner, he's not like that now. He's good to me,' she asserted.

'I finished with Alf when he was sent down for six years,' she confided, her blonde hair falling down one side of her face, as she tossed her head defiantly.

Malson had been living with Evelyn Hopper for over two years. He had first seen her when she'd visited her husband Alf in Lincoln prison. They'd been talking, or more like arguing at the next table in the visitors' room. He was due out the following week. His sister Mabel had come to see him to tell him he could stay with her and her husband for a few weeks until he could fix himself up with lodgings. He hadn't much time for Alf Hopper, he was a sneaky swine. But he did like the look of Evelyn. After he got out of prison he looked her up. Then after taking her out a few times he moved in with her.

'You won't have to worry about that little bleeder any more,' he had assured her.

It was obvious to Laxton that Evelyn Hopper wasn't going to lose any sleep over the demise of her husband Alf. What surprised him most was the way she looked so shocked when she heard of his murder.

'Were you informed that he was to be released yesterday?' he put to her.

She hesitated for a couple of seconds before replying in a low voice...

'Yes I was told a few weeks ago that he was coming out, but I wrote a letter to him, telling him that I didn't want anything more to do with him, and that I wasn't going to meet him. I told him all about Bernard. As I've just said. I'm finished with him now.'

'What did he say to that?' queried Bullyn.

'He made a few threats,' she answered. Then gave a shrug of her shoulders. 'But I didn't let it bother me, now that I've got Bernie,' she added, giving the big man's brawny arm an affectionate squeeze.

Laxton, rubbing his jaw reflectively, with the back of his hand, asked them.

'Where were you yesterday evening at around six p.m?' The question, which was directed at both of them, took them by surprise.

Malson's eyes narrowed menacingly.

'Hold on a minute,' he growled. 'You're not trying to pin his murder on us are you?'

Laxton straightened up to his full height. There was an icy expression on his face as his eyes hardened.

'Just answer the question,' he snapped back. There was a note of antagonism in his voice. Malson backed off. Evelyn Hopper intervened.

'We were down at the supermarket,' she declared. 'Weren't we Bernie?'

Malson nodded. 'That's right. And we can prove it," he said confidently, pulling in his beer belly and sticking out his chest.

He walked over to a sideboard and opened a drawer. After a couple of minutes rummaging around, he produced a slip of paper and threw it on the table.

'There you are,' he announced triumphantly. 'That's the receipt that we got from the supermarket with yesterday's date written on it. The woman at the checkout will verify it, she knows us well.'

He stuck his chin out aggressively as he leaned towards the Inspector.

'If you don't believe us, there's the phone,' he added, pointing with his finger.

Laxton nodded at Bullyn, who picked up the receipt from the table, went to the phone and lifted the receiver. After dialling the number printed on the receipt, she asked the person from the supermarket if the couple were there between six-o-clock and six fifteen p.m. on the date in question. A few seconds later she received a reply. She thanked the person on the other end of the phone and glanced up at the Inspector.

'The woman at the supermarket verified it,' she declared as she put the phone down.

Laxton turned to Bullyn.

'I reckon that will do us for now,' he concluded. Then with a cursory nod, they thanked the couple and were just about to leave, when Bernie called after them.

'By the way,' he rasped, 'how did Alf get it?'

'As far as we know, he was knifed,' replied the Inspector

coldly.

Bernie gave a callous laugh.

'If it had been me, copper,' he growled, 'I would have broken his bloody neck.'

Bullyn, who had been taking notes throughout the interview, turned to Laxton as they returned to the car.

'That's another one with a strong motive and a good alibi,' she asserted.

'I know that, but it's pretty obvious they didn't have anything to do with the killing of Alf Hopper. Having said that, there's something not quite right,' he mused. Then went on... 'Evelyn Hopper seemed to be too uptight. She knows something.'

His brow wrinkled as he pondered for a moment. 'Why would anyone want to kill Alf Hopper? It doesn't make sense,' he said with a grunt.

'Well, there's Malson for one, he wouldn't hesitate if he thought he could get away with it. Although it seems to me Hopper's wife is the one with the motive, she couldn't stand the sight of him,' suggested Jane Bullyn. 'Maybe she was afraid he would come between her and Malson when he was released from prison.'

'I agree with what you say,' Laxton rejoined, climbing into the car and reaching across to open the car door for her, adding as she sat down... 'But with their alibi, I repeat, they couldn't have done it.'

Arriving back at headquarters around half an hour later, they explained the current situation to Wilberton. The Chief asked them to follow him into the room at the back of his office, where they took a seat as he referred to his wallboard. With marker in one hand, and a cane in the other, he went through all that had happened so far.

'First we have Rose Drawell, murdered. We discover that an insurance has been taken out on her for a large amount by her estranged husband. Up to now this is the strongest motive for killing her that we have uncovered. The problem is, James Drawell, her husband, has a cast iron alibi. He was at the hospital at the time of the incident.'

The Chief paused to let the facts sink in. Then continued, lowering the tip of the cane to point out the facts that were written on the wallboard.

'Next we have the murder of Rebecca Moristone. Although we haven't any clues as to who perpetrated this crime, forensics have come up with the strip of cloth which possibly came from the killer's clothing. I repeat 'possibly'. We know that her grandson Richard would be the sole benefactor from her death. The fact that he was deeply in debt being a very strong motive, making him the obvious suspect. Again he has an unbreakable alibi.'

Wilberton paused as one of the staff brought in a tray holding three cups of coffee, and placed them on the desk. He picked up one of the cups and took a sip of the hot liquid, then went on to another set of statistics.

'Next, is the murder of John Basser, pushed in front of a train by what we know now was a blonde haired woman. The persons who stood to gain most from his death were his wife and his partner, Charles Insten, who was in dire trouble as regards their business. It seems less likely that his wife was involved. Incidentally, as far as we can make out, they both have a solid alibi.'

Laxton, who had been listening with great interest, butted in at this point.

'We haven't totally taken Gloria Basser out of the equation yet, Chief, although I must admit I don't think that she had anything to do with her husband's murder.'

Wilberton ran the cane through his fingers as he waited for the Inspector to finish. Then turned back to the board.

'Point taken, Robert,' he conceded as he carried on with his deductions.

'Now we have the murder of Alfred Hopper. His wife admits that she hates him. Whether that is a strong enough motive to kill him is debatable. Of course, she may have feared him. If so, that would be a different matter altogether.'

He stopped again, reached out for his cup and finished his lukewarm coffee; he pulled his face as he placed the cup back on the tray and proceeded with his summing up.

'Then again she couldn't have done the deed personally, she was nowhere near the scene of the crime at the time it happened.'

He stood back from the board, the cane in his hand held out like a headmaster preparing to punish some intransigent school boy. Then he asked them for their comments.

'Can we see the close up of the incident at the Railway Station again?' requested Laxton.

'Yes,' replied the Chief, 'I've got it here. In fact it is to be shown on television tonight, and the newspapers will be printing it tomorrow morning. It isn't very clear, but it may give us a lead,' he suggested.

Wilberton's tone of voice didn't carry much conviction. He gave the order for the film to be switched on. As it came to the crucial moment when the woman was seen to have pushed Basser in front of the train, Laxton's back suddenly straightened, as the woman's blonde hair fell back from her face as she reached out.

'Chief, that woman bears a strong resemblance to Evelyn Hopper.'

'I can't see her being involved in John Basser's murder,' declared Wilberton shaking his head. 'What motive would she have? From your description of her, she wouldn't move in the same circles as John Basser.'

After going over the film three more times, they came to the conclusion that there wasn't much more they could get from it, and switched it off. After another ten minutes or so discussing the situation, they decided to call it a day. Getting to their feet the two detectives left the office.

'I've got a strong feeling about this,' confided Laxton to his partner, as they walked to the car, telling her...

'We'll go to Louth tomorrow and question Evelyn Hopper again.'

Laxton drove most of the way to Dalesworth in silence, as he mulled over in his mind, the day's events. As they approached Gunby roundabout he spoke.

'What's puzzling me,' he said stopping to allow a car from

his right, to go through.

'Is the fact that, first of all Alf Hopper is murdered, and if Evelyn Hopper was the woman who pushed Basser in front of the train. What is the connection? What reason would she have to do it?'

Bullyn, who had been listening intently to the Inspector's comments, turned towards him.

'As you've just stated. *If* she was the woman who was involved in Basser's murder,' she emphasised. 'We don't know for certain it was her. The best thing we can do is to ask her where she was at the time John Basser was killed.'

Laxton nodded in agreement as he stopped the car and the two of them climbed out and made their way up the garden path. Nancy greeted them as they walked through the door. He put his arm around her and kissed her affectionately on the forehead, before following her into the warm comfortable lounge.

'Are you going to stop for a cup of tea, Robert?' asked Nancy, smilingly.

Laxton, returning her smile, nodded his head, telling her…

'I'll have half an hour.'

Three quarters of an hour later, after exchanging endearments with her, (oblivious to Jane's presence), he decided that it was time to go. He felt a warm glow in his chest as he got to his feet and reluctantly went out of the door. After waving goodbye he raised his collar and sunk his hands deep into his coat pockets and made his way to his car. Giving another wave he climbed in and drove off. Nancy stood in the doorway watching until the rear lights disappeared into the heavy mist that had come down like a blanket since he had arrived. Giving a deep sigh she closed the door.

Chapter Sixteen

Evelyn Hopper cleared the table after the lunchtime meal. Bernie went into the lounge, flopped down on the settee, and switched the television on. She followed him a few minutes later with two mugs of tea. They both settled down to watch the one-o-clock news. She wasn't taking much notice, when a picture flashed on the screen, showing a woman, apparently pushing a man in front of a train. The newsreader was making an appeal. A blurred close up picture of the woman was shown.

'Do you know this woman?' asked the newsreader.

Evelyn Hopper froze. Bernard Malson turned and looked straight at her.

'Evie, that woman looks like you!' he exclaimed.

'Don't be silly, Bernie, she's nothing like me,' she retorted, her face reddening as she got up to take the mugs away and wash the dinner dishes. Twenty minutes later, after she had just finished drying the crockery, the phone rang.

'I'll answer it,' she called to Bernie. She picked up the receiver and placed it to her ear.

'Evelyn Hopper?' a man's voice enquired.

'Speaking,' she replied. There was a touch of anxiety in her voice.

'You bloody fool,' the voice rasped. 'Why didn't you make sure that you couldn't be seen by the surveillance cameras that were installed at the railway station?'

'Now look here. Who are you?' she snapped, looking over her shoulder in the direction of the lounge where Bernie was watching television, as she kept her voice low.

'Never mind who I am,' the voice on the other end of the phone retorted. 'Be at the roundabout at the top of Station Road at six-o-clock tonight. We'll sort it out then.'

The phone clicked and went dead.

'Who was that?' called Bernie from the lounge.

'Oh just a friend,' she lied as she replaced the phone and joined him in the lounge.

'By the sound of your voice it didn't sound much like a friend,' he remarked, a puzzled look on his face, as she sat on the settee beside him.

'Let's see what other programmes are on the telly,' he grunted, reaching out for the morning paper.

Putting his glasses on, he scanned through the pages.

'Ah, here we are!' he exclaimed, running his finger down the list of programmes.

'There's a good western on I.T.V. at half past one, Evie,' he announced, his eyes lighting up as he picked up the control and switched the channel.

Evelyn Hopper, deep in thought, just nodded her head in reply. She had more serious matters to think about. After the film had been running for about half an hour, she was getting bored. Westerns weren't her favourites.

'I'm not very interested in this film, Bernie, I'm going to lay on the bed and have a nap,' she told him, as she got up and made her way to the bedroom.

Bernie, who was deeply engrossed in the film, just nodded his head, to let her know that he had heard her.

Her mind was in turmoil as she closed the bedroom door behind her. She felt a strong feeling of foreboding, as she flopped down on the bed and buried her face in her hands.

'It had all seemed so simple,' she told herself, shaking her head.

She was beginning to have second thoughts about the terrible deed that she had done.

Burying her face in the pillow, she fell into a deep, troubled sleep.

'Evie! Evie!' a distant voice called.

She opened her eyes and saw Bernie leaning over her. He was carrying a cup of tea.

'I've made you a cup of tea,' he told her, softening his voice.

'What time is it?' she mumbled sleepily, as she sat up.

Bernie looked at his watch.

'It's half-past-five,' he informed her.

'Half-past-five!' she repeated, suddenly coming to her senses. 'I've got to meet someone at six-o-clock.

Jumping off the bed, she took a long drink of the tea that Bernie had brought her. Then putting on her coat she turned to leave.

'Aren't you taking the car?' he enquired, noticing that she hadn't picked up the car keys.

'No, Bernie,' she replied. 'I'm not going far. Anyway the walk will do me good.'

She could feel spots of rain on her face as she walked briskly to the roundabout, which was about twenty minutes walk. She stopped about fifty yards from it. It was dark and cold as she waited. She pulled her coat collar tight around her neck. After what seemed an eternity a car's headlights showed in the distance. She stepped out into the road, so that she could be seen clearly. She held her arm out. The car came nearer, flashing its main beam.

'Good,' she thought, 'he's seen me.'

She stepped back onto the footpath and waited for the car to stop. The car didn't slow as it pulled in towards the kerb, on the contrary, it speeded up and swerved, mounting the kerb. She realised too late, what was happening. She screamed as the car hit her with full force, throwing her high into the air, then sped on, turned right at the roundabout, and headed along the Louth bypass, leaving her broken body in a crumpled heap.

Henry Shawlyn drove steadily up to the roundabout and braked, as a car, flashing its headlights almost blinding him, approached from the right. He stopped his car and waited. He saw a woman standing on the side of the road, her arm held out. It seemed as though she was expecting the oncoming vehicle to stop. It didn't. She stepped back. The car mounted the kerb and smashed into her. Shawlyn's jaw dropped in horror at what seemed a deliberate act.

'Good grief,' he gasped, hardly daring to believe his eyes. 'That looked deliberate.'

He switched on his main beam as he tried to catch sight of the car's registration number, as it flashed by in front of him, then carried on, along the Louth bypass. He couldn't make it out. But he did see the make and colour of the car. It was a black Volvo. As far as he could see, there was only one person in it. He jumped out of his car and ran over to the stricken woman. He wiped away the blood that was running from her nose with his handkerchief; then lifting her bloodied head gently with the palm of his hand, he tried to make her more comfortable. She gripped his wrist, her lips moving as she struggled to say something. Laying her head back on to the grass, he took out his mobile phone and called an ambulance and the police.

'All right, my dear, hang on, help is on the way,' he whispered to her in a comforting tone.

He wasn't very skilled at first aid. There wasn't much he could do to help her. He did know she mustn't go to sleep. Blood was bubbling out of the corner of her mouth. She mumbled some words. Placing his ear close to her lips, he attempted to hear what she was trying to say. He picked up one word out of the jumbled sentence.

'Basser's...' Her weak voice faded away. It was all he could understand.

'Come on, my dear,' he urged. 'Keep talking. Basser's what?' To no avail, her grip on his wrist weakened as she passed out.

At that moment an ambulance arrived, closely followed by a police car. The ambulance drove as close as possible to the injured woman. The paramedics very carefully lifted her on to a stretcher and swiftly carried her into the ambulance, then drove off at speed, with sirens wailing. The whole operation was completed in three minutes.

It was eight p.m. Robert Laxton was stretched out in his usual position, on the long settee, his eyes half closed; he had a glass of whisky and soda on the table beside him, with Horatio purring contentedly in his lap. He was watching a video tape of the London Philharmonic Orchestra playing The Blue Danube, one of his favourite pieces of music. He was conducting with his long forefinger, when the phone rang. Stretching out his hand, he picked it up and placed it to his ear. It was Chief Inspector Wilberton. There was a note of urgency in his voice.

'Robert, there's been an accident. Evelyn Hopper has been seriously injured. She's been taken to Lincoln hospital. It looks as though it may have been deliberate.'

'Okay I'll be there as quick as I can,' Laxton told him as he switched off the music. Swinging his long legs off the settee, he jumped up, dumping Horatio unceremoniously on the floor. Putting his coat on hurriedly, he rushed out of the house, clambered into his car and with a screech of tyres, drove out of the gate. Twenty minutes later he arrived at Dalesworth, where he picked up Bullyn on his way to the hospital in Lincoln. He explained the situation to her as he drove along. They arrived at the hospital at nine p.m.; they were directed to the accident ward.

"We're looking for Evelyn Hopper. She was involved in a car accident tonight. We'd like to ask her a few questions if that's possible," Bullyn told the staff nurse in charge.

'I'm afraid you can't,' the staff nurse replied, telling them...

'She died from her injuries fifteen minutes ago without regaining consciousness.'

'What do you mean by, regaining?' Bullyn asked her.

'Well she was conscious for a couple of minutes before the ambulance arrived at the scene of the accident. Then she passed out.' The nurse shook her head; she had a solemn look on her face as she went on... 'I'm afraid we weren't able to resuscitate her. There's a gentleman in the recovery room. He was with her just after the accident.'

The two detectives thanked her and went to the recovery room, where they approached the man in question, who looked to be in his early sixties; he was sitting in a chair, holding his head in his hands; the man was obviously distressed. He looked up at them through his fingers as they came over to him and introduced themselves.

'Now then, sir, can you tell us your name?' asked Laxton, noticing streaks of dried blood on the side of the man's face.

'Henry Shawlyn,' he told them, his hands shaking as he nervously straightened his tie.

'Can you describe to us, in your own words, what you saw?' requested Bullyn, pen and notebook in hand.

Shawlyn ran his fingers through his thick grey hair, which had fallen over his forehead. He paused for a few seconds as he gathered himself, then he took a deep breath before commencing to describe what he had seen.

'Well,' he began, his voice quavering, 'as I approached the junction to the roundabout, I saw a woman standing on the side of the road, as if she was waiting for someone, when a car approaching from the right drew near flashing its main beam. She stepped back on to the kerb as if expecting it to stop. Then the car suddenly swerved and hit her. I couldn't believe my eyes, it was horrendous.' His voice rose hysterically. 'It looked as though it was deliberate.'

'All right, all right, calm down, sir,' coaxed Laxton soothingly. Then asked, 'Did the woman who was hit, say anything?'

'Well. Yes,' replied Shawlyn, pulling out a handkerchief and wiping the sweat from his brow, before carrying on. The two detectives listened intently.

'She was mumbling something. I couldn't quite catch what she was saying. I just picked up one word. Bassers... and then she passed out.'

'Bassers?' repeated the Inspector, questioningly. 'In what context did she say it?'

Shawlyn's brow furrowed; there was a questioning look in his eyes. 'What do you mean?'

'Well,' explained Laxton patiently, 'did it sound like the beginning of a sentence and did it sound plural?'

'Oh!' exclaimed Shawlyn. 'I see what you mean now. Yes, it was the first word, it sounded as though she was trying to add to it. As far as it being plural or singular...'

He shrugged his shoulders.

'Did you manage to get the car's registration number?' enquired the Inspector.

'No,' he replied with a shake of his head, adding. 'I tried but it was moving too fast.'

'Can you describe the car and the driver?' asked Bullyn.

'The car was a large black Volvo. I couldn't see the driver, it was too dark,' he told her, stammering nervously and shaking his head.

After taking down his name and address, they thanked him for his help and informed him that he may be needed at a later date.

'Can I go now?' asked Henry Shawlyn tentatively.

Laxton nodded. The man got up out of his chair and hurried off down the corridor to the exit, as the two police officers followed him and made their way to the car. Before turning on the ignition, the Inspector, a thoughtful expression on his face, turned to his companion.

'We'll call and have a word with Bernard Malson, he may be able to enlighten us as to why she had gone to the roundabout in the first place.'

Ten minutes later they arrived at the home of Evelyn Hopper. A worried Malson answered the door and asked them into the house.

'Can you tell us why Mrs Hopper went out tonight?' enquired the Inspector, deliberately declining to tell the big man that she was dead.

'She didn't tell me,' replied Malson, shaking his head. 'The phone rang and she answered it, then told me that she had to go out.' He scratched the back of his head. There was a worried look on his face.

'That's over two hours ago,' he grunted. 'I don't know when she'll be back. She did say she wouldn't be long.'

The two detectives exchanged glances. It was obvious by his remarks, that Malson hadn't heard about the fatal incident.

'She won't be coming back, Mr Malson,' Bullyn informed him in a sombre voice as she looked down at the floor. She raised her eyebrows and looked up at the big man in front of her, telling him…'I'm afraid she's dead.'

Malson took a step backwards and sat down in a chair, slowly shaking his head from side to side; he was in a state of shock.

'Dead?' he gasped, a look of disbelief on his face. 'How?' he spluttered. 'She only left here a short time ago. What's happened. Has there been an accident?'

'She was hit by a car,' Laxton told him. 'We believe it may have been deliberate.'

'Deliberate!' repeated Malson, his eyes hardening. 'That means she was murdered.'

Laxton nodded his head in agreement.

'Do you own, or do you know anyone that owns a black Volvo?' he enquired.

'A black Volvo?' repeated Malson, shaking his head negatively. 'Why do you ask?'

'That's the make of car that was involved in the incident.'

Malson's eyes narrowed as he looked at him, then he jumped up and eyeballed Laxton.

'Are you accusing me of killing the one woman in my life?' he exploded, his fists clenched menacingly in front of him.

'No I'm not accusing you, Mr Malson, calm down,' advised the Inspector in a passive voice. 'But I had to ask you so that I could check your reaction.'

The big man took a deep breath and cooled down. The anger in him slowly dissipating. But the hurt was still showing in his eyes. Laxton couldn't help feeling sorry for him.

'What I would like to know,' he demanded. 'Who would want to kill my Evie?'

'That is what we intend to find out,' Laxton told him.

'Did she ever mention the name, Basser,' asked Bullyn.

'No,' mumbled Malson, shaking his head. He turned his troubled eyes to Laxton.

'Get the bastard, Inspector. If you don't... So help me, I'll find him...'

He left the sentence unfinished. He held his big fists up in front of him as he squeezed his eyes tightly shut. A tear ran down his cheek. Laxton laid a hand on his shoulder.

'Don't worry,' he told him in a low voice. 'We'll get whoever did it.'

The Inspector exchanged glances with D. C. Bullyn. It was obvious they weren't going to get any more out of the distraught man. After making sure he was going to be okay, they left and returned to headquarters. Wilberton was waiting for them. He looked up as the two detectives walked in. Laxton explained to him what she had told the man who had reported the incident. The one word 'Basser's'

'Did you get anything out of Malson?' he enquired.

'No,' replied Laxton. 'But I'm certain now that Evelyn Hopper did have some connection with Basser's death; but who was she referring to when she said 'Basser's?'

'She could have been about to say, Basser's wife,' suggested Bullyn, adding… 'Maybe she was describing the driver of the car.'

'Mmm…' muttered Wilberton. 'Gloria Basser does have long blonde hair. I wonder.'

He paused for a moment, then turned to Laxton. 'There's one way to find out. You'll have to question her again tomorrow.'

The Inspector looked at his watch as they stepped out into the dark night; it was eight fifteen p.m. as they walked wearily to the car. They'd had a long day. He drove Jane back to her home in Dalesworth. Nancy was waiting at the door as they arrived.

'Come in, Robert,' she told him, seeing the tired look in his eyes. She put her arms around him and gave him a gentle kiss on the cheek. 'I'll make you a nice cup of tea.' He smiled his thanks, as he sunk into a comfortable easy chair. After drinking the welcome beverage, he took his leave of them and made his way back to his cottage.

Chapter Seventeen

Laxton with Bullyn at his side, was deep in thought as he drove the car on his way to the home of Gloria Basser in Wardingham. He couldn't see how she could be involved in the incident at the roundabout just off the Louth Bypass, but logic told him that there must be some connection between her husband's death and Evelyn Hopper, or else why would she mention Basser, and if she didn't mean Basser's wife; then what the hell did she mean?

It was around eleven a.m. when the Inspector, and his partner, drove into Gloria Basser's driveway. There was a look of surprise on her face when she answered the door bell. She was wearing a silk dressing gown and holding a large hair comb in her hand as she invited them in, her lovely blonde hair cascading over her shoulders.

'How can I help you, Inspector?' she asked questioningly, as she lifted a well plucked eyebrow and looked up at him.

'Would you mind answering a few more questions?' asked Laxton, his voice softening.

'Go ahead, I've got nothing to hide,' she told him, the pain still showing in her eyes, as she looked into the long ornate mirror in the hallway and ran the comb through her hair.

'Where were you between six and six thirty p.m. yesterday evening?" he queried, as Bullyn, pen and notebook in hand, stood at his side taking notes.

She stopped combing for a moment; there was a questioning frown on her forehead as she turned away from the mirror and walked into the lounge, followed by the two detectives.

'Why do you want to know what I was doing yesterday evening,' she retorted, adding…

'My husband's death was seven days ago. Anyway I thought we'd agreed that I didn't have anything to do with it.'

'This isn't about your husband's death,' he replied, adding

in a strict tone of voice…

'I repeat, Mrs Basser, where were you between the hours of six and six thirty p.m. yesterday evening?'

Gloria Basser shrugged her shoulders. 'I stayed in last night.' She paused for a moment the comb half way through her hair, as she cast her mind back. 'I was in the bath just after six,' she confided, then continued taking the comb all the way through her hair.

'Was there anyone here with you?' he followed up, giving her a long probing look.

'No,' she replied, glancing at herself in the mirror that hung on the wall over the stone fireplace. 'I was alone.'

'So there wasn't anyone to prove you were here!' exclaimed Laxton.

'Are you calling me a liar, Inspector?' she rejoined sharply; tossing her golden locks defiantly, as she turned to face him.

'No,' he declared, with a shake of his head. 'I'm just trying to clarify the situation.'

'Anyway,' she countered, 'I'm asking you again, why are you questioning me about what I was doing last night?' There was a mystified expression on her face.

Bullyn glanced across at Laxton, he nodded his head. There was a serious look in his eyes.

'A woman was deliberately run down and killed just outside Louth yesterday between six p.m. and six-thirty. The last word she spoke before she died was 'Basser's.' The only person who seemed to fit the bill was you, his wife.' Bullyn explained in a sombre voice, adding…

'We would like to eliminate you from our enquiries if we can. But we can't do that until we get some proof that you couldn't have been there.'

Gloria Basser, an exasperated expression on her face, shook her head slowly from side to side, she couldn't believe what she was hearing.

'What was her name?' she asked, her voice softening at the thought of the woman dying.

'Evelyn Hopper,' Bullyn informed her.

'Evelyn Hopper,' Gloria Basser repeated, as she studied her

long, painted finger nails. 'I've never heard of her. Why would I want to kill someone I don't know?'

'Mrs Basser,' interrupted the Inspector, 'there have been many strange happenings recently, which take some explaining. You must understand that we have to ask these questions.'

'Hold on a minute,' she said, casting her mind back. 'I had a phone call at around six-fifteen from the Good Samaritans, asking me if I needed any help. That should prove to you that I was here.'

She gave them a number and pointed to the phone on a small table. Bullyn picked the phone up and checked Gloria Basser's statement. She nodded into the receiver as the woman on the other end spoke; then she turned to Laxton.

'They say Mrs Basser's statement is correct.'

Laxton thanked her for her co-operation and told her that he was sorry for not accepting her word. She gave him an understanding nod.

He was just on the point of leaving, when he suddenly stopped and turned to face her.

'I would like to ask you one more question,' he informed her as she tied her hair in a ponytail. 'Do you know anyone who drives a black Volvo?'

'Yes,' was her swift reply. 'Charles Insten, my husband's partner.'

Laxton looked at Bullyn. 'Of course, that's it!' he exclaimed, hitting the palm of his hand with his fist excitedly. 'Basser's partner. That's what Evelyn Hopper was trying to say.'

'Why would Charles want to kill this woman?' Gloria Basser asked confusedly.

'That's what we want to find out,' returned Laxton. 'We have reason to believe she may have been involved in the death of your husband.'

He turned back to Mrs Basser. 'Do you have his home address?'

She went to a drawer and took out an address book. A mystified Gloria Basser gave the two officers a questioning look as she read out Charles Insten's address in Hackney, London.

They turned and went to the door. The Inspector stopped and looked at her, his hand on the door handle.

'Thank you, Mrs Basser, you've been a great help,' he informed her. Then as an after-thought, he told her he was sorry if they had upset her.

Still mystified, she bid them goodbye. After telling her that they would keep her informed if there were any further developments, they thanked her and left. On returning to Lincoln they went through her statement with Wilberton.

'At last we're getting somewhere,' he announced, his eyes lighting up, as he rubbed his hands together with anticipation.

'I want you to go to London tomorrow and interview Insten again. I'll get on to Scotland Yard and inform them that you're coming,' he told the two detectives as they turned to leave the office. It was getting misty as they stepped out on to the headquarters car park and approached the car. Laxton checked his wrist watch. It was two-thirty p.m.

The heavy November mist was beginning to close in as Laxton stopped the car to drop Bullyn off at her home. Nancy was standing in the doorway. She had seen the car arrive.

'Aren't you coming in for a cup of tea?' Jane Bullyn put to him as she climbed out of the car.

He looked across at Nancy, a warm feeling swept through him. He nodded his head.

'Okay, Jane,' he told her, a broad smile on his face he disembarked and followed her down the crazy paved path.

He put his arm around Nancy's shoulder and gave her a long lingering kiss as he stepped into the warm inviting bungalow. Jane went into the kitchen and put the kettle on, as he and Nancy made their way into the spacious lounge, their eyes only for each other as they sat down on the comfortable settee. She looked deep into his eyes.

'I love you, Robert,' she whispered huskily as she reached up and offered her lips to him.

He paused for a second as he beheld her haunting beauty. Leaning forward, he put his arms around her and pressed his lips passionately against hers. He didn't need to reply.

At that moment Jane gave a deep cough; a knowing smile

on her face, as she entered the lounge carrying a tray, on it were three cups of tea and a plate full of buttered scones.

The couple disengaged self consciously, as she placed the tray on a coffee table in front of them, breaking the magic spell that had consumed them.

'Right!' she exclaimed, taking a seat on the settee, by the side of her mother.

'Now we'll have something to eat.'

Robert, full of feeling, took a deep breath, then letting it out slowly, he reached out, took one of the scones and without much enthusiasm, bit into it. Eating was just about the last things he had on his mind at the moment.

Nancy, her face flushed, reached down below the level of the table and squeezed his other hand affectionately, before picking up a cup of tea from the tray and taking a sip.

When an hour or so of somewhat, muted conversation had gone by, Laxton reluctantly decided it was time to leave. After informing Jane that he would pick her up around ten-o-clock the following morning, he gave Nancy a peck on the forehead and went out of the door into the dark cold evening, the heavy November fog swallowing him up, as the two women watched him climb into his car and drive off.

The journey to Old Bolingbroke was almost incident free except for having to slow almost to stop, as a hare bounded out of the long grass that lined the, by now, dark, fog shrouded country lane: it stopped, transfixed in the bright fog lights for a few seconds, turning its head to observe the approaching car, its eyes reflecting the lights. Laxton was almost upon the petrified hare. He cursed as he came down heavily on the foot brake and the car came to a juddering halt. The offending animal took one leap and disappeared into the undergrowth. Shaking his head in frustration he restarted the engine and carefully continued his hazardous journey. He gave a sigh of relief when he eventually turned into his driveway and switched off the ignition. He checked his watch; it showed ten minutes to six.

'Just in time for the six-o-clock news,' he thought, as he hurriedly opened the door and went into the kitchen. He smiled to himself and closed his eyes as the mouth watering aroma of braised steak met his nostrils.

'Annie, you are a gem,' he muttered to himself, as Horatio was circling his feet meowing, almost tripping him up as he walked across the kitchen. Going to the fridge, he took out a plateful of pilchards and put them on the floor for the cat, then, rubbing his hands in anticipation he placed the plateful of braised steak and mashed potatoes on the table. A few minutes later he was tucking in with gusto, as he listened to the news. After finishing his meal, he leaned back in his chair and massaged his stomach.

'That was really good,' he told himself contentedly.

Getting to his feet he switched off the television and carried the dirty dishes to the sink, then he retired to the lounge, where he sprawled out on the settee and relaxed to the sound of one of his favourite pieces of music by Johann Strauss. This was followed by the rest of the evening being taken up with his summing up and attempting to make sense of the facts that were known so far about the four killings. To no avail. Taking a deep breath and with a shake of his head, he got to his feet and wearily made his way upstairs for a quick shower and bed.

The following morning, he opened the flowered curtains and looked out over the Bolingbroke castle ruins. The autumn sun was just beginning to break through the mist that hung over the fields that surrounded the village. He stretched his arms out wide and took a deep breath.

'It feels good to be alive,' he told himself, as he turned away and made his way to the bathroom.

This was followed by a good breakfast, then, after making sure that Horatio was fed, he went out to the car and set off to pick up Jane Bullyn.

Half an hour later they were on their way to London.

The drive, although long and boring, was uneventful. They arrived at New Scotland Yard in the late afternoon. They briefed D. C. I. Walkner, who immediately made plans to interview Charles Insten. A decision was made not to inform him of why they wanted to interview him. As Walkner said. 'Just in case he tries to do a runner.'

Laxton and Bullyn, accompanied by Walkner, arrived at Insten's flat in Hackney and rang the door bell. There was no answer. The janitor, after some persuasion from the officers, opened the door with a pass-key. The room was in a shambles. It was obvious that he had made a hurried exit. A short man in his fifties, from one of the neighbouring flats, on hearing a commotion, popped his head through the open door.

'Are you looking for Charles,' he called out to them.

The detectives turned looked at the little man and asked him if he knew where he was.

'Well, all I can tell you is that he left about twenty minutes ago with a case in his hand,' he told them. Then after a slight pause he added… 'But I have no idea where he's gone.'

A quick search of the flat revealed a torn luggage tag for Gatwick. Thanking the man, they returned to the car and sent a message to the airport police, who were armed, giving them a description of Charles Insten, with orders to apprehend him. Then with sirens wailing, they wended their way through the heavy London traffic to Gatwick airport. After having a word with the Chief of the airport police for permission to apprehend Insten. Chief Inspector Walkner gave out instructions.

'We'll spread out and cover the entrances, and try not to be too conspicuous,' ordered the thick set Walkner in a gruff voice, on arrival at the airport, after being informed that the man they wished to apprehend hadn't been seen. Ten minutes went by.

'There he is,' called out Laxton, pointing to one of the entrances, where the fat man could be seen, scurrying across the car park towards the glass entrance doors, his eyes glancing nervously from side to side.

'Let him come through the entrance door first. Then we'll cut off his escape,' Walkner ordered as Insten put his forearm against the glass door to push it open.

Bullyn raced to get behind the heavily built Insten. The others moved discreetly towards him. The wanted man, who had a walking stick in one hand and his suitcase in the other, spotted them advancing on him, as he made his way across the spacious reception area, after entering through the large glass doors. Looking over his shoulder he saw Bullyn blocking his retreat.

Not fancying tackling the two big men from the airport police in front of him, he turned and went for the easier option, Jane Bullyn. She reached out in an attempt to grab him as he closed in. She just managed to get a hand on to his coat pocket; hanging on to it as he struggled to get by her. He tried in vain to shake her off; then he swung the walking stick, catching her a glancing blow on the side of her head and knocking her to the ground. She reached out and managed to grab his ankle as he went past. He staggered, and fell over his suitcase. Scrambling up, he threw the case to one side and ran on, in an attempt to go out of the glass doors and back into the airport car park; Laxton, who had outstripped the broad shouldered Walkner, was almost on him. Insten stopped and turned as he saw the Inspector gaining on him. He raised his stick, swinging it from side to side menacingly. Laxton taking a quick look, went straight in. He ducked under the heavy walking stick and threw a well timed right hook, which caught Insten flush on the jaw. He went down as if pole-axed.

'Well done,' gasped a breathless Walkner, showing his admiration, as he wiped the sweat from his forehead with a handkerchief.

'Sorry I couldn't hold him,' gasped Bullyn as she rubbed the side of her head and vigorously massaged her hip at the same time.

'Are you okay,' the Inspector asked her, concern in his voice as he rubbed his knuckles.

She looked up at him and nodded. 'Except for a little soreness, I'll be all right.'

Insten, getting unsteadily to his feet, shook his head. 'What's this all about?' he mumbled, feeling his bruised jaw.

'I'm arresting you on suspicion of murder," Laxton told him, then read him his rights.

He was led through the crowd that had gathered, to the police car and taken to New Scotland Yard for further questioning. Chief Inspector Walkner left it to Laxton to lead the interrogation. Insten agreed that he owned a black Volvo car, but denied any involvement in the killing of Evelyn Hopper.

'Give me one good reason why I would want to kill her,' he

blustered, banging his fist on the table in front of him, to emphasise his point. 'I didn't even know the woman,'

The Inspector looked down at the floor as he paced slowly back and forth; then he stopped and turned to Insten.

' You've admitted that you own a black Volvo?' he told him pointedly.

The fat man's face paled. Beads of sweat stood out on his forehead, as he looked around the room nervously. Something was obviously troubling him.

'I refuse to say another word without the presence of my lawyer,' he muttered, his double chin wobbling as he shook his head.

At that moment a constable popped his head round the door and Laxton was called out of the room. He was told that the black Volvo had been located in the airport car park. There was extensive damage to the near side front wing, and blood had been found on the damaged bonnet. He stroked his chin thoughtfully as he went back into the interrogation room and confronted Insten with the evidence, that the front wing of the Volvo, which had been traced to him, was badly damaged, and there was blood on the bonnet.

'It will go better for you if you tell us all you can about the incident. If the blood on the bonnet matches that of Evelyn Hopper's, you won't stand a chance,' advised Laxton, taking a seat opposite the accused man.

Insten held his head in his hands. He was clearly shaken. Slowly dropping his hands, he raised his head, the defeated expression on his face telling it all as he looked up at the Inspector. He paused for a few seconds, took a deep breath, then told him...

'Okay you've got me,' he confessed, as he gently massaged his bruised and painful jaw.

'I killed her because she'd stupidly given the game away. I had to stop her talking.'

Laxton, leaning his elbows on the table, moved closer, his eyes like chips of ice. He now had the quarry in his sights.

'What game?' he demanded, staring Insten in the eyes.

'I can't tell you any more, I won't tell you,' Insten spat out, taking a large handkerchief out of his pocket and mopping his brow, as he shook his head from side to side.

'I want my lawyer,' he demanded, his voice muffled by the handkerchief.

Laxton leaned back in his chair, his fingers pressed together, forming a pyramid, as he focussed his eyes on the troubled man in front of him. The room went deathly quiet: the ticking of the old clock on the wall was like a sharp regular beat of a kettle drum. Suddenly the silence was broken.

'Would you like a drink of coffee?' the Inspector asked him quietly, changing the tone of his voice. Insten, looking down at his interlocked fingers, nodded his head.

Jane Bullyn brought the drinks in on a tray and placed it on the table, then, leaning over Laxton's shoulder, she whispered in his ear. He rose from his seat and left the room. He went into the reception, where a constable at the desk handed him the phone.

'Laxton here,' he announced, going quiet as he listened carefully.

'Yes I've got that. On top of the bonnet you say, and what about the blood on the stick?' He nodded his head at the phone. Then thanking the person at the other end, he replaced the phone on the receiver. Deep in thought, he returned to confront Insten. There was a steely glint in his eye as he took his seat again.

'We now know that the blood on the car matches the blood of Evelyn Hopper,' he told Insten. Then he leaned forward across the table, taking the weight on his forearms, adding in a low penetrating voice.

'But the blood on your walking stick doesn't.'

The words dripped from his lips like acid, as Insten's fat jowls quivered. His eyes half closed, slid from side to side, as if looking for an escape route. But there wasn't one.

'We know that you've already killed one innocent person. Evelyn Hopper. Who else have you attacked?' snapped Laxton, his tone of voice demanding an answer from the accused man in front of him.

'She wasn't as innocent as you think,' sneered Insten, a mirthless grin on his face.

'Oh!' exclaimed Laxton, a hard edge to his voice, as he

resisted the urge to wipe the smile from Insten's face with the back of his hand. 'Why was that?'

Charles Insten, realising he was saying too much, stopped talking. At that moment his lawyer, Mr Brinxham entered the room, and asked to be left alone with his client. They were led to a secure room. Ten minutes later they came out. The lawyer informed them that his client had nothing more to say at present. Insten was formally charged with the murder of Evelyn Hopper, and placed in custody. Walkner turned to the two officers and asked them if they would like something to eat, before they set off on the long journey back to Lincoln police headquarters. After a quick meal of ham sandwiches and a cup of tea, Laxton and Bullyn made their way to the car and set about the task of negotiating the heavy London traffic, Laxton breathed a sigh of relief as they drove out of the area and joined the A1. From there it was a comparatively comfortable journey back to Lincoln. They arrived back at six thirty p.m. Wilberton, who had been waiting patiently in his office for them to return, asked for three coffees to be brought in, then listened intently as the Inspector laid out all the facts in detail.

'Mmm, so we've got him for the Evelyn Hopper killing,' he mused. 'But what about the bloodstains on his walking stick, who do they belong to?' He stroked his chin, as he carefully thought over the facts that Laxton and Bullyn had brought back with them from the interview with Insten in London.

'There's also his comments, that she wasn't as innocent as we think.'

'Rebecca Moristone was possibly beaten to death with a walking stick. Could there be any connection there?' interjected Bullyn.

'It does seem to point that way, but I'm not so sure,' rejoined Laxton, as three steaming mugs of coffee were placed on the desk. 'First of all,' he put to them. 'What motive would he have for killing Rebecca Moristone, also for instance, why would he travel all the way from London to murder someone he didn't know?' He shook his head as a look of bewilderment clouded his face. 'It just doesn't add up.'

There was a pause in the discussion as they each picked up a mug of coffee.

'Well we've had a few strange happenings,' muttered Wilberton, taking a sip of his hot drink, before turning to his wallboard, the obligatory cane in his hand.

'First of all,' he began, pointing his cane at the wallboard. 'We've had five murders. Insten has admitted to one of them. We know he killed Evelyn Hopper because he was afraid of her talking. But the other four are without an obvious motive. It's possible Evelyn Hopper was the blonde woman who pushed John Basser in front of the train, also seemingly without a motive. Yet her own utterances connect her to it.' Scratching the back of his ear, he looked up at Laxton and gave a shrug of his shoulders.

'What the hell's going on?' he breathed. At that moment the phone rang. Wilberton picked it up, his attitude giving nothing away as he listened intently to the message.

'Yes, yes. I've got that, thank you,' he said, putting the phone down. He turned to Laxton, a serious expression on his face.

'Forensics have opened Insten's suitcase. They've found a blue striped suit. The sleeve of the jacket has a strip torn out of it. It matches the strip of cloth found near Rebecca Moristone's body. All we are waiting for now is for them to match the blood on Insten's walking stick with hers and we've got him on two counts of murder.' With this he concluded the briefing.

Laxton stretched his arms and yawned tiredly as they walked to the car and climbed in.

He was in deep contemplation as he switched on the ignition and started the engine, then engaging the gear he set off on the journey to Dalesworth. Jane Bullyn looking at him out of the corner of her eye, broke in on his thoughts.

'Oh, by the way, I almost forgot,' she told him. 'Mum's told me to tell you she's preparing a meal for you tonight.'

He pushed the recent happenings to the back of his mind and glanced across at her. His face broadened into a smile.

'That'll be great!" he exclaimed. "I'll really look forward to that.'

Twenty minutes later he stopped the car outside the

bungalow where Jane and her mother lived, and followed her up the path.

Nancy greeted him with a long hug and a kiss as he walked through the door. Robert Laxton looked down at her with deep affection. The meal, followed by a fine wine, was delicious. He went into the kitchen, where Nancy was washing the dishes. Placing his arms around her waist from behind, he buried his face in her hair and kissed her affectionately on the back of the neck. She felt a shiver go down her spine.

'Nancy I reckon I'm going to have to marry you before someone else gets you,' he whispered in her ear.

She turned round and faced him, her green eyes looking straight up into his.

'Is that a proposal Robert?' she asked him, her voice full of emotion.

He didn't have to answer, the love for her that showed in his eyes said it all.

'Oh darling,' she gushed, throwing her arms round him and giving him a long lingering kiss. Then she gave him a tea towel, telling him. 'We'd better start you right then.'

Jane entered the kitchen and burst out laughing at the sight of the big man drying the dishes, and her mum, a happy smile on her face, washing them. When they told her that they were to be married, she was ecstatic, dancing around the kitchen. She reached up and kissed an embarrassed Laxton on the cheek, almost knocking the plate he was drying out of his hand. He placed it on the table and stood looking at them for a few seconds; then, putting his arms around them both, he breathed in deeply and gave a contented sigh.

Chapter Eighteen

Chief Inspector Wilberton checked his watch as he entered the police station, then addressed the Constable at the reception desk.

'When Inspector Laxton arrives send him straight into my office.'

Ten minutes later the Inspector and D.C. Bullyn arrived. The young Constable gave them the message. They carried on through to Wilberton's office. The Chief looked up from his seat behind the desk where he'd been studying some papers. He took off his glasses and looked up at them as they opened his office door and stood in front of him.

'Ah Robert!' he exclaimed, an air of expectancy in his voice. 'Forensics have been in touch. They've informed me that the blood on Insten's walking stick matches that of Rebecca Moristone. We now have Insten for a double murder.'

He placed his glasses back on his nose and looked down at his entwined fingers. There was a deep frown on his forehead as he directed his gaze at the Inspector.

'What I can't understand is, why did he kill Rebecca Moristone. What could be his motive? Up to now we haven't uncovered any connection between them.' He shook his head in puzzlement. 'We're almost certain Evelyn Hopper pushed Basser in front of the train. Again, why? As far as we know they didn't know each other either. Then there is the murder of Alf Hopper, connected to the other two by his wife's murder.'

Pausing for a moment, his eyes half closed, he tried to mentally untangle the web of evidence that confronted them, running his finger along the bridge of his nose as he did so.

'There's only one way to find out.' he suddenly decided. 'We'll have to go to London to interview Insten again, and confront him with the evidence. When he sees we've got him for Rebecca Moristone's murder as well as Evelyn Hopper's he should crack.'

New Scotland Yard was informed that they were coming to interview Insten again. When the trio arrived they went to the interrogation room, where Insten, accompanied by his lawyer Brinxham, was sat at a table waiting for them. Inspector Laxton, a calculated look on his face directed his gaze at the broken man, as he stared transfixed, at his clasped hands on the table in front of him. There was a defeated look on his face as he dejectedly lifted his head and met the Inspector's steely grey eyes.

'We have received information that the bloodstains on your walking stick match the blood of the murdered woman, Rebecca Moristone,' he stated grimly. 'Can you explain to us, how it came to be there?'

Charles Insten, still clasping his hands, broke down, beads of sweat standing out on his forehead. His hands were trembling as he answered.

'Okay,' he mumbled, his voice quavering. 'I'll tell you everything I can.'

He turned to Brinxham, leaning towards him as he and spoke for a couple of minutes in a low voice in the lawyer's ear, Brinxham, a serious expression on his face, nodded occasionally as he listened intently to what Insten was saying. Then he switched the focus of his attention to the police officers.

'I want the fact that my client is helping the police with their enquiries, to be taken into account,' he announced.

Wilberton nodded his head in agreement.

A stenographer was brought in to take down the statement, which was also taped.

'Right!' Wilberton exclaimed, looking at his watch. 'The time is exactly twelve-thirty p.m. We'll start from the beginning. First of all, what led you to commit the murders?'

Insten took a deep breath, then proceeded in almost a whisper, to tell them of a cold-blooded plan which was almost unbelievable.

'It all started with my being deeply in debt, resulting in me using the firm's cash to gamble on the stock market. As you will know, the F.T.S.E, has been in free fall for the last six months. The cash that I invested almost halved in value.' He stopped and looked into the eyes of the listeners; he was gratified to see their imperceptible nods as he carried on with his statement. 'Then I turned to other forms of gambling to try to recoup my losses quickly.' He shrugged his shoulders. 'Unfortunately it didn't work.'

Insten paused for a moment, taking out his handkerchief and wiping his brow, then after loosening his tie and unbuttoning his collar, he took a deep breath and continued.

'I was reading the newspaper, when I came across a message. Advertising for persons to make up a group. It stated...'

If you are in trouble and want a way out, contact this number.

'I got in touch and told the person of my predicament. If I didn't clear the debts that I'd incurred in the name of our joint investment business, my partner John Basser, would take over and I would be declared bankrupt.' He lifted his rounded shoulders in a gesture of helplessness. 'This meant I would be finished.' He shook his head. 'I couldn't stand that.'

He paused and took another deep breath, the sweat slowly spreading from under his armpits, as he looked down at his clenched hands. Wilberton leaned across the table.

'You're doing fine. Take your time,' he told Insten, attempting to give him some encouragement. The fat man, after taking a drink of water, sat up in his chair, pulled himself together and carried on with his statement.

'The person asked me bluntly, would I be in the clear if my partner were dead? Well, yes, I told him. Thinking at the time, what a ridiculous statement. The man took my address and phone number and I was told that I would be contacted at a later date. I put the phone down thinking to myself. 'Another bloody crank.' I thought no more of it. A week went by, then I had a phone call from the same person, giving me instructions.' Insten stopped talking for a moment as he reached again for the glass of water. After taking another drink he continued.

'I gave the idea a lot of thought before going through with it. But being desperate I said to myself. 'What the hell. What have I got to lose,' so I decided to go along.' He shrugged his shoulders again. 'If only to find out what it was all about.'

After a few seconds to gather his thoughts he took a deep breath, then carried on.

'The man told me I was to be at the Bell Inn, it was situated just outside Spawlsby, a village in Lincolnshire. I was instructed to be there at seven p.m. on the third of October. I was to bring a red envelope containing details and a description of my partner John Basser sealed in it. There was to be nothing written on the outside of the envelope. Following instructions I arrived at the Bell Inn just after seven p.m. There were three people sat at a table in a secluded corner. I could hardly make them out. Their faces were hidden, but I could see one of them was a woman, her long blonde hair was hanging over her shoulder.'

He paused again and took another drink of water. After a few moments he went on. With the others round the table hanging on to his every word.

'One of the two men at the table was doing all the talking. He was obviously the person who'd organised the meeting.'

'Did you know what the names of the others were,' enquired Laxton.

'There were no names mentioned.' he answered, raising his head and looking straight at the Inspector. 'We were told it would be better if we were unknown to each other,'

He coughed into his hand noisily to clear his throat. After swallowing, he continued with his statement, keeping his voice low.

'Each of the participants brought a different coloured envelope, which we placed on the table. The one, who'd been doing all the talking, shuffled the envelopes around, then asked each one of us to select an envelope that *wasn't their colour.*'

'Which one did you select?' interjected Laxton, adding…

'And who was designated as your target?'

'I selected the blue envelope,' replied Insten. 'My assignment was …' He hesitated and swallowed hard as he closed his eyes momentarily; there was a solemn look on his heavy, fleshy face, as he completed the sentence almost in a whisper, as if talking to himself, 'to kill Rebecca Moristone.'

He sat back in his chair and stretched his shoulders, his eyes sweeping from side to side at the four that were listening to him attentively.

'What was your reward for er... doing this?' persisted Laxton.

'Whichever one of the other three chose my envelope, would execute the assignment that was written in it.' the fat man told them, his jowls wobbling as he spoke.

'What you mean is, they had to eliminate John Basser?' interrupted Wilberton in an attempt to clarify the situation.

'Yes,' replied a dejected Insten, dropping his chin on his chest and looking at his fingers.

'Do you know which one of the other three drew your envelope?' asked Laxton.

'Yes, it was the woman. I saw her long blonde hair as she reached out to pick the red one, which was mine.' He ran his tongue from side to side across his lips, as he gathered his thoughts, then continued.

'I followed her home, and made a few discreet inquiries locally. I found out her name was Evelyn Hopper.'

'What was the reason you followed her?'

'I wanted to make sure she fulfilled the assignment.'

'Did you inform her that John Basser would be catching that train?'

'Well,' replied Insten. 'I rang her the night before and told her that I had asked him to come up to London the following day, and that he would be catching the twelve-o-clock train from Lincoln.' He shrugged his shoulders. 'From then on it was up to her.'

'Why did you kill her?' queried the Inspector. 'She wasn't a target was she?'

'No, but when I saw the police message on television, I knew it was only a matter of time before she would be caught, and there was the strong possibility that she would have led the police to me. I couldn't take that risk.'

He paused for a moment, collecting his thoughts. D.C.

Bullyn asked him if he wanted another drink. He shook his head. Wilberton got out of his chair and paced up and down the room for a few seconds, gazing at the floor.

'Can you identify the other two men who were at the table?' asked Wilberton.

'No,' he replied. 'They had their faces covered. We were told that we wouldn't be suspected as there would be nothing to connect us to the target or each other.'

'What about your affinity or relationship to the person you wanted, er… For want of a better word, *removed*. Didn't that put you off?' asked Laxton.

Insten gave a shrug of his shoulders. 'We were told that if we made sure that at all times we had a good solid alibi, and were discreet, we wouldn't be suspected.'

At this point Insten sat back in his chair and held his face in his hands, sweat was running down his forehead. Leaning his head back, he looked up at the ceiling He didn't look too well. His lawyer Brinxham intervened, calling a halt to the proceedings.

'My client has told you all he knows,' he announced.

Wilberton nodded his head in agreement and formally closed the interview. It was one forty five p.m. Insten, his shoulders hunched, looked down at his feet, as he was taken back into custody. He was a broken man. After thanking the New Scotland Yard police for their co-operation, the trio left the building.

Heavy spots of rain were falling as they walked to the car. Laxton pulled his coat collar up around his neck and looked up at the darkening sky, grimacing as he eyed the black clouds that were gathering.

'At last we now have some idea of what's going on,' Wilberton remarked as they drove back to Lincoln, adding…

'We must find out the names of the other two men in the group.'

He tugged at his ear lobe, as he contemplated the situation. The sound of heavy rain beating incessantly on the roof of the car and the windscreen wipers relentlessly swishing backward and forward across the windscreen, were the only sounds that could be heard as they drove along the A.1. Laxton broke the silence. Glancing over his shoulder and addressing Bullyn who was sitting in the rear seat, he spoke up.

'What did you do with those two cigarette butts.'

'I handed them over to forensics,' she replied, leaning forward, and speaking in his ear.

'Okay,' he told her. 'We'll talk to them tomorrow and see if they have any significance.'

Laxton looked across at Wilberton.

'What about you, Chief,' he asked. 'Do you want me to drop you off at your home?'

The Chief Inspector nodded to him. 'Yes Robert that will suit me fine,' he replied.

Chapter Nineteen

James Drawell paced up and down the lounge of his home, a deep frown creasing his forehead: he was apprehensive. The police had interviewed him, regarding the death of his estranged wife, Rose. He was wondering if the recent murders would do anything to jeopardise the clever plan that he was involved in. He stopped pacing and took a deep breath, then he relaxed.

'What am I worried about? he asked himself. 'They can't blame me for her murder. I was in hospital when it occurred.' He smiled grimly to himself. All he had to do now, was to keep his head, then he would be comfortably off, with one hundred thousand pounds in the bank. He rubbed his hands at the thought of it. Going to the drinks cabinet, he took out a decanter and a glass, then poured himself a whisky; he stopped as he heard the door bell ring. Frowning, he put the whisky decanter down on a small coffee table.

'Who can that be?' he asked himself. He wasn't expecting anyone. He went out into the hallway and opened the door. A man stood in the doorway. Drawell, the glass of whisky in his hand, had a strange feeling that he'd seen him or had come into contact with him at some time in the past.

'Can I help you,' asked Drawell, a puzzled look on his face.

'I'm from the Insurance company, I'd like to discuss a problem that has arisen regarding the insurance you've taken out on your wife, Mr Drawell?' the man told him, his eyes seemingly cold despite the friendly smile on his countenance.

'It's a bit late to be calling about the Insurance isn't it,' said Drawell, with a look of annoyance on his face at being disturbed; he looked at his wristwatch. It showed nine p.m.

'Well I was passing, so I thought I'd clear up a few points of interest,' the man explained apologetically, still smiling. 'It will only take a few minutes,'

'Okay,' he muttered, standing back to let the man in, telling him...

'If it doesn't take too long.'

Drawell took a long hard look at the man, there was something about the voice.

'Haven't we met?' he asked pointedly as he led his visitor into the lounge.

The man shook his head and glanced away evasively. 'No I don't think so.' he said letting his eyes wander around the somewhat spacious hallway as he passed through. He seemed to take special notice of the stairway with its banister rail. He stepped into the large room.

James Drawell hesitated, checking his watch again. He was on the point of telling the man that he had changed his mind and to come back tomorrow morning; then again, he told himself. He would like to know what the problem was with the insurance. He didn't want any snags at this stage.'

'Oh well, okay, but don't take too long, I want to have an early night,' he growled irritably, taking a swig at the drink in his hand.

'Don't worry Mr Drawell, you'll get your early night,' the stranger told him, the patronising smile still on his face.

'Before we start, may I use your toilet?'

Drawell grunted his assent, pointing to the bathroom door and tossing the remainder of his whisky back. The stranger went through it. Closing the door behind him he took a bottle and a handkerchief out of his pocket. He poured liquid out of the bottle on to the handkerchief; then reaching up he took the light bulb out of its socket and smashed it on the floor. James Drawell, who was in the lounge putting the decanter away, heard the crash and rushed towards the bathroom.

"What the hell are you doing in there,' he shouted.

There was no answer as he tried the door. It swung open. The bathroom was in darkness as he entered. Suddenly a cloth was clamped over his nose and mouth. He struggled to free himself as he was dragged backwards. He felt his strength waning as the room spun round. There was a sweet smell before he passed out.

The man looked down at the limp body of James Drawell. Bending down, he dragged the unconscious man into the hallway and propped him up against the wall below the banister. He took a length of rope from around his waist, and fashioned a noose at one end of it. Placing the noose around Drawell's neck, he climbed the stairs and passed the rope through the banister rail, then heaved on it, hoisting the unconscious Drawell until his feet were clear of the floor. His legs gave a few jerks, almost like a puppet being manipulated on a string, as the life was throttled out of him. After a bit of a struggle the man tied the end of the rope to the rail. Breathing heavily from his exertions he descended the stairway. Drawell's leg jerked involuntarily, and his feet gave a couple of twitches, as the man took out a handkerchief and wiped the sweat from his brow. There was a cruel glint in his eyes as he took a step back and studied his handiwork. Something was missing, he told himself, scratching the back of his head. Then it dawned on him, a stool. He searched the kitchen, eventually finding a small one in the closet. 'That will just fit the bill,' he muttered to himself, as he placed it on its side near the dangling feet of the, by now, dead man.

'That should do the trick,' he murmured out loud, rubbing his gloved palms together, as he stood back and surveyed his handiwork. There was a look of satisfaction on his face, for a job well done. He had one more task to perform, a suicide note. He found a writing pad in a drawer in the lounge and scribbled a few words on it, then placed it in Drawell's pocket. After a quick check round to make sure he wasn't leaving any incriminating evidence, he slipped out of the door and melted into the dark night.

Robert Laxton with the Chief Inspector at his side and Jane in the rear, drew up at the home of Henry Wilberton, stopping the car in the wide drive. His wife, 'a handsome woman' thought Laxton, came out to greet them, her black hair was tied back. She was of Spanish origin, her even white teeth flashing as she met them with a broad smile.

"Hello Henry darling," she addressed her husband

affectionately, as he took her hand in his and gave her a kiss. Their son was with her. He was fiercely proud of her and their four children, one son and three daughters. The son was the only one of their children at home now, the daughters having got married. He introduced them to his companions.

'You've met Maria. And this is my son Spencer,' he said, a hint of pride in his voice as he introduced them to the two detectives. Laxton clumsily shook her hand. Jane Bullyn was received with open arms and a hug.

'Would you like a cup of tea?' Maria asked them smilingly.

Henry Wilberton held up his hand.

'Robert and I will have something a little stronger,' he said, then turned to his son. 'What about you Spencer?' The tall young man smiled and shook his head. He seemed more interested in Jane Bullyn.

Henry Wilberton gave him an enquiring look, then laughed good naturedly as he beckoned Laxton into the lounge. Going over to an ornate drinking cabinet, he took out a decanter and two glasses. Pulling out a coffee table, from a set of three, he placed them on the table and poured two generous tots of whisky, topped up with a squirt of soda. He handed one to Laxton, as they both sat on the settee. Wilberton leaned back and took a sip of his drink.

'Well Robert, what's your summing up of the case so far?' he remarked in a conversational tone of voice.

Robert Laxton, his elbows on his knees, leaned forward over the coffee table and looked into his glass for a few seconds, swilling the amber liquid round and round, while he was thinking up a reply. Then he raised an eyebrow at the Chief, there was a studious look in his eyes as he gave his opinion.

'Well,' he started. 'We are now almost certain that all five murders are in some way connected, according to the information given by Charles Insten. We know that he killed Rebecca Moristone and Evelyn Hopper, and that Evelyn Hopper killed John Basser. We don't know yet who killed Rose Drawell, and Alf Hopper, Evelyn's husband, or why. Does that make sense?' queried Laxton, sipping his drink, as he gave a sideways glance at Wilberton.

'Mmm,' muttered the Chief, shuffling his backside on the soft cushion of the settee to get more comfortable. 'It seems to me that the whole plot was concocted by one person; the problem is... we don't know for certain who he is. At the moment I have only a vague idea of what the plot is. If my idea is anywhere near the truth, then we are dealing with a cold blooded killer, who will stop at nothing.'

He tipped his head back, emptied his glass and placed it on the table.

Having also finished his drink, Laxton got up from his seat and stretched his arms out wide, then followed Wilberton into the kitchen, where Jane Bullyn was talking animatedly to Maria and their son Spencer, who, at twenty five was a handsome six-footer. He was showing a lot of interest in Jane, who, in turn was laughing happily in his presence.

'Spencer has invited Jane to have dinner with him.' exclaimed Maria. 'But I've got a better idea, Jane has told me that Robert has asked Nancy to marry him, so we'll celebrate. I'd like to invite all of them to have dinner with us. What do you think Henry?'

'That's okay by me,' rejoined her husband with a shrug of his shoulders, adding... 'It would be really nice.'

Then she turned to Robert Laxton and congratulated him on his forthcoming marriage.

The Inspector smiled his thanks. Then, addressing Wilberton, he told him.

'Henry, I want you to be my best man.'

'I'd be honoured,' he rejoined, with a slight nod of his head.

Laxton checked his watch, it was getting late.

'We'd better be off now,' he told them.

With this Henry Wilberton and his wife said goodbye to Laxton and Bullyn.

'What a nice woman,' said Jane Bullyn, of Maria, as they made their way along the crazy paved path, to the car.

Nancy was waiting at the door for them when Laxton stopped the car to drop Jane off. He told her about their calling at Henry Wilberton's home, and the invitation from Maria.

'What a lovely offer,' she enthused, clasping her hands in

front of her.

Then after a hot drink and a few endearing words, he gave her a kiss and set off back to his cottage in Old Bolingbroke. Annie was just coming out of the driveway, pushing her old bike, as he slowed down to manoeuvre the car into the driveway.

'Your dinner is in the oven, Mr Laxton!' she called out to him, a beaming smile on her round face as she mounted the bike.

He wound the window down, calling out, as she pedalled off along the lane...

'Thank you, Annie.'

After putting the car away, he walked across the wide, block-paved drive. He smiled to himself as he observed a house sparrow, checking out the wooden replica of a house that he had placed high on the cottage wall during the previous January. He took a deep breath as he opened the door and entered the cottage. The smell from his dinner made his mouth water. Going into the kitchen, he opened the oven door and 'gingerly' took out the plate full of stew and dumplings that Annie had prepared for him earlier.

'As my old grandma used to say,' he told himself as he placed the steaming hot, tasty looking meal on the table, 'the way to a man's heart is through his stomach.'

He rubbed his hands together in anticipation as he muttered...

'Annie has surely got the message.'

With this, he picked up his knife and fork and tucked in. This was followed by a satisfying glass of Guinness, drank to a background of music by Strauss, as he stretched his long frame on the settee. Then after a couple of hours of watching the news on the television, he wearily climbed the stairs to the bathroom and bed.

The next morning, after rubbing his eyes and stretching, he went to the window and gazed down at the mist covered remains of Bolingbroke Castle. Raising his eyes, he looked at the weak November sun, as it fought to break through the heavy mist as it rose over the distant hills.

'It's going to be a cold, fine day,' he told himself as he stretched his arms out wide and took a deep breath. After a shower, he quickly dressed, made himself a pot of tea and a couple of slices of toast, then he strode out of the cottage, ducking his head under the bamboo chimes that hung just outside the back door as he passed through on his way to the garage; where he climbed into the car and drove out on to the lane. The fields were blanketed in a light covering of frost as he drove through the open countryside, along the narrow, winding lanes on his way to Dalesworth to pick up Jane. After a cup of tea and a few minutes chat with Nancy, the two detectives set off on their journey to Lincoln, arriving at headquarters, some half an hour later. Wilberton beckoned them into his office, greeting them as they opened the glass door and walked in. He was sat at his desk, poring over some official documents. He looked up at both of them as they entered. Then focussing his eyes on Laxton, he told him…

'I want you to interview James Drawell again and see if we can come up with a little more information on the killing of his wife, and the insurance he's taken out on her. I have a feeling that he knows more about her murder than he's shown so far.'

Laxton acknowledged his superior's request with a nod of his head.

'What about the cigarette butts from Moristone, which were handed in?' enquired Bullyn, as they were about to leave.

'I'll get on to forensics and find out what they've come up with,' replied Wilberton.

Laxton turned, raised his right hand in a parting gesture as they walked out of the office, Jane Bullyn following him to his car. They drew up outside the home of James Drawell some twenty minutes later. Bullyn rang the door bell. There was no answer. Laxton banged on the door with his fist, to no avail. The two detectives looked at each other. Shrugging his shoulders the Inspector turned to leave, saying…

'We'll have to call again later when he's at home.'

They were just turning away when the next door neighbour came out, rubbing his nicotine stained fingers over his balding head. His bleary eyes showing that he had just got out of bed.

He called out to them…

'Isn't he answering?' he queried.

Laxton, turning his attention to the man, shook his head negatively.

'That's strange, he was at home last night, he had a visitor,' he told them in a puzzled tone of voice, as he stroked his bristly chin.

'Oh!' exclaimed the Inspector, a quizzical expression on his face. 'And what time would that be?'

'I would say about nine-o-clock,' answered the neighbour, hitching his trousers up over his fat paunch. He paused for a moment before adding with a slight shake of his head…

'As far as I know, he hasn't been out at all this morning.'

Laxton looked the man in the eyes; he smiled to himself, it was obvious that he didn't miss much. He bent down and peered through the letterbox, into the shadowed hallway beyond. He scanned the stairs on the left, then turned his eyes through to the kitchen. Something in the hallway was blocking his view. He couldn't quite make it out. Suddenly his body stiffened.

'Good grief,' he gasped.

He straightened up, his face had turned pale. He took two steps back, then hurled himself forward, smashing the door in. James Drawell's body was hanging from the banister rail by a rope that was fastened round his neck, his face purple. His eyes were wide open, almost popping out of their sockets. A footstool lay on the floor under the dangling body, seemingly kicked over on the floor by the hanged man. Laxton grabbed Drawell's legs and lifted his body up. Bullyn scrambled up the stairs and reached through the banister rails; after a struggle she pulled open the tight noose and lifted it from around Drawell's neck, then taking out her mobile, she phoned for an ambulance, and informed Wilberton of the incident, as the Inspector gently lowered the body to the floor, and checked Drawell's pulse, then he pressed his ear to the prostrate man's chest. He couldn't detect any sign of life. He looked up at Bullyn, shaking his head, a grave expression on his face.

'He's dead,' he muttered.

He then proceeded to thoroughly search the immediate area

for clues. Fifteen minutes later the ambulance arrived, followed by the Chief and forensics. After examining the body the paramedics duly pronounced James Drawell dead, and then forensics went through his pockets. Among other things, they found a note. On it were written the words, 'I can't bear the guilt any longer. I killed my wife and Alfred Hopper. I'm ending it all.'

After reading it they handed it to the Chief.

Wilberton studied the note for a few moments, then turned his eyes to the banister and back down to the floor. Bullyn and Laxton exchanged glances, she shrugged her shoulders, a non-committal expression on her face, as the Chief bent down and stood the stool on its legs. Then he stood back from the morbid scene and studied it carefully, biting the knuckles of his clenched fist, his eyes half closed.

'What do you think?' he muttered, turning to Laxton and handing him the note.

The Inspector stroked his chin for a few seconds, as he perused the slip of paper. Then he turned his attention the scene in front of him, before speaking. He shrugged his shoulders.

'Well it does seem to clear up two of the murders, Chief,' he replied, a little inadequately.

'I'm not so sure,' intoned Wilberton, shaking his head slowly from side to side.

'Something doesn't look right. It all looks too neat,' he said quietly as if he was talking to himself. 'He told you he didn't smoke, yet we're almost sure the killer of Rose Drawell smoked Lucky Strikes.'

'Well not exactly,' contradicted Laxton forcefully. 'The person who stood in the bushes smoked them, but he wasn't necessarily the one who murdered her.'

'I know that,' replied Wilberton testily, as he shook his head in annoyance. 'But it's a fair assumption that he was the killer.'

He looked at the stool again, then stepped on to it and stood up straight. He looked again at the bottom of the banister rail where the rope was still fastened.

'Would you say James Drawell and me were about the same height?' he asked Laxton.

The Inspector, his arms folded, frowned deeply, as he thought for a moment before answering. 'About an inch taller I would say,' was his reply.

'Well!' Wilberton exclaimed questioningly; exasperation creeping into his voice again. 'Who is?'

Laxton shrugged his shoulders, as his gaze moved from the Chief to Jane Bullyn and back, he had a blank look on his face.

'Which one would you say is the taller?' asked the Chief with a weary air of resignation. 'Me or him?'

'Oh,' replied the Inspector, suddenly realising what he meant. 'I would say he was about an inch taller than you.'

Wilberton shook his head from side to side as he hopped down from the stool.

He turned to one of the forensics team, who had been watching him with some interest.

'Do one of you have a measuring tape?' he requested.

They looked at each other, searching their pockets and shaking their heads.

'No, Chief,' one of them told him. 'But I can get you one.' With this he left. A couple of minutes later he returned.

'There you are,' he declared, handing Wilberton a fifteen metre tape. Thanking the man, he proceeded to climb to the top of the stairs; to where the rope was hanging from the banister. Reaching through the banister rails, he called out to Bullyn, 'Can you hold the measure level with the bottom of the noose?'

Laxton held her arm to steady her, as she climbed on the stool and reached up to do as the Chief had instructed. Carefully he checked the measurement of the rope from where it was fastened to the rail on the landing, to the bottom of the loop where Bullyn was holding it. He jotted the measurement down on a note pad.

'Mmm, eighteen inches,' he muttered, reading it out loud. Turning to Bullyn again, he asked her to hold the end of the tape to the floor, whilst he held it to where the rope was fastened to the banister. He chewed on his bottom lip for a few seconds, his eyes half shut in concentration, as he worked out the measurements.

'Just under nine-foot; let's say eight-foot eleven inches. The footstool is twelve inches. That leaves seven-foot eleven inches. Still muttering to himself he jotted more figures down. 'The rope to the bottom of the noose, at full stretch is eighteen inches. That leaves six-foot-five.' He glanced at Laxton. 'You say that James Drawell is about five-foot-ten.' The ball point pen in his fingers moved swiftly across the page of the note pad. He paused for a moment and chewed on the end of the pen as he made a quick calculation in his head. His eyes narrowed for a few seconds, then he looked up at the Inspector, a triumphant expression on his face.

'That means he would have to jump seven inches to put his head in the noose to hang himself.' Wilberton looked Laxton in the eyes. They both spoke in unison.

'He was murdered.'

After checking the handwriting on the note with other correspondence in the house, it was obvious to them that Drawell couldn't have written the confession. The person who had written it was the murderer. A few minutes later, after deciding that there was no point in them hanging about, they concluded it was time to leave.

Arriving back at headquarters, Wilberton led them into his back room and stood in front of his wall board, marking pen in hand. Laxton, his arms folded as he sat on the edge of the desk, and Bullyn were watching him. Wilberton turned his attention to the Inspector.

'What is your summing up of the facts so far, Robert?' he asked him.

Laxton pushed himself off the desk and walked over to the wall board. He studied it for a few moments then began his summary.

'Well,' he started. 'Let's go through the evidence at hand. First of all, Rose Drawell was murdered by persons unknown. Number one suspect, James Drawell, her estranged husband, has a perfect alibi so we know he didn't murder his wife.' He paused for a moment as he reached for a glass of water, then carried on.

'Next... John Basser was pushed in front of a train, we know now, by Evelyn Hopper, a complete stranger. We have no idea why she did it. Indeed it's quite possible that John Basser didn't even know her. The one who had most to lose if Basser had stayed alive, was his partner, Charles Insten, who, as far as we know, would be the most likely suspect; again he has an unbreakable alibi. So once again, we know he couldn't have committed the crime.' He paused again, taking another sip of water.

'Then we have the murder of Rebecca Moristone. Her one beneficiary is her only relative, her grandson, Richard Moristone. He is once again the main suspect. He also has a solid alibi, so we can leave him out of the reckoning.'

Laxton plucked at his bottom lip for a moment, as he gathered his thoughts and surveyed the faces in front of him. Then he went on with his summary.

'Following that incident, we have the killing of Alfred Hopper, just after he was released from Lincoln prison. His wife, Evelyn Hopper who had every reason to get rid of him, because she thought he threatened her life, also has a good alibi, making her innocent of his murder. One of the factors in all of these killings, is that all of them seem to have been done by strangers.'

He stopped for few seconds as he picked at a spot on his chin. Then went on...

'Evelyn Hopper was the next victim. She was killed by Insten, because she was careless enough to be seen pushing John Basser in front of a train.'

Laxton stopped talking for a moment as hot drinks were brought in. After taking a good drink of one of the mugs of tea, he continued with his summing up.

'Now we come to James Drawell, who was found hanged. He was almost certainly another of the four conspirators that Charles Insten referred to. The only conclusion that I can come to, is that he was considered a risk by the fourth member, who was the person who thought up the scheme in the first place, and eliminated him.'

The Inspector stopped for a moment and let his eyes settle on his two companions, who were listening attentively, then, tipping his head back, he swallowed the remainder of his tea.

For a few seconds he looked down at the dregs in the bottom of the mug, as if he was trying to read something in them. Placing it down on the table, he took a deep breath and carried on.

'Now let's see if we can work out why all these people were killed,' he said, turning and referring to the Chief's wall-board again.

'Charles Insten has confessed to killing Rebecca Moristone, so we'll start there. His reward for that deed was almost certainly the killing of his partner John Basser, who was despatched by Evelyn Hopper. Her reward in turn, would have been the removal of her husband Alfred Hopper, who, we know, she hated. She was then taken out by Insten, because she'd become a danger to him by letting herself be seen. The murderer of Alfred Hopper is almost certainly James Drawell, whose wife Rose was killed as his reward. He in turn was eliminated by persons unknown. If my calculations are correct, that leaves just one person who makes up the group of killers.'

He stopped and looked at the other two for effect. Then, his voice dropped in volume as he spelled it out.

'The beneficiary from the death of Rebecca Moristone.'

Laxton looked straight at the other two. They both spoke at the same time.

'Richard Moristone.'

'Dead right,' agreed the Inspector.

The Chief, reaching out, gave Laxton a pat on the shoulder and congratulated him.

'Well thought out, Robert,' he told him, adding...

'We'll go to Hull right away and interview him.'

'Before we go, Chief, I'd like to hear what forensics have to say about the Lucky Strike cigarette butts that Jane handed in,' stated Laxton, telling him...

'They may give us a little more leverage.'

Wilberton nodded his head in agreement as he picked up the phone and inquired after the information. His brow creased as he listened to the reply.

'Yes, okay, let me know as soon as you get the result,' he said, replacing the phone.

He turned to Laxton and Bullyn.

'Forensics are getting on to it now, they're going to let me know shortly,' he told them.

A couple of minutes later, the three of them left the office and made their way to the car.

Robert Laxton got into the driver's seat, manoeuvred the car out of the Station car park and set off for Hull.

Chapter Twenty

Laxton squinted his eyes against the misty autumn sunlight that was reflecting off the Humber, as they negotiated the bridge. The police car was waved through with a nod from the officer manning the toll gate. After calling at Hull police headquarters to inform them that they wished to interview Richard Moristone again, they were accompanied by the redoubtable Sergeant Melner.

Arriving at Richard Moristone's flat, their knock on the partially open door was greeted by a flippant, 'Enter.' The four officers stepped into the flat. A voice called out.

'Now then, Inspector. What can I do for you?' It was Moristone.

They entered the lounge, the top of his head could just be seen above the back of the settee, in which he was reclining. A large mirror hanging over the stone fireplace on the wall in front of Moristone showed him, cigarette in one hand and a glass in the other, his legs stretched out and his feet up on a small stool. He took a deep drag on his cigarette and exhaled. A perfectly formed smoke ring drifted to the ceiling.

'To what do I owe the pleasure of your company, Inspector?' he asked insolently. There was a hint of sarcasm in his voice.

'We'd like to ask you a few questions sir,' requested Laxton, walking round the settee and looking down at him.

'Fire away,' said Moristone, waving his cigarette in the air.

'Where were you on October the twenty seventh at around ten p.m.?' queried Laxton.

'October the twenty seventh,' he repeated, with a nonchalant shrug of his shoulders. 'Why do you ask?'

'A woman named Rose Drawell was murdered,' rasped the Inspector, annoyed at Moristone's flippant attitude.

Moristone took a long pull on his cigarette, rested the back of his head on the settee and half closed his eyes as if casting his mind back, then, after blowing a stream of smoke across the room, he opened his eyes and looked straight at the Inspector.

'I was here with my girlfriend. Ask her, she'll verify it,' he answered, raising his glass to his lips and taking a good swig, His eyes slightly screwing up as the fiery liquid went down.

'We will,' rejoined Laxton sharply.

'Anyway, I don't know anyone by the name of Rose Drawell,' Moristone replied; his answer lacking conviction, as he got up from the settee and poured himself another drink.

'Would anyone else like a drink?' he asked, holding out the decanter.

The four officers shook their heads, declining his offer.

At that moment Wilberton's mobile phone, which was in his pocket, buzzed, breaking the silence. He took it out and put it to his ear.

'Yes, yes, I've got that,' he replied, a frown on his forehead as he switched the mobile phone off. After placing it back in his pocket, he rubbed the side of his face with the palm of his hand for a few seconds, before turning to Moristone, giving him a long probing look.

'I see that you smoke Lucky Strike cigarettes?' inferred the Chief Inspector, eyeing the one in Moristone's fingers.

'Yes I do,' snapped Moristone nastily. 'What's so unusual about that, so do many others, including my girlfriend, Monica.'

Wilberton, ignoring his outburst, pressed on. 'What size shoes do you take?'

'Size eight, but then again, so do lots of people.' He sat up and looked down at the chief's feet. A mirthless grin on his face. 'By the look of it, even you. What has that got to do with your investigation?'

Wilberton let the remark go. He kept his eyes unblinkingly on the, by now worried-looking man in front of him, and carried on.

'Size eight footprints and two Lucky Strike cigarette butts were found at the scene of the murder of Rose Drawell.'

'That doesn't prove a thing,' insisted Moristone, getting up from the settee and pacing round. He took another deep pull on his cigarette. He was beginning to look agitated. He laughed shakily, throwing his arms wide. 'Those facts could apply to many people.'

'I've just been informed that the cigarettes found at the scene of Rose Drawell's murder had traces of your saliva on them,' interjected the Chief. 'I doubt if anyone else would have that,' he added meaningfully, his eyes hardening.

Moristone stopped in his tracks. The colour suddenly drained from his face, his cockiness visibly subsiding as the implication of what the Chief had just announced sunk in. His eyes narrowed, as he quickly glanced away.

'I would like you to accompany us to the police station, sir, to help us with our enquiries,' Wilberton told him. There was a note of authority in his voice.

Moristone stubbed out his cigarette in the ashtray on the table, then raised his eyebrows and looked up at the Chief.

'Do you mind if I just nip to the toilet?" he asked him, then before the Chief could object he disappeared through a door at the back of the lounge.

The four officers waited for Moristone to return. Three minutes went by. Wilberton looked at his watch, then at Laxton and Bullyn. They suddenly realised that Moristone had done a runner. Springing into action, the three of them rushed to the door through which Moristone had gone. Sergeant Melner, who had been covering the only door to the flat, ran to another door which had been left ajar, this one led to a balcony, overlooking the alley at the back of the flat.

'Look, sir, over there,' he shouted, pointing as he looked out over the balcony.

Wilberton ran to the Sergeant's side, his eyes following the direction in which the big man was indicating. A motor cycle engine was revving up. Glancing down to the end of the alley, they could just make out Moristone disappearing in the distance in a cloud of exhaust fumes. The Chief, closely followed by the other three, charged out of the flat and ran to the car. They quickly clambered in and Laxton gunned the engine. Wilberton instructed Bullyn to send out a message, alerting all police cars, instructing them to detain Moristone. A call came in informing them that he had been seen heading towards the Humber Bridge. After dropping Melner off at Hull police station, they set off after Richard Moristone.

It was just going dark as Moristone stopped on the approach road to the bridge, and weighed up his chances. The cold night air cut into his lungs as he breathed deeply to clear his head. He looked out over to where the long suspension bridge spanned the Humber, then turned his thoughts to the distant sound of police sirens. He revved the powerful engine, then rearing up on the back wheel, he surged forward to the bridge, where he paid the man at the toll booth, who barely looked up as he went through. Heaving a sigh of relief, Moristone threaded his way through the slow traffic. He looked over his shoulder and saw that the police were following him and that they had just reached the bridge, with lights flashing and sirens wailing. Ahead of him two police cars were creating a road block at the exit. Spinning the bike round, the desperate man cast his eyes around him wildly. He gunned the engine as he decided what to do next. He looked first one way and then the other. The cars behind him were relentlessly closing in. The exit was blocked off by two police cars; there was no way out that way he told himself desperately. He figured he had one chance to escape, if he could get through the vehicles that were following him, and back to the entry point. Putting the engine into gear, he turned the bike round and accelerated, taking the outside lane where there was less traffic, swerving in and out of the slow moving cars heading towards him. Bemused drivers were shouting angrily through open windows.

'Bloody idiot,' and one or two other choice words.

Laxton spotted Moristone at the opposite end of the bridge, as he spun the bike round and sped towards them. Cars were twisting and turning as they attempted to avoid the madman.

Making his way to the outside lane, the Inspector was now in the motor bike's path. They were on collision course as Moristone leaned forward over the petrol tank, a maniacal look on his face. He was certain that Laxton would swerve round him. He couldn't have been more wrong. When they were

211

almost within striking distance, Laxton slammed his foot on the brakes and spun the steering wheel. The car skidded to a stop sideways on, in front of the bike. There was a shocked look on Moristone's face as he braked hard, causing the bike to skid into the side of the car. The motor bike came to a crunching stop. Moristone didn't. His mouth opened in a scream as he sailed through the air, landing on the tarmac with a resounding thump. His body bounced and rolled among the vehicles which were swerving and skidding to prevent their cars from smashing into him. Miraculously he wasn't hit. Laxton and Wilberton, who had already taken evasive action as Moristone sailed over them, jumped out of the car, followed by Bullyn, who held up the traffic. They ran over to Moristone, who was groaning with pain. He had a badly cut face and his leg was bent in an unnatural position. It was obviously broken. Within ten minutes an ambulance arrived. Paramedics strapped his leg and lifted him on to a stretcher. Blood ran from the nasty gash in his forehead; he scowled at Laxton as he leaned over him.

'You've got me, Inspector, but I gave you a run for your money,' he mocked.

Laxton ignored his comments, telling him he was under arrest for the murder of Rose and James Drawell, then read him his rights, before he was carried into the ambulance and taken away. After watching the ambulance disappear in the distance, the trio drove across the bridge and continued their journey back to Lincoln, where they dropped the Chief off at headquarters, Laxton took Jane Bullyn home. He had a word with Nancy, who was thrilled when he talked over with her the invitation from Maria Wilberton. After putting his arms around her and giving her a lingering kiss, he bid them goodbye. It was a weary Robert Laxton who wended his way in the dark, along the narrow, undulating country lanes, his main beam lighting up the countryside as he made his way to his home in Old Bolingbroke. He looked at his watch as he climbed out of the car, it showed eight p.m. He shook his head as he opened the door and entered the kitchen with Horatio, as usual, almost tripping him up as he weaved in and out of his feet, as he made his way across the kitchen to the fridge. Smiling to himself, Laxton bent down, picked the cat up and stroked him and whispering in his ear...

'Okay! Okay! I've got the message.'

Opening the fridge door he took out a tin of cat food and placed it on the floor. Then after taking a deep breath, he flopped down on the settee, laid his head back, closed his eyes and relaxed for a few minutes. It had been a long tiring day. Getting to his feet he poured himself a can of Guinness, then he went to the oven and took out the meal that Annie had prepared for him. He smiled ruefully to himself, as he surveyed the plate full of dried up sausage and mash. With a shrug of his shoulders, he placed it on the table, pulled up a chair and proceeded to wolf it down, dried up or not. He *was* hungry. After taking a shower, he decided to have an early night. Pulling on his pyjamas, he climbed into bed and within seconds he was out.

The next morning Laxton woke up after a solid night's sleep. Pushing the blankets back, he sat up in bed, rubbed his eyes and peered out of the window. A heavy mist was blocking out the sun. Throwing the blankets off him, he climbed out of bed. Stretching his arms out wide, he yawned loudly as he went into the bathroom. After a good wash and shave he felt a new man. Fifteen minutes later, after a quick breakfast, he was on his way to his car. Annie was just arriving on her bike as he opened the car door.

'Did you enjoy your dinner when you got home, Mr Laxton?' she called out cheerily.

He nodded his head and smiled.

'Yes thank you, Annie,' he lied, as he got into the car and started the engine. A few seconds later, he pulled out of the driveway, waving to her as he left.

The sun was just beginning to break through the thick mist that hung over the countryside as he made his way to Dalesworth to pick up Jane Bullyn. After stopping for a cup of tea with Nancy, he and Jane made their way to headquarters. On arrival they went into the incident room, where Wilberton was waiting for them.

'We've had a full confession from Richard Moristone. He's admitted devising the whole scheme,' he told them, then paused to let them absorb the implications, as they took a seat opposite him, then he went on…

'It seems that although he had a legacy coming to him from his grandmother, he was so heavily in debt that he couldn't wait for her to die, but there was a problem. He couldn't see any way that he could do anything about er…' his brow creased as he searched for the right words, '*getting rid of her*, without it leading straight back to him. What he needed was someone to do the deed. Someone,' he reiterated, 'who had no connections to her or him whatsoever. Short of hiring a… 'hit man', which he thought would be very risky, and expensive, he couldn't think of any way to overcome that obstacle. That was *if* he could get someone to do the killing for him in the first place, which he doubted very much.'

He paused again as a cup of coffee for each of them was brought in, then after reaching out, picking up his coffee and taking a drink, he continued with his summary.

'Then Moristone had what he thought was a brilliant idea. First of all he had to recruit three more besides himself. He advertised for persons who were in deep trouble. He promised them a way out of their difficulties.'

He took another sip of his coffee, then carried on.

'Out of the numerous contacts he had, he chose the three he needed. The three most likely to go through with his plan. He asked them, if someone who had no connection with them, did their bidding, would they accept? After hearing what he had to say, they all agreed to the plan. They were to meet at the Bell Inn, situated near Spawsby in Lincolnshire. It was chosen because of its relatively out of the way position. Each of them were told to bring a specific coloured envelope, containing the details of the person they wanted eliminating. There was to be nothing written on the outside of the envelope. They each were to choose one of the envelopes at random, which wasn't their colour. It was what you might call a '**blind stab**'. Wilberton paused for a second as he picked up his cup and took another drink of his coffee, looking at the other two as he did so. After clearing his throat, he proceeded with his summing up…

'Moristone told them, providing they were careful, and they

made sure that they had fixed themselves up with good alibis, they wouldn't have anything to worry about, as there wouldn't be anything to connect them to their target. Evelyn Hopper made the cardinal error of being seen committing the act. Insten saw her as a danger to himself and killed her. Richard Moristone sensed that events were not going exactly to plan, so to speak. He could see the murder of Rose Drawell being traced back to him. He had to shift the blame, and James Drawell, her husband was the obvious scapegoat.'

The Chief Inspector looked at the two detectives out of the corner of his eye as he finished off his coffee. There was a grim smile on his face as he told them,

'If he had taken a tape measure with him, he might have got away with it. But, as is often the case. Murderers always seem to make one mistake.'

Then after thanking Inspector Laxton and D.C. Bullyn for their part in apprehending the killers, he told them, 'That will be it for today.'

Jane Bullyn, a frown on her forehead, looked up at Laxton as they walked to the car.

'What I can't understand is, how Moristone thought he could get away with it.'

Robert Laxton clicked his seat belt and glanced across at her.

'Well,' he rejoined, after giving it a little thought. 'The idea *was* a clever one,' he reminded her before continuing…

'We hadn't a clue as to what was going on until Insten panicked and killed Evelyn Hopper. There was no way that we could have proved beyond a shadow of doubt that she was the woman seen on the video tape, pushing Basser in front of the train.'

He paused as he reached out and switched on the ignition, telling her…

'It was too vague,' as he started the engine and pulled out into the main stream of traffic.

'Then Moristone blew it when he bumped off James Drawell. If he and Insten had kept their cool, we would have had one hell of a job nailing them.'

An hour later he drew up outside the bungalow in Dalesworth where he joined Jane and went into the bungalow, where Nancy was waiting for them. She placed her arms around his shoulders and gave him a loving kiss. Then after giving a deep sigh, she told him…

'I hope you are staying for lunch, Robert.'

He gave her a kiss on her forehead and whispered in her ear…

'I certainly am.'

After the meal he leaned back in his chair and massaged his stomach.

'That was really good!' he exclaimed, a satisfied smile on his face.

'Good,' rejoined Nancy, informing him…

'Then you won't mind drying the dishes.'

Then after spending the rest of the afternoon with them, discussing the forthcoming wedding, it was just beginning to go dark as he reluctantly set off to his cottage in Old Bolingbroke. Wending his way across the Wolds, he was deep in thought as he attempted to visualise what the future held for him. He gave a deep sigh.

Nancy Bullyn and Robert Laxton went ahead with their wedding arrangements. The wedding was to be held in the second week in March at the church in Dalesworth. Henry Wilberton was to be best man. After the arrest of both Moristone, who was in hospital, and Insten, things went quiet. Christmas came and went without a hitch. There were the usual petty crimes caused mainly by boisterous revellers. But on the whole it was uneventful.

It was the second week in January and everyone was beginning to settle down after the New Year celebrations.

'Well!' exclaimed Wilberton, to Laxton and Bullyn, who had just walked into his office out of the icy cold air. 'We've been informed that Moristone won't be fit to stand trial until the end of March.'

'That'll give us plenty of time to get the wedding over with,' said Laxton, rubbing his hands in front of the electric fire that stood in the middle of the room for extra heat.

The Inspector sat on the edge of the desk and picked up the report that the Chief had been reading. He plucked at his bottom lip as he studiously went through it.

'It looks as though we've got a cast iron case against the both of them,' he concluded, placing the paper back on the desk and looking up at Wilberton. Then standing up he turned to go out of the office.

'Oh by the way, Robert,' called the Chief, just as he was about to go through the door, 'I've received a call from Hull. They want you to attend the trial of Gregory Mendois.'

Laxton's eyes went up into his head. 'What do they need me for? They've got all the evidence they need.' There was a note of annoyance in his voice. He needed this like a hole in the head, he thought.

'I should think they want you as a material witness,' replied Wilberton.

'When is the trial starting?' he asked, without much enthusiasm.

The Chief Inspector paused and looked away, suppressing a half smile. 'This afternoon at one thirty p.m.,' he told him with a straight face.

There was a look of incredulity on Laxton face. 'This afternoon?' he repeated. 'That's short notice isn't it?'

Wilberton shrugged his shoulders. 'It can't be helped,' he said apologetically. 'It's been delayed because of the Christmas and New Year break. Oh and leave Bullyn here with me. I could do with some help straightening this lot up.' He waved his hand indicating all the paper work strewn about his desk. Laxton stormed out, a look of extreme annoyance on his face at the thought of his afternoon being taken up, for a few minutes in court.

The journey to Hull wasn't very pleasant. The sleet rattled on the windscreen like tracer bullets in the strong wind as he carefully made his way along the busy highway. He turned up the heat in the car and hunched over the steering wheel as he looked out over the Humber when he was negotiating the bridge. The heavy mist hanging over the murky water didn't do much for his temper as he showed his credentials and drove through the toll.

The Hull court room was a hive of activity as he arrived. He was taken to a room where he had to wait to be called. He checked his watch; it was almost one-twenty. He'd just made it, he told himself with a sigh of relief. The judge didn't take kindly to latecomers. Twenty minutes later he was called in. His eyes swept the court room. Mendois was sat with his counsel, a smirk on his face, confident in the fact that he was going to get off lightly. Probably a hefty fine he thought. After being sworn in, Laxton gave his evidence, directing his eyes at the bewigged judge. After answering one or two questions, he was escorted out of the court room. An hour later the case was over. The lawyer representing the prosecution came out of the courtroom and approached him, a wide smile on his face.

'Guilty on all counts,' he pronounced.

'What did he get?' asked the Inspector.

'One hundred thousand pounds fine, and three years incarceration,' was the reply.

Laxton nodded his head, a look of satisfaction on his face, as he turned to leave.

The sleet had turned to heavy snow as he did the return journey over the Humber Bridge; a white blanket of snow covered the countryside, as the wipers fought to keep the windscreen clear, making the going extremely difficult as he drove back to Lincoln.

Wilberton, rubbing his hands together, smiled with satisfaction as he was informed of the sentence that had been dealt out to Mendois.

'That should keep him quiet for some time,' he remarked, as he congratulated Laxton on the successful conclusion.

Picking up Jane Bullyn, the Inspector set off for home with the feeling of a job well done.

Driving was tricky, as the roads and country lanes were becoming almost impassable as the snow drifted. He was relieved when he eventually arrived at Dalesworth where he dropped Jane off and had a word with Nancy.

'Will you be all right in this bad weather, Robert?' she asked him, concern in her voice. 'Why don't you stay here till tomorrow morning?'

He shook his head with a smile. 'It will be just as bad in the morning,' he told her, looking down into her eyes and kissing her gently on her cheek.

'In fact it will probably be worse,' he added as he opened the door to leave, letting a blast of cold air and a flurry of snow through the door. Stepping outside, he quickly closed it behind him. Leaning into the blizzard he trudged through the six inches of snow that covered the garden path. Climbing into his car he turned the heating on and carefully drove off, as Nancy and Jane watched concernedly through the window, as his rear lights slowly disappeared into the snowy night.

The drive across the country lanes was horrendous as the big car ploughed its way through the small drifts that were beginning to form. Reaching out, he switched on the radio. He smiled to himself as he looked at the windscreen wipers struggling to cope with the heavy snowflakes that were falling, as he listened to a deep, rich, baritone voice, singing the words...

'In the bleak midwinter, softly falls the snow.'

'It couldn't be more appropriate.' he muttered, as he struggled to keep control of the car as it slid about on the freezing surface.

Breathing a sigh of relief, he finally arrived at his cottage in Old Bolingbroke. The castle ruins were almost invisible under the heavy fall of snow as he turned into his driveway and put the car in the garage. Trudging through the, by now, eight inches or so of snow, that lay on the drive, to the back door, the smell of home cooking invaded his nostrils as he walked through the door. He quickly closed it behind him as the cold wind and snow blasted into the kitchen. A note on the table from Annie, told him that his dinner was in the oven. He looked in the oven and rubbed his hands with anticipation. Stew and dumplings.

'Good old, Annie,' he muttered to himself, a smile on his face, as he took the hot meal out of the oven and placed it on the table. His affection for the little woman knew no bounds. Horatio was circling him as he smelled the meal. Robert Laxton reached into the fridge and took out a saucer full of fish and placed it on the floor for a not very grateful cat. Then he tucked into his meal with gusto.

Chapter Twenty-One

The two and a half months to the big day passed quickly. The snow disappeared as winter changed to spring. First the snowdrops showed, then the crocuses followed by the daffodils sprang up. To the happy couple, Robert Laxton and Nancy Bullyn, it was a good time to be alive. It seemed no time at all before the wedding day was upon them.

In the meantime Richard Moristone was still in care, slowly recovering from his injuries. He'd spent all the time he was in hospital plotting how he could escape and take his revenge on the Inspector. There was hatred in his eyes as he read in the local newspaper that was supplied to the hospital, that Robert Laxton and Nancy Bullyn were to be married on the Saturday at Dalesworth church at ten a.m. Today was Friday.

'If I could just get out of here,' he told himself with a grim smile on his face, 'I would give them a wedding present to remember.'

He had been in hospital since his arrest before Christmas. After numerous operations, the plaster had been removed from his leg, and he was now able to get about with the aid of two metal walking sticks. He looked through the mirror at his bedside and ran his fingers gently over the cuts to his face, which were, by now, almost healed.

'I'll carry these scars for the rest of my life,' he muttered to himself, a look of anger in his eyes. Actually he was in better condition than he'd led the doctors to believe. A police constable was standing guard outside the door of the ward. Moristone quietly checked his bedside locker. He saw that his clothes were still there, together with a twenty-pound note.

After waiting for everyone to settle down for the night, he reached into the locker, taking extra care not to make a noise as he took out his clothes, then with some difficulty he carefully dressed. Picking up one of the metal walking sticks, he hobbled to the door and called out; stepping back behind the door as he did so. The guard, who had dozed off, woke with a start. Cursing to himself, he got up out of the chair.

'What the hell do you want now?" he mumbled, scratching his head as he shuffled wearily into the ward.

As he came through the door Moristone hit him over the back of the head with the heavy handle of the metal walking stick. The guard gave a moan and fell to the floor unconscious. After quickly tying him up and pushing a paper handkerchief in his mouth to gag him, Moristone, after a struggle, dragged the unconscious guard's body across the hospital ward to get him to the bed. He paused for a moment to catch his breath and listen to check if he had been heard. All he could hear was the pounding of his heart. Bending down, he placed his arms under the unconscious man's limp body, then with some difficulty and a lot of grunting at the effort he was putting into it, he hoisted the guard on to the bed. After covering the guard with the blankets, giving the impression that he was still in the bed, he stood back and checked his handiwork. He had a grim smile on his face as he nodded with satisfaction. Poking his head out of the door of the ward, he checked the corridor. There was no one in sight. Making as little noise as possible, Moristone carefully hobbled past the office, where the nurse, who was on night duty, had her head down, busy checking through some papers. Taking a deep breath, he made his way to the exit. He breathed a sigh of relief when he saw a taxi parked outside the entrance. Approaching the taxi driver, he asked him if he was available. The driver, who had just brought a pregnant woman in, and was having a fag before setting off back to the office, looked him up and down. There was a look of doubt in his eyes.

'I've been waiting for a friend to pick me up,' Moristone lied. 'He's just phoned to tell me he can't make it.' He shrugged his shoulders in a gesture of helplessness.

The taxi driver tossed the cigarette through the open car window.

'Jump in. I'll drop you off on my way back to the office,' he told the crippled man reluctantly, after deciding it would be better for him to go back with a fare. Moristone gave the driver instructions on where to take him. The driver's reluctance was soon settled when Moristone gave him the twenty-pound note and told him to keep the change; then he clambered into the rear seat of the taxi. When they were some fifty yards from his destination, he leaned over and told the driver to stop. After a struggle he disembarked from the taxi; he thanked the driver and told him he would be able to manage from there.

'Are you sure, sir?' enquired the driver concernedly, holding the crippled man's metal walking stick as he leaned on the bonnet of the car for support.

Moristone nodded his head and took the metal stick from him.

'I'll be okay,' he assured the driver.

The man reluctantly climbed back behind the steering wheel and drove slowly away.

Dawn was just breaking, as Moristone watched the taxi disappear into the heavy early morning mist. The road was deserted as he hobbled a hundred yards to a row of garages where he housed his car. Removing a loose brick in the wall, he pulled out two keys, one was for the garage and the other one for the car. Opening the boot of the car, he took out a piece of sacking, that he unrolled, to reveal a double-barrelled sawn-off shotgun, which he'd acquired for protection after Mendois's two heavies had beaten him up. He had a cruel expression on his face as he slid two cartridges into the breech, then, climbing into his car he drove off towards the Humber Bridge. Thirty minutes later after negotiating the bridge, he made his way to Dalesworth which was around one and a half hours journey. Stopping the car in a lay by about half a mile away from the village, he checked his wrist watch, which showed seven thirty a.m. He laid the gun in his lap and closed his eyes. He had two and a half hours to kill, he told himself, his face widening in a grim smile, at the pun.

Robert Laxton and Henry Wilberton, both smartly dressed and sporting a carnation in their lapels, arrived at the church in Dalesworth. A constable approached them. He gave the chief a note. He read it and passed it to Laxton. It informed them that Moristone had escaped from hospital and was on the run. He turned to Wilberton.

'You don't think he'll come here, do you?' he asked, a worried expression on his face.

'I shouldn't think so. If he's got any sense he'll be miles away by now,' the Chief replied, unconvincingly, adding in a low voice…

'He won't get far in his condition.'

The guests, who were already there, congratulated the prospective groom, giving him their best wishes. He nodded his head in acknowledgement, a nervy smile playing on his lips. He looked down at his best man, standing beside him, and whispered in his ear.

'Have you got the ring in a safe place?' he asked anxiously.

'Stop worrying, Robert, everything is under control,' Wilberton assured him, raising his hand and patting his waistcoat pocket.

Standing in front of the altar, Robert Laxton waited nervously for his bride to arrive.

The organ echoed through the church, as it struck up with the wedding march, signalling her arrival. He gave a glance over his shoulder as she walked down the aisle. A proud smile played on his face as he saw how lovely she looked. Nancy took her place beside him. He reached out and gave her hand a reassuring squeeze. She was dressed in a powder blue two-piece, and a hat with a veil covering her face. Robert looked down at her, his heart full of love and pride, as the organ stopped playing. The vicar started the proceedings. A few minutes later Robert Laxton placed the ring on her finger and gave her a gentle kiss.

They were man and wife. After the signing of the register they walked out of the church into the bright sunlight. Nancy, her arm linked through Robert's, was smiling happily as they made their way through the crowded church yard to the wedding car that was to take them the short journey to the local pub, where the reception was being held. As they went through the church gates and approached the car, a man stepped out in front of them.

'So! You thought you'd seen the last of me did you?' a familiar voice called loudly.

Robert Laxton's eyes narrowed when he saw it was Richard Moristone. He was standing in the middle of the lane in front of them, leaning on a metal walking stick. In his other hand he held a sawn off shotgun. He had a cruel smile on his face.

'Put the gun down, this isn't going to help you, and innocent people could get hurt,' Laxton told him sharply.

Moristone limped awkwardly towards the Inspector, a sneer on his face.

'The only person who's going to get hurt is you,' he snarled, hatred in his cold eyes, as he pointed the gun at Laxton's chest. His finger closed on the trigger. Nancy screamed.

'No! No!' she cried, her arms outstretched as she ran towards Richard Moristone.

'Nancy, get out of the way,' called a horrified Laxton. His shout almost drowned out by the blast from the shotgun, which reverberated around the village. Nancy Bullyn slumped to the floor. She'd taken one barrel of the shotgun in her chest at point blank range. The crowd closed in on Moristone. He swung the gun round, forcing them back. Then, realising he had only one shot left, he slowly backed away from them. He turned, his weight on the walking stick as he hobbled away from the scene. Robert Laxton went down on his knees and placed his arm tenderly under Nancy's head, and kissed her. Then, with a look of hatred in his eyes he went after the man who'd shot her. In the meantime Wilberton had called for an ambulance and back up.

'Look after Nancy,' Laxton called to Jane, as he went after the cold blooded killer.

Moristone, with the aid of the metal stick in one hand and the shot gun in the other, limped away from the threatening crowd and made his way along the lane that led through the centre of the village, towards where he had parked his car, with the Inspector in hot pursuit. Laxton caught a glimpse of the desperate gunman, as he turned up a side lane. Keeping his head down, he followed him. Moristone, a stranger to the area, looked back and saw that the Inspector was gaining ground on him. It was obvious to him that he had no chance of making it to where his car was parked. Looking frantically for somewhere to hide, he made his way up a side road to where he could see an old dilapidated cottage. On reaching it he stopped for a couple of minutes and ran his eyes over it. A sign had been placed on the site, with instructions that no one was to enter it; warning them that the property was in an extremely dangerous condition and was shortly to be demolished. Moristone stroked his chin for a few seconds, then suddenly made his mind up, deciding that it was the only place he could hide. He hobbled across the muddy frontage, towards the open doorway (the door had long since fallen off). Taking tentative steps he ducked his head and entered the gloomy crumbling room. A strong smell of dry rot assailed his nostrils as he made his way to the rear of the cottage. Maybe there was a way through he thought, as he entered the shadows beyond.

Laxton, who had seen Moristone turn up the lane, was a few minutes behind him. He had reached the bottom of the lane and was just in time to see him approach the cottage. He had a grim expression on his face as he ran up the lane and stopped outside the crumbling building which he figured Moristone must be in, deep footprints in the heavy mud proving the point. He was consumed with hatred for the callous brute as he took a deep breath and entered the property. Stopping for a moment to allow his eyes to get accustomed to the gloomy interior, he took note of the ceiling that was in a state of collapse. Stepping carefully on the floor boards that were riddled with woodworm and dry rot, he tentatively made his way across the dark room, to another doorway which led to the rear of the cottage. On his left there was a flight of broken stairs that led up to the bedrooms. He strained his eyes to check whether there was any chance that Moristone could be up there. After assuring himself that it was impossible for anyone to have negotiated them, owing to the fact that they had collapsed half way up, he carried on. There was a ghostly silence as he entered the back room; all that could be heard was the creaking of the rotting, unsafe floorboards. He had just passed into the room when he felt something dig into the back of his neck. It was the barrel of the shotgun. His body went rigid.

'Walked right into my little trap didn't you, Inspector?' a voice growled as Moristone stepped from around the edge of the doorway and stood behind Laxton.

There was a sudden crack as the rotten floorboards under Moristone's feet collapsed, throwing him off balance, causing him to reach out to save himself from falling. Laxton felt the gun barrel leave his neck. He swung round, knocking the hand that held the gun to one side, then, seeing his opportunity, he reached out and wrapped his left arm around the killer's neck, grabbing the barrel of the shotgun with his right hand.

'Got you, you murdering bastard,' he growled, as he strengthened his arm hold on Moristone's neck.

'Not yet, you haven't," snarled the killer hoarsely, as he struggled to get out of the stranglehold that Laxton had on him. Then, with the power of a desperate man, he managed to train the shot gun on the Inspector, who, in turn grabbed the twin barrelled gun and forced it away from his head. Then mustering all his strength, he drove it under Moristone's chin, and rammed it upward into his throat. Moristone's eyes rolled in terror as Laxton placed his thumb over his adversary's forefinger, which was on the trigger. He let out a choked scream, as he was almost impaled.

'Now pull the trigger, you piece of slime,' hissed Laxton, his eyes showing his revulsion as he put pressure on Moristone's trigger finger.

There was a loud blast, which threatened to demolish the crumbling cottage. The top of Moristone's head disintegrated, splattering Laxton with blood and fragments of bone. The shot man's legs twitched involuntarily as Laxton lowered the lifeless body of the callous murderer to the floor. The dim light was suddenly blocked out as Wilberton appeared in the doorway.

'Are you okay, Robert?' he inquired apprehensively.

'Yes, Henry I'm okay. I got the swine,' he replied Then asked, after wiping the blood from his face with a handkerchief, his voice full of emotion, 'How is Nancy?'

'She's not so good I'm afraid,' Henry Wilberton told him, shaking his head. 'But she won't give up, she's a battler. She's been taken to Pilgrim Hospital in Boston, where she will be in good hands.'

Laxton took a deep breath as he walked wearily through the doorway that led out of the cottage, his hand shaking uncontrollably, as he reached into his pocket and gave his badge to Wilberton.

'What's that for?' asked the Chief as the badge was placed in his hand.

'For killing Moristone,' he replied unfeelingly. There was a note of finality in his voice.

'I saw the whole thing,' volunteered the Chief as he dropped the badge back into Laxton's pocket, telling him…

'As far as I could see he shot himself. Now let forensics and the paramedics in, so that they can clear this mess up.'

Half an hour later they arrived at Pilgrim Hospital. Laxton was taken to where Nancy lay in intensive care. The doctors and staff that surrounded the bed were working hard to save her. Laxton asked if he could see her. The doctor paused for a moment, as he looked down at her, then he turned and looked at him; the expression on his face telling it all as he nodded his head and stood aside. Her skin was like marble as Robert Laxton approached the bed. He looked down at her pale face, she looked as though she had just fallen asleep, then, his eyes full of heartfelt pain, he leaned over and kissed her gently on the forehead. A few seconds later her eyes fluttered open and her lips moved.

'Don't leave me, darling,' she murmured.

'I won't, dearest,' he told her, shaking his head; tears welling up in his eyes as he gently held her hand in his.

Suddenly her eyes opened wide as she looked up at him. He felt her fingers tighten, as she gripped his hand.

'I love you, darling,' she whispered, then her head sank back on to the pillow. At that moment the doctor came in and leaned over her. He shook his head, a sombre expression on his face as he looked up into the heart broken man's eyes.

'I'm afraid she's gone, sir,' he declared, a sombre tone to his voice.

Laxton nodded his head dejectedly. He gave one last look at

her lovely face, then turned away, his shoulders shaking. He was overcome with grief. Jane leaned over and kissed her mother, tears streaming down her face.

'Why, why?' she sobbed, as Robert Laxton put his arm around her comfortingly and led her away. He was silent as he asked himself the same question.

The funeral was held on the following Sunday, in the same church that they were married in. Robert Laxton stood quietly at the front of the small crowd that were gathered around, as he watched her interred in a quiet corner of the churchyard next to her late husband. Then, after giving a deep, heart-felt sigh, he turned his back on the proceedings, and walked slowly away, telling himself that his reason to carry on with his life had gone.

Three weeks went by and Robert Laxton hadn't been seen. He didn't answer his phone. Wilberton was beginning to get worried. He called Jane Bullyn into his office.

'Has Robert been in touch with you?' he asked her worriedly.

She shook her head. 'No,' she told him, adding concernedly...

'I've tried to phone him but there's no answer, I didn't want to intrude. I thought the best thing to do, was to leave him alone and let him get it out of his system.'

Wilberton tapped on his desk with his forefinger for a couple of seconds, a thoughtful expression on his face. Then he looked up at her and made a decision.

'I reckon three weeks is long enough, I want you to contact Robert and see if he's okay,' he told her.

'I'll get down there right away,' she informed the Chief determinedly.

He nodded his approval as she walked out of the office and went to her car.

Half an hour later, Jane Bullyn drove into the driveway of Laxton's cottage in Old Bolingbroke. A plump figure approached her as she opened the car door. It was his daily help Annie.

'How is he, Annie?' she asked as she climbed out of the car.

The usually jolly little woman shook her head, a worried frown wrinkling her brow.

'I'm glad you've come, Miss. I'm worried to death about him. He won't let me in. Every time I go through the door he tells me to get out and he won't eat anything. I've tried to help him but he just tells me to leave him alone,' she confided.

'I've fed the cat,' she added, as Horatio came out to meet them.

Jane patted her on the arm sympathetically as they walked side by side up the path.

'We'll see what we can do, shall we?'

Annie followed her to the door of the cottage. Jane Bullyn rang the door bell, there was no answer. She tried the door and it swung open. Stepping inside the cottage, she entered the lounge, wrinkling her nose at the smell of stale sweat and alcohol. Laxton was slumped on the settee. Empty whisky bottles were strewn around on the floor. He was almost unrecognisable, with his unshaven face and unkempt hair, giving him the semblance of a tramp. Jane and Annie set about tidying up, beginning by piling all the dirty pots in the sink and the empty bottles in the bin. Annie washed the pots, as Jane stood over him, her hands on her hips. He looked up at her through bloodshot eyes.

'Go away,' he mumbled, waving his left hand as he reached out with his right and grabbed the half full bottle of whisky that stood on the table.

'Oh no you don't,' she snapped, snatching the bottle out of his hand and emptying it down the sink and telling him…

'It's time you pulled yourself together.'

'I can't go on without her, Jane,' he groaned, holding his head in his hands.

'Don't talk silly, Robert!' Jane retorted, looking down at the dejected figure, telling him feelingly…

'She was my mum and I loved her dearly, but life goes on.'

He got up from the settee and stood up. Taking a deep breath he stretched his arms out wide; then he ran his fingers through his wiry hair. Looking down at the young woman who looked so much like Nancy, he could see the hurt in her hazel eyes. He could also see the strength. He knew in his heart that she was right. She squeezed his big hands, and stood on tiptoe to kiss him on the cheek, his whiskers prickling her lips. His mouth slowly broadened into a smile. He took another deep breath. Then exhaled slowly; there was a rasping sound as he scratched his bristly chin.

'Okay, Constable,' he quipped, 'I'll get cleaned up.'

With this he disappeared into the bathroom, to return twenty minutes later looking a new man, albeit a stone lighter. Jane finished cleaning the pots as Annie cooked him a plate full of bacon and eggs. Then they both watched him devour the food ravenously. She knew then, he was going to be all right. Annie squeezed past him as she went to the door. He put his arm around her and gave her an affectionate hug as she left.

'Thank you, Annie,' he told her, looking up at her with a smile. 'You're a gem.'

She smiled back at him, wiping a tear from her eye, with the back of her hand.

'That's... that's all right, Mr Laxton,' she sighed, her voice breaking with emotion. 'So long as I know you are getting well again.'

He nodded his head and told her...

'I'll be okay, Annie,'

'I'll be off now,' Jane told him as he polished off his sixth slice of bread.

'Tell the Chief I'll be back on duty in the morning,' he called after her, as he gave the bacon rind to a hungry Horatio, who was fussing around him.

It was a bright sunny morning, as Robert Laxton walked out of his cottage to his car. He glanced up at two blue tits who had taken up residence in the house box and were, by now feeding their young, flying back and forth across the garden, their beaks full of bugs and caterpillars. He turned and looked up at the blue sky, as he climbed into the car with a heavy heart, and sat for a few seconds deep in thought. Then with a determined expression on his face, he gave a deep sigh and pulled himself together. Annie was just turning into the drive as he switched on the ignition and started the engine. After giving a parting wave to a smiling Annie, he engaged the gear and drove out of the double gates and on to the lane.

He arrived at the Lincoln headquarters an hour later to clapping and cheering from all the staff. Chief Inspector Wilberton shook his hand.

'Welcome back, Robert.'

End